OUT OF
TIME

What others are saying about this book . . .

"A dangerous mission, a family curse, and a smart and tenacious protagonist—*Out of Time* has all the ingredients to keep you up well past your bedtime."

—Maria V. Snyder, *New York Times* best-selling author of *Poison Study*

OUT OF
TIME

ELIZABETH A. DRYSDALE

SWEETWATER BOOKS
An imprint of Cedar Fort, Inc.
Springville, Utah

ISBN 13: 978-1-4621-4082-4

Published by Sweetwater Books, an imprint of Cedar Fort, Inc.
2373 W. 700 S., Springville, UT 84663
Distributed by Cedar Fort, Inc., www.cedarfort.com

Library of Congress Control Number: 2021939457

Cover design by Shawnda T. Craig
Cover design © 2021 Cedar Fort, Inc.
Edited and typeset by Valene Wood

Printed in the United States of America

10 9 8 7 6 5 4 3 2 1

Printed on acid-free paper

To Mom and Dad.
You were right.

ALSO BY ELIZABETH A. DRYSDALE

Curse of the Forgotten

CHAPTER ONE

I tap my pencil against the top of my battered desk with increasing frequency. The old analogue clock on the wall ticks slower and slower as I sneak glances at where it's perched up on the old brick wall. The whisperings of my schoolmates pick up as we get closer to two o'clock. The sub hasn't left her chair since we came in, her glazed eyes watching us without seeing. It's the last period and she's obviously given up. I can't say I blame her.

The room is warm, chalk-filled air sitting heavy in my lungs. Leaning forward, I try to read the pop quiz in front of me. The words swirl together in a jumble of meaningless drivel. Sighing, I stop trying with the quiz and start a nervous doodle on the corner of the page instead. I'm a senior with no real thoughts about college, so I highly doubt this quiz is going to make or break me. Plus, art is one of my favorite subjects and I'm kind of good at it, even if my teacher says it doesn't have enough "feeling" in it, whatever that means. Anyway, I'd rather give art my attention than history. Those classes seem pointless when my aunts have practically lived through all of it and love to share what political figures were really like.

But it's not enough to fully distract me, nothing has been today.

Panic I've been trying to hold back all week threatens to rear its ugly head and take over, making my breaths shallow. "Coven Meeting" has been an ugly stain on the calendar hanging on the fridge since Mom got the call on Sunday. And now it's here.

It's not like coven meetings are that unusual. My family are all members, everyone but me. So the meetings happen, the coven leaves, and everything is fine. But today is different. Mom hasn't given up hope on getting me in and I can't take another failure. With only one gift—to travel back in time—it's near impossible to get in, especially when that one gift is as useless as mine.

The bell rings, shaking me out of my thoughts so hard that I knock my elbow against the desk. Sharp jabs of pain travel up my arm as I gather up my books and shove the summons from the guidance counselor the sub handed me earlier into the deepest reaches of my backpack.

"You going to the party tonight?" Jessica asks, and I glance up at her in surprise.

"Oh, I hadn't even heard about it." I try to skirt around saying a direct no.

It's been a long time since I was even invited to anything that I almost want to figure out a way to go. Living in the same town all through school has made it pretty easy for my classmates to figure out certain things about my family. Like we're not joiners, not at all. I guess that's what happens when you can't love anyone. It makes getting real friends impossible and makes wanting to keep trying a distant memory.

Jessica, a pretty blonde girl in a tight skirt, laughs as her gaze flicks over me. She's leaning on Mike's desk next to me. My cheeks heat up. She was never inviting me.

"Of course, like I'd miss one of Bobby's parties. It'd be social suicide." He gives me a meaningful side glance.

Yeah, yeah, I know. I'm a loner and that's okay. It's not like I could ever really care about these kids anyway. Unfortunately, I'm still about to commit social suicide, just not one they would ever care about. No, I'm going to commit the ultimate sin of not fitting in among my own kind.

I cross the floor, dodging desks and other students like a waif. My feet slow as I leave the imposing four-story brick school behind, all thoughts of school and parties flitting away. I know what the coven is going to ask me to do and I already know I won't be able to do it.

Closing my eyes, I focus on the swirling pool of magical thread that fills my well of power, bringing my magic to the surface. Sparks of purple flash along my hands but nothing more than that. Parlor tricks. That's all I'm good for. Good thing they're going to ask me for a real presentation of traveling through time instead of a few pretty colors. No, that would be too easy.

Leaves scrape along the broken sidewalk in a crisp fall wind. Everything in this town is falling apart, why not my family's status with it? This will be my last chance. I already know that. There's no way Mom can convince them to test me again.

The quarter mile walk is far too short today and before I'm ready, the house looms in front of me. Its familiar sagging appearance brings none of the warmth it usually does. Instead of the relief I usually feel when getting home, a trail of cold sweat works its way down my back. I won't find any tenderness in there today.

≈≈≈

Blood pumps thick through my veins as I make my way through the tangle of uncut grass that's my yard. I try not to look at the house as my knees threaten to lock up in anticipation. Avoiding the front walk, and with it the front door with its layers of peeling yellow paint, I make for the side door instead. Cars from every different era sit piled in the driveway, announcing our less than welcome guests.

I pull open the warped screen door, sneaking into the kitchen before letting it slowly close behind me. It's almost completely closed when the rusty spring lets out a low moan. Flinching, I back away from the door and press myself against the long pantry cupboard. If I can make it up the stairs, I'll be safe. I just have to make it from this room to the hallway without any of the women I can hear in the sitting room seeing me. Piece of cake.

"We've been waiting for you, Sophronia."

My shoulders slump, backpack falling out of my hands to the floor. "Just Soph. Why bother waiting for me?" I groan, slipping my worn converse off onto the cracked linoleum.

"You'll always be Sophronia, no matter what Americanizing you try to do." Mom ignores my question, gripping my arm in her plump hands to lead me out of the kitchen. "I'm glad you weren't too late. You know how agitated Rebecca can be."

I'm sure my tardiness has no bearing on Rebecca's emotional state. If anything, my not showing up would make everyone happier. Mom yammers in my ear, blathering on about what they've already discussed. There's nothing these old biddies like more than to brag about their children.

"Iole, so good of your daughter to finally join us," Rebecca says with a thin-lipped smile.

She stands in front of the group in my already crowded living room. Every available surface is filled with sagging couches, old curio cabinets, and a few yard-sale-scavenged chairs. The women utilizing our furniture turn toward me as one.

"I told you she'd have school, Rebecca. You can't expect her to be here on time when you set the meeting for two," Mom says, face smooth, betraying neither her age nor her emotions as she tips herself into an empty chair.

Rebecca turns towards the other women. "Now that we're all assembled, I think we can skip our membership requirements. Sophronia knows she needs to show proficiency in her one magical gift in order to join our numbers."

"Just get on with it," Grandma says, perched on a barstool in the corner of the room. "No need to make this girl suffer more than necessary."

Smoothing her grey hair back, ensuring her bun is perfect, Rebecca turns her hawk eyes on me. "As this is your fourth attempt, I'm going to assume you are already familiar with the rules."

Sighing, I ignore her smirk. There really aren't any rules, just requirements. Rules Mom knows I'll never be able to meet, despite all her prodding.

"Now, your only gift is still time travel. Is that correct?" she glances at me over the binder clenched in her long fingers.

"Yes."

"And you're aware that the qualifications of your gift will be steep as you have no other talents to supplement our coven?"

Of course. How could I forget how little I have to offer when the coven is constantly so willing to remind me? Shrugging my shoulders, I ignore the smile dimpling my mother's face.

"Today you're going to go back to 1950. You're going to find me and tap me twice on my right shoulder. Failure to accomplish this will once again lead to refusal of your application by the coven." She gives me a curling smile. "You may begin."

Standing in the middle of the room, I close my eyes. Focusing on the date Rebecca has given me, I tune out the nervous titters of my aunts from their place on the floral couch under the bay window. I tune out the snide smiles I know must be growing around me. The other women in this room made their minds up about me a long time ago.

My first test happened when I was five, which is pretty standard. That's when gifts show up and can be assessed. Rebecca just loved that I only had one. It's harder to get in with only one gift. Instead of showing basic skills over a few magical skills, I had to show complete control over the only one I had.

That day I couldn't move even seconds back in time, let alone the two months they asked of me. I was always terrified that I'd get stuck in the past, unable to find my family again. And my simple failure was all Rebecca needed to gain control over the coven, something she'd been trying to do for years.

I try to focus back on the task at hand, despite my rapidly beating heart and the headache I'm growing from all the old lady perfume filling the too small room.

1950s, 1950s. She didn't even give me a specific year. I have a whole decade to go back to. I can do this.

Eyes closed, I focus on drawing out the strings of power from the well I built up earlier today. There's actually quite a bit there, I've never had so much during a test before. The tension in my chest starts to loosen and focusing becomes easier.

My magic surges out of me, purple tendrils forming in the air, creating a heavy wooden door a foot away. I open my eyes and reach for the cool knob. Maybe it will actually work this time. I catch a glimpse of Mom clasping her hands together and its all the urging I need to wrench it open.

A twisting purple tube shifts ahead of me, its colors morphing while bright spots like stars shoot across its expanse. Taking an unsteady step through the door, it disappears behind me. I'm left alone in the cosmic tunnel, heartbeat echoing in my ears as I sprint through the shifting semidarkness.

It's out of my hands now. The tunnel is made now, the magic has done its job and created its shift in time and I can't change it. If I've done everything right, this tunnel will end in the 1950s. If not, it doesn't matter where I end up.

The tunnel narrows the farther I run, my breath coming in short gasps. Muscles tightening as I leap through the emptiness expanding where the tunnel ends. Free falling through the air, I hold back a scream. I've done this before but every time is still terrifying. Mom says if I let myself practice more, it wouldn't scare me as much. She's probably right, but I try not to touch my magic more than once a month.

The world around me fades to black and then I'm blinking, near blinded by bright light. Holding my head as I sit up from the cool blades of long grass. The heady smell of charcoal fills the air. Vision clearing, I peer at the swing set across from me, rusty chains squeaking in the heavy breeze.

Standing, my shadow barely reaches past my feet. Sweat drips down my spine as the temperature climbs. Well, I guess this is better than showing up in the middle of winter.

I exhale, allowing my lungs to completely empty while I spin in a small circle. Nothing looks *too* different. No sign leaping out declaring the year.

Muscles aching, I trudge barefoot through the silky strands of long grass and onto the cracked sidewalk. I keep my gaze glued to the ground in front of me. The last thing I need is to develop tetanus while wandering through time.

The cuff of my jeans catches on a jagged piece of sidewalk sticking up, sending me sprawling to the uneven ground. I sit back and yank my burnt gold hair into a ponytail, peeling it away from where it's stuck to the side of my face. Staring at the house across the street, I check for anything familiar. Anything that could tell me when I am.

A wide porch wraps around the old farmhouse, the windows dark from the sun blaring against them. The driveway sits vacant. If a car would just drive by, I'd be able to tell immediately when I am.

Pressing my hands into my knees, I pull myself to my feet. Forcing one foot in front of the other, I make it another half a mile, nothing around me looking familiar. My chest feels light. I might have actually done it this time.

"Soph? Is that you?"

I lower my head, shoulders drooping. Turning, I recognize the sandy haired kid that sat behind me in homeroom last year.

"Hey," my voice stays even, foot kicking against the ground.

"I thought you were going out of town this summer. Did you change your mind?" he asks. He watches me with wide eyes, hands slung in his short's pockets.

"Just got back."

He nods. "Cool. See you around then."

Plodding past me, he heads up the front steps of a house to the left. He gives me a small wave before disappearing into the dark house.

So much for making it this time. My heart sinks in my chest as I realize I've only gone back in time three months. I went on a vacation with my mom this last summer, something I was excited enough about that I told anyone that would listen before school got out, a grand total of three people. That's what happens when you have no friends.

Mom and I had traveled up the coast together. Blissfully alone for one of the first times I can remember.

No point in looking for Rebecca, I summon anything left in my magic stores and form a door again. Tumbling through it, I stand before the women I'd just left. For them I've only been gone about two minutes, not the fifteen I lived through. Time is a funny thing.

Rebecca stands before me, the skin of her face stretched back from the tightness of her severe bun. She holds out her clipboard, my notes in full view as she places a red 'X' next to my test date.

"Another waste of time, Iole," she says with a sneer.

Mom wilts into the couch and I don't give her another look before vaulting up the creaky stairs and slamming the door to my room behind me, cheeks on fire.

⁓ɷ⁓

Hiding under the worn blankets, only the rich, tangy smell of Chinese food tickling my nose could draw me out of bed.

Muted voices travel up the stairs as I slip a threadbare bathrobe on, my toes curling as they make contact with the cold floor. The stairs creak with every step like an alarm.

Mom meets me in the living room and gives my face a pat. Heading into the kitchen, she goes back to her take-out box. I grab one of our mismatched plates and load up from the already mostly empty containers.

"You couldn't have waited for me?"

"Like one pig waits for another," Aunt Daphne says, red hair standing out in all directions as she hands me an egg roll.

Slumping into the worn stool, I dip the roll into a mixture of sweet and sour sauce and hot mustard before taking a big bite. The sauce drips down my chin, Mom wiping it away with a crumpled napkin while my aunts chatter around us.

"I'm just saying, a conversation about mashed potatoes isn't a good indicator of love," Aunt Tanis says with a sly smile to Aunt Agathe, whose thin shoulders stoop.

"You weren't there, how would you know?" she demands, stern face belying the submission in her shoulders.

Aunt Daphne flings a dumpling at Aunt Tanis. "It's not real love anyway, you know that. Let Agathe have her fun."

"It could be love," Mom says, eyes wistful as fried rice falls from her relaxed chopsticks.

Tuning them out, I dig through my leftovers. They have this conversation almost every month. Someone thinks they're in love, and someone else has to remind them that they aren't. I'm just glad they aren't talking about the coven meeting.

My foot taps against the faded yellow cabinet under the island. As far as I know, nothing in this house has been updated since the 1970s. The linoleum peeling up around the cabinets grows every year, and the upper cabinets have begun to sag. I shrug. They'll worry about it if it's a problem.

"How was school, Sophronia?" Mom asks, patting my knee to get my attention.

"Fine." I put my plate in the chipped sink. "Another day of busy work that doesn't make sense."

Mom laughs. "It's to help you learn. Repetition is good for you."

"As the last eleven years has proven."

"It's your last year, enjoy it, or at least try to enjoy it," she amends as I cross my arms.

"Soon you'll have to grow up and join the real world with us." Aunt Tanis's large chest hits the table as she leans over.

"I'm not sure I'd call where you're living the 'real world,'" Aunt Daphne teases. Aunt Tanis gives her a half-hearted punch on the shoulder.

Mom hands me the dirty spoons as she tosses the empty containers into the trash. "You'll be grown up soon enough."

I give her a small smile. Her eyes narrow with concern. Shrugging, I climb the metal spiral staircase to the third floor. Shrieking laugher travels up the stairs behind me, and my lips twitch.

The top floor is all mine, has been since Mom moved us back home over ten years ago. The pointed ceiling stretches to the sky, exposed wooden beams warm in the afternoon light coming through the round window. Sinking onto my bed, the metal frame squeaks a protest. Pictures of my aunts, Mom, and I line a silver mirror hung over fading floral wallpaper. The years of smiles mocking me as I sink further into the bed. I dig a finger into one of the larger holes in my quilt.

I meant it when I said school was fine. There's absolutely nothing wrong with it. Which is why I have no idea why the guidance counselor wants to see me. It's not like I get in fights or have bad grades. I'm perfectly normal as far as they're concerned.

So why does it matter to them if I have friends or not? I certainly don't care. If you can't love someone, how can you truly care about anyone? I learned pretty early in Kindergarten that even little kids can tell if you don't truly care about them.

Telling Ms. Brown I didn't care only made her more concerned. Apparently not caring about other people is a sign of being a sociopath.

But I can't tell her the truth. I can only imagine how she would've reacted, voice high and squeaky, brown eyes blinking more than normal as she tries to reason out my explanation.

I've been cursed. Well, not just me personally, it's my whole family actually. Starting with Grandma Damaris.

It's the curse's fault I'm not interested in making friends. With the curse firmly in place, I have no desire to even try to care about anyone else. I won't be like Mom and my aunts.

I can't be blamed for something that happened before I was born. I'm just doing my best to live with the consequences.

⚬⟋⟋⟍⟍⚬

Dragging my feet down the stairs the next morning, my body tenses in the uncharacteristic silence coming from the kitchen. Peering around the corner as I climb down the last stair, the room is empty. The clock above the sink blinks 6:00 a.m. at me. It's early enough that they could be in bed.

"Mom? Aunt Daphne? Aunt Tanis? Aunt Agathe?" my voice echoes through the empty space.

"They're not down here, darling." I start when Grandma Damaris speaks up from behind the leaning pantry cabinet.

"They're always here."

Grandma gives me a smile, her forehead just barely wrinkling with the movement, looking more like a woman in her forties than should be possible at her age. "Aunt Tanis had a dream last night."

"A dream?" I ask with parted lips, blue eyes wide.

Grandma slides onto one of the island stools, grabbing a dented box of cereal and pouring it into a clean bowl. Cereal pieces ping off the bowl, making my chest clench.

"She dreamed of *him*," Grandma says, braiding her rich brown hair down her back.

"The warlock?"

She grabs my hand, her olive skin a perfect match for mine. "He talked to her about the curse."

"So?" I pull my hand away with a grimace.

"He told her how to break it," Grandma says, her tone hushed as she leans closer to me, my reflection small in her dark brown eyes.

I grab the counter for support, digging my fingers into the hard wood. My skin tingles. "But you said we'd never break the curse."

"I didn't think it was possible. He told me he'd never forgive me," she says with a sigh. "I guess a few hundred life cycles were finally enough to thaw that man."

Grandma met the warlock a few thousand years ago. Life cycles are what we call an average lifespan. In another fifty years, my family will probably have to move, starting a new life cycle somewhere else.

"Do you really think it was him?"

She takes a bite of cereal, chewing as she thinks. "It doesn't really matter if it was him or not. Tanis always dreams true."

That's one of Aunt Tanis's gifts. Her dreams always come true, no matter how crazy they are. She dreamed we'd have a snowstorm once, not anything interesting most months, but this was in July. We stocked up water, ramen, and chocolate, all the necessities, and bunkered down. We were the only ones ready when the storm hit. Ten people died in that storm just from car accidents.

"So, what do we have to do?" I ask, getting the feeling back in my fingers as I rub my hands together. "How do we break the curse?"

"There's not going to be an us," she tells me, reaching out for my hand again before dropping it in her lap.

"What do you mean?"

She looks away, tapping her spoon against the counter. "Remember how I told you to practice your gift more? That practicing could help it to grow in strength?"

"Yes . . ."

"Well, your gift is the one we need," she says with a weak laugh.

"You've got to be kidding me."

With twelve other gifts in the house, there's never once been a time when mine was needed. My one little gift.

"To break the curse, you have to go back in time and save a man from dying."

After what happened earlier, I don't have anything to say. Grandma knows no amount of practice will make me ready for this task. She stares at me for a moment before continuing.

"He died when his ship sunk in the Atlantic in 1640."

CHAPTER TWO

◦⟋⟋⟋◦

My hands grow cold. "I don't understand, you've always told me I wasn't allowed to go to that time. And you know I can't do that. I couldn't even pass the test!"

Grandma's eyes narrow in sympathy, her brow forming the beginnings of wrinkles. "Wouldn't you do anything to break this curse?"

I would, and she knows it too. Any of us would. My grandma had laughed when she'd first been cursed; the idea of never knowing true love something only heard of in fairy tales. But as time had passed, she'd found it much less funny, especially as she'd watched each one of her daughters falling prey to its power.

"You know I would, Grandma." My chest deflates as she grabs my hand again.

"I told them we could count on you," she says, breathless as her face smooths out again. "I knew when you came to us with only this gift that it had to be for a reason."

Body tensing, I pull away but her grip on me is like a vice. Her nails dig into my skin even as she goes over my biggest shame.

"A witch with only one gift is such a rare thing. It had to be for a reason. Now look! You're the only one of us that can go back to break this curse!"

I'm not sure I have as much confidence as she does. Hundreds of years seems crazy to even think of traveling to when I couldn't do the apparently simple fifty Rebecca asked for. It's going to take days, maybe even weeks to try and build enough magic for that.

I sigh. "Are you sure this is a true dream? There've been a few of Aunt Tanis's dreams that have been . . . less than true."

Like the time she dreamed we would win the lottery. I still find old tickets in the back of drawers, part of our fruitless attempts to make it come true. Aunt Tanis reminds us it will eventually happen, there's just no telling when.

"She's not the only one that says it." Grandma's pert lips twitch into a side smile.

"Aunt Daphne?"

Grandma nods. "She wrote it three days ago."

Aunt Daphne is more of a typical oracle, glassy eyed and soft of speech, she tends to write down her prophecies. She's never seen the future though.

Grandma releases me, going back to her bowl of now soggy cereal, time taking the crunch out of it. "We weren't sure what to do with her prophesy about a man that could reverse the curse who died four hundred years ago until Tanis had her dream. Now it's confirmed. You must go back and save him."

"Do we have a name?" I pour a glass of lukewarm milk. "Do we know where he is? How about what he looks like?"

Grandma waves off my concerns. "We have your mother to figure that out."

Taking a sip to resist the urge to grind my teeth together, I point out the obvious. "Without a name, Mom can't find anyone."

"Fine, fine. Why're you so irritable this morning?" Grandma runs a hand through my burnt gold hair. "His name is Matthew. Your Mom was able to track him to a small settlement named Nantasket."

"Matthew." The name is clunky in my mouth as I stand up to rinse out my glass. "But why now? This guy's been dead for hundreds of years and now the warlock wants to save him?"

Grandma taps a long finger against her chin. "Obviously we don't know exactly what the reason was for the urgency now, but it's my guess that he only just found out about you."

"Me?"

"About your ability to travel through time. It's a very rare power. I'm confident that once he found out about what you can do, he made his move to save Matthew."

I knead my fingers into my forehead, feeling a headache building. "He must not have done his homework then. There's no way I can save that guy."

"You'll do fine. I know you will. Why don't you stay home today?" Grandma asks, joining me at the sink. "You'll need some time to get prepared. This is a big jump for you."

And to a time period I've been forbidden from jumping to. I don't bother adding this little objection, Grandma's too fixated now. She rocks back and forth on her heels, humming under her breath as she thinks.

"Tanis said if his life were saved, our curse would immediately be broken. Can you imagine?" she asks, eyes wistful as she stares through me.

Grandma has been living without being able to love a man for almost two thousand years, I'd get a little dreamy eyed too if it were me. Not that she didn't try. For hundreds of years she tried to find love despite the curse, my mother and aunts the evidence of her efforts. After Grandma's many failed attempts, my aunts decided not to try. Mom was the only one tempted by the fairytale of love. And so here I am, the only third generation Magissa daughter.

"After all this time," Grandma whispers, gaze turning to the hazed over window above the sink. "I stopped dreaming it would ever happen again."

Giving her a pat on the arm and a sympathetic smile, I drift through the swinging butler door and into the living room. The air in the whole front of the house is a swirl of potpourri and incense. Knickknacks line every available surface, some ancient and actually worth something, others garbage Aunt Tanis picked up off the street for no other reason than it "was pretty and shouldn't be thrown away."

I sink into the faded old floral couch facing the bay window, the cushions conforming to my body, and think over Grandma's words.

I could break the curse.

My one gift is the only one that can break it. The irony sends silent ripples of laughter through my body.

No matter what Grandma says, my one gift has been a disappointment since my birth seventeen years ago. Most witches are born with at least two gifts, ranging from reading palms to controlling the elements. Grandma's even so powerful that she can lend gifts to others. The magic shows up when the girl is a child, leading to her testing. The vary rare had new gifts develop through their teens. And then there was me.

But for the lucky ones with magic, the more gifts you had, the more power you had. With only one gift, I lowered my family's status in our community. I'm a walking example of how the curse has affected us the longer my family has suffered under it. At least that's the explanation my family came up with. Maybe love was needed for real magic to work and without it my family has been reduced to watered-down versions of what we could have been.

The front door bangs open and Aunt Agathe breezes into the room. A flush of cool air comes in with her, throwing her larger-than-life hair around her head.

"Hey, baby girl." She swoops me onto her lap as she climbs on the couch. We curl into the cushions, her lavender perfume lulling me to sleep. "How are you handling everything?"

"I don't even know where to begin." I rest my head against her shoulder.

She lays her head on mine. "Tanis is still upstairs talking about her dream. She and Daphne are going crazy with the possibilities of what this might mean."

"What exactly *did* she dream?"

Aunt Agathe sighs. "She dreamed of him, the warlock."

"The one Grandma was in love with?"

"The last man any Magissa woman loved," Aunt Agathe says in a low voice, arms tight around me. "Tanis said he looked just like your Grandma said he did, although he wasn't wearing the toga she remembered." Aunt Agathe laughs. "Still a handsome man though, tall, broad chest, dark eyes, bronzed skin. Tanis said she understands why your Grandma loved him."

"Why did he come to Aunt Tanis? Why not just come here and talk to Grandma himself?" My voice is muffled against Aunt Agathe's narrow chest as I burrow in deeper to her.

"I don't know," she says, running a hand through my hair, pulling out the braid I'd put in yesterday. "His son died, and he has no way to save him. I guess he's not a time traveler like our special girl."

"Ha."

She pulls me closer. "It's true. Anyway, in the dream he told her we had to save his son."

"How did he die?"

"Drowned when his boat went down crossing the Atlantic," she says with a shrug.

"That's not bad, I just need to make sure he doesn't get on the boat."

Aunt Agathe shakes her head. "It's not that simple. It never is."

The floorboards squeak behind us. Mom pads into the room. "You're going to be late for school, Sophronia."

Aunt Agathe squeezes my shoulder as I climb off her lap. "Grandma said I didn't have to go."

Walking around the couch, Mom ties her faded blue bathrobe over a bright pink flower nightgown. "I don't know if that's such a good idea."

"Grandma said I needed time to get ready for my trip."

Birds chirp in the front yard, and I watch them clinging to the old stone birdbath as Mom stares me down. Her dark brown hair lies in twisted tangles against her shoulders as she chews her bottom lip. "I haven't decided if you're going through time yet."

"It's not really your decision," Aunt Agathe says with a tsk.

Mom closes her eyes, mouth moving as she counts to ten. "It's not your decision, Agathe."

"This affects all of us," Aunt Agathe says in a harder tone than I've ever heard from her before.

"I'm not sending her on a death trip through time so you can love that boy you met!" Mom yells, covering her mouth with plump hands as she finishes.

"Why don't you go back upstairs?" Aunt Agathe says to me.

I leap from the couch as quick as I can to not detract from their argument. Scuttling up the stairs, their argument echoes through the bones of the house.

"You can't take this away from us because you're scared."

"You can't sacrifice my daughter because you're tired of living like this," Mom hisses.

"You're scared," Aunt Agathe presses as I linger in the cramped upstairs hallway. "You're scared of what it would be like to be free. To be just like everyone else. You're afraid of what it would be like to have a man that wouldn't run from you after a few months like Soph's father!"

"If I'm afraid of anything, it wouldn't be complications from stupid men, it would be losing my daughter to a witch hunt! And you promised never to bring John up again!"

I cringe. Bringing up my father is never a good idea. She still carries around an open wound from him, not that she would admit it.

"She's a smart girl, she's not going to get caught up in all that."

"She might not get a choice!"

"Eavesdropping?" Aunt Daphne asks from behind me.

Her narrow frame fits seamlessly behind one of the many dressers lining the hallway, only her out-of-this-world hair casting a distinct shadow from where she peers at me. I lean against the wall, peeling wallpaper pressed against my back.

"They're talking about me," I point out as she raises an eyebrow.

"Let's not worry about that now," she says, gripping me by the elbow as she directs me to my room. "Why don't you get ready for school. By the time you get back, they'll have sorted everything out."

Just another way of telling me I'm not welcome. No matter how old I get, I'm convinced they'll always think of me as a baby. It doesn't help that they're literally hundreds of years older than me. I'll never catch up. Maybe one day I'll move out on my own just like Mom did and make my own decisions without their committee. I just hope I won't have to wait until I'm already 200 years old for that. We live a long time, usually dying from accidents or actual intent instead of old age, but that doesn't mean I want to waste my years unnecessarily.

Without bothering to close the door behind me, I strip out of my pajamas and into the worn jeans and plain blue t-shirt I'd laid out last night. Hair thrown in a ponytail, I sling my backpack over my shoulder and march down the creaking stairs.

"Goodbye!" I call out to my still arguing family, Grandma now firmly ensconced between Mom and Aunt Agathe.

"Have a great day, dear," Mom says with a wave, her focus never leaving Aunt Agathe.

Stepping out onto the street, I begin the walk to school, wishing I'd grabbed my sweatshirt as a cool fall breeze brushes against my skin, leaving goosebumps in its wake. I trudge along, sneakers squeaking against the wet concrete. The road seems to stretch on forever the longer I walk, the old 18th century homes looming over the sidewalk on both sides, their once stately porches sunk into gap-toothed grins.

School isn't much better. The whole town is in need of a good facelift. The red brick of the high school looking more like a prison, complete with a fence around the football field. The ringing of first bell burns in my ears, letting me know that I'm late. I leap up the front steps, heading towards the office now that I've missed homeroom.

"Sophronia," the receptionist says with a catlike grin as I drop into one of the red cracked plastic chairs. She's been working here only the last year, hired after graduating high school in the next town over, and we're already on a first name basis. "Late again?"

"Yep." I adjust the straps on my bag.

Her gold bracelets clink against the counter as she leans over to stare at me. "What's your excuse this time?"

"Tardiness." I make sure to clearly enunciate every syllable.

Her crisp red lips dip into a frown. "And rudeness."

Shrugging, I stand and hold my hand out for my slip. She holds it out but doesn't let go right away, forcing us into a game of tug of war. "You'd better watch yourself, Sophronia, or you're going to end up a loser just like them."

It's not uncommon for people to be so open about their dislike of my family. We're weird. We don't go to events and there's been the occasional fire at the house from potions getting out of control, but we've never done anything to make us "losers." And today is not the day to mess with me.

"Only if I'm lucky," I say with a grin, walking out the door as she lets go of the slip.

I tuck into my favorite lunch spot, a concrete wall lining the small bit of grass the seniors have been granted, and pick at the fries on my plate. The chicken sandwich that came with them didn't even make it through the double doors.

A few football guys lay out in the grass, jackets thrown off to impress the girls sitting around the only table out here. The girls don't even look, too busy reapplying their lip gloss and complaining about the food.

"Hey," a guy with dark curly hair throws a fry, hitting me in the shoulder.

This gets the girls' attention.

"Don't bother with that one," Mary says, lips half pink as she stops mid-glossing. "She doesn't have time for anyone."

He gets up, slinking over to me. The 'V' of his shirt is pulled down just far enough to see the smooth planes of his chest. "I'm sure that's not true. You'd make time for me, wouldn't you?"

My smile feels like a grimace.

"See! She's been like this since third grade, so weird," Mary continues, crossing her arms over her underdeveloped chest. "Soph doesn't have friends, especially *boy* friends."

"Maybe she just hasn't been around the right kind of people. I'm Bobby," he says, extending his hand toward me. "I'm new here."

Mary huffs as he sits on the wall next to me. Spreading out his shoulders, he tilts his head back into the weak, fall, afternoon sunlight.

"I think we have English together," I comment, more to make Mary irritated than because I actually care about his company.

"With Ms. Guertin? Yeah, you sit behind Amy," he says, leaning closer to me.

The girls turn back to their lunch, Mary shooting me one last glare before picking up her ham sandwich. Our little charade over, I grab my tray to take back in.

"Don't leave so fast," he says, hand shooting out to grab me by the wrist. "Let's talk."

"I have to get going."

His hand stays firmly wrapped around my arm, keeping me from walking any further without losing my tray. He rubs his thumb against the inside of my wrist. "Then let me go with you."

I shake my head no. Mary tilts back to face me, a smile twitching on the glossless side of her mouth, waiting for me to prove her right.

"Fine," I say through clenched teeth.

Slinging his black leather jacket over his shoulder, he lets his hand trail down my waist as we walk back into the cafeteria. Whispers spring up around us, my cheeks burning as I catch my name being thrown around.

"Don't listen to them," Bobby says, leaning down to whisper in my ear.

"I don't care what they say." It's mostly true.

He chuckles, pulling me closer to him as I dump my tray. My heart pounds in my chest.

"Hey Bobby, taking on that frigid prude in your first week?" another guy in a football jersey asks, eyes roaming over me as I pull free from Bobby's embrace. "You ought to get a medal."

Bobby laughs with him, and I use the distraction to slip out the side door and up the stairs to the library. Their laughter echoes in my mind, the word "frigid" repeating over and over.

Hiding in a back corner with only dusty abandoned books to watch me, I press my face into my hands and breathe deep. My eyes burn, but no tears fall.

How could they? I'd have to actually have emotions about my classmates to feel any real pain. It's one of the great ironies of the curse, to feel the pain of missing something without ever being given the chance to feel what you're missing.

∿ℓℓℓℓ∾

Before heading back to class, I drift over to the line of ancient computers sitting dusty and forgotten against the back wall. Most kids have their own computers, so I guess the school never felt the need to update their turn of the century relics. Not my family though. I don't know if Mom would ever think buying a computer was a good use of our limited funds.

I push the power button and the monitor blinks blearily at me as it takes a full two minutes to wake up. Not that it matters. I don't have anywhere better to be.

I pull up a glacial internet page, my mind drifts over what I could possibly search. I have two names, one of a boy I'm sure is lost to time and one for a town. That's probably what I should go with.

The cursor mocks me as I type out "Nantasket" in blocky letters. The computer whirs as I push enter. Tingles of anxiety trickle up through my spine while I wait. Wait for what, I'm still not sure. I don't know what I'm hoping to accomplish here.

I was drawn to the computers as they whispered to me through the heavy air of the answers to forgotten questions. But now I'm not sure I'm ready to figure out what they know.

A Wikipedia page blinks into existence and I click on it before I can change my mind. The top of the page is filled with a black and white map of a town filling a small peninsula in Massachusetts. Scanning the first paragraph, I snort out a sigh. The town doesn't even exist anymore. I'm supposed to be saving the life of a boy who died from a town that's also been wiped away by time. That's pretty ironic.

Settled in 1622 by a group of Puritans, its name meant "low-tide" and it was known for its acres of sandy pools. The settlers fished, traded with the natives, and salvaged shipwrecks for their economy. I wonder if they profited off the ship that Matthew died on.

Thinking his name sends goosebumps up my arms. Clearing my search bar, I type in "Matthew Nantasket." Not surprisingly, it pulls up nothing. I go back, seeing a link advertising the list of original inhabitants of Nantasket. My focus narrows as I search for his name and come up empty. How unremarkable do you have to be for history to forget you even while it remembers others who surely lived around you?

I type in "people of Nantasket" and the search results come much quicker. There's drawings of the first settlers and a list of names I scan through looking for Matthew's. I scroll past a Mercy when the name Thomas pops up with an asterisk next to it. Intrigued, I lean forward and click on the name. A sketch of a man with dark hair and a broad brim hat comes up along with accounts of his disappearance during a witch trial. I press the back button quickly to get away from the chills that travel up my spine. Those trials are the biggest reason why this time period has been off limits.

The computer fritzes out as I slam my hands down on the keyboard. Whatever, there's nothing more to learn here.

No one asks me about my day as I throw open the front door and collapse onto the couch. Their voices drift in from the kitchen but contain none of the joviality from yesterday.

Picking at a stray thread coming out of a sagging pillow, I try not to think about what they've been talking about all day. Their tense voices imply the same topic that had them riled up only eight hours before.

"Everything okay?" Aunt Daphne asks, drifting down the stairs with a lighter than air gauze gown floating around her. "You seem different."

"Reading my aura is an unfair tactic." I pull the thread free, leaving a two-inch trail of frayed material behind. She can't read minds, but she can tell emotional states which at this point feels like an intrusion.

Aunt Daphne shrugs, settling in beside me and sending off a wave of lemon-scented cleaner. "It's your decision to make, no matter what they decide."

"Somehow I don't believe that."

She sniffs, crossing her arms with a serious expression that her frazzled red hair ruins. "You're the maker of your own destiny. If you don't want to save that boy, you don't have to."

"Wouldn't that be selfish?"

Aunt Daphne sighs. "I don't know if selfish is the right word, but we've lived a long time without love. I don't know how much of a difference it can make at this point. What I want is for *you* to experience it. I want to look into your eyes and see a star-crossed dreamer." She smooths my brassy hair from my face. "This curse aged you way too fast, my darling."

"I don't understand why I should even care about breaking the curse at this point. All love seems to do is ruin lives and encourage people to make bad decisions."

"Love is about more than just silly behavior, Soph, it's about finding joy in the people around you. The world is constantly changed by the power humans have of loving each other."

I sit up. "You think it's a power? Like a gift?"

"It's the closest thing to magic I've ever heard of."

Leaning back against the couch, I puzzle out her daydream. Aunt Daphne can be pretty flighty, but she seems so present right now. Too with it to be rambling.

"Oh, Sophronia! You're home!" Mom says with a gasp as she marches into the living room, blue bathrobe still in place despite the afternoon hour.

"That's what happens when it's three." I turn away from her to face the window.

Mom must silently ask Aunt Daphne what's going on because she shrugs, her shoulder knocking into me. "Is everything okay?"

"Are you still trying to plan my life for me?"

Mom releases a slow breath. "Whatever we decide, just know that I'm doing my best to protect you."

"You don't even know what you're protecting me from. Why are you so afraid of being able to feel true love?" I meet her gaze as I stand.

"Just because what I felt wasn't true love doesn't mean that it didn't feel real," she says, voice broken. "I can't imagine the pain you would go through if you experienced something like that with a person you really loved."

My father left us before I was born. Ordinarily I know enough to stay away from the subject of him, but today has made me hard. "How could you expect a man to stay with you when you never loved him?"

Her fingers tense into fists, soft tears roll down her plump cheeks.

"Iole," Aunt Daphne whispers, moving to grab her hand. Mom wrenches it away, her eyes boring into me.

"You're too young to understand what you're talking about," she snaps, walking into the kitchen with a straight back.

The cold bites at my arms. Relishing the pain, I keep to the winding path through the woods behind our house, the perfect place for me right now.

Mind spinning, I can't calm my racing heart. Mom thinks something bad will happen to me on this trip and my aunts are ready to send me anyway. Mom's the only one who doesn't want me to go. She's the only one saying what I want, and I had to go and bite her head off for it.

Falling to my knees, jeans soaking up the moist leaves, I draw in a ragged breath. This isn't what I want. None of this is what I want. I didn't ask for any of this.

If Grandma had just stayed with the warlock, none of this would have happened. My aunts would be happy. Mom would be happy. I'd be free to live like a normal teenager. Well, a normal teenage witch.

A normal witch who'd be allowed in the coven. I've dreamed of being a part of them, our long dark robes joining us in sisterhood. My family was in our local group, but that was before me. Before their magically stunted offspring made them an embarrassment.

Wind whips through the trees, raining dried leaves on my head. Blowing them off my face, I push to standing. Thinking of the coven clears my mind. If I did this, if I were able to travel back so far and change the course of history, would the coven consider me powerful enough to join them? Could I redeem my family's reputation while breaking the curse binding them?

A deeper whisper tells me I should do it for my mom. Despite the fact that she doesn't want me to do it at all, I know my father leaving still eats at her.

It's one of the things we're not supposed to talk about, stories I've only heard murmured behind closed doors.

Mom picked up and left in the middle of the night nineteen years ago. Just left without telling anyone. It really didn't go over well with the rest of my family. They've pretty much always lived together.

Through the centuries, it's been my grandma and her daughters. Then Mom was gone without so much as a hint of goodbye.

They didn't hear from her again for two years.

She'd thought it was true love. A love like the fairy tales stacked on dusty bookshelves lining her room. With the opportunity for love lying right in front of her despite the promises of an ancient warlock's curse, Mom felt she had to take it.

Following my father to Washington, she'd put the rest of her life behind her. They'd had a courthouse wedding and Mom had turned into the perfect 1950s wife. House clean, hair done, and an elaborate warm meal ready for my father every night. With no example of how to be a wife from her mother, she'd copied things she'd seen on tv.

But copying wasn't enough.

I've often thought it was a cruel twist of the curse to make her capable of having something akin to a crush when she had no ability to follow through. Eventually, it became too hard. Too hard to cook and clean and give up her magic for surface level feelings. And, given enough time, even a stupid man knows when a woman doesn't love him.

So he did to her what only two years earlier Mom had done to her family. Left.

A week later Mom learned she was pregnant.

Even so, she waited. She stayed in their mildew riddled apartment, waiting for him to come back.

She gave birth to me alone in a hospital. Seeing me convinced her it was time to go home. So she gave up on my father coming back and moved back in with her family. She's never professed to be in love again.

Mom showed up on the porch with a tear-streaked face and an infant in her shaking arms. Grandma took me right away, ushering Mom into the house. They haven't asked Mom a lot about my father, worried perhaps that they would scare her away again. But even so, what Mom has shared pushes me toward this impossible journey.

Sighing, I trudge the mile back down the now dark path and toward the backdoor. A single low-watt bulb droops over the door leading off the kitchen, its pale light promising the forgiveness waiting for me inside.

My footsteps on the porch set off a cacophony of creaking, so it's not surprising when the door swings open before I can reach the handle.

"Soph, baby!" Aunt Agathe says, blue eyes shining in the weak light as she grips my hand and pulls me into her embrace. "You shouldn't leave like that. We had no idea where you were."

"I didn't think you guys would care." My words are muffled as she presses me into her chest.

She runs a hand down my back. "It wouldn't matter what circumstances you left in, we'll always care."

Aunt Agathe releases me, and I peel off my muddy sneakers and place them by the door.

"What's everyone doing?"

"We've been worried about you." She doesn't meet my gaze. "And Tanis has been busy sewing you new clothes."

"Clothes?"

"Well, you know, petticoats and shifts," Aunt Agathe says as she shifts from foot to foot. "She thought we should be ready for you to go, if you chose to do that. Tanis thinks you'll need everything to be hand stitched and authentic."

"Doesn't that seem like overkill for a rescue mission?" I ask with an uneasy laugh.

She wrings her slim hands together. "You don't understand, we've already lived through this, well, everyone but your mother. It was a dangerous time, we spent much of it in hiding. You don't want to have anything on you that would make them think you're a witch."

"It's not like I'll have a sign around my neck proclaiming 'witch!' or anything." The hair on the back of my neck rises.

"You'll have to go there to understand," she says, voice becoming weaker. "It doesn't take much of anything for them to say you're a witch."

Settling onto the island stool, I grab a granola bar out of the old wooden bowl on the counter. "Well, if I decide to go, which is a big *if*, and there's any trouble, I can just use my gift."

"You'd think that," Aunt Agathe says. "But in that moment, you might not have the strength. We have no idea how long it will take for your magic to build back up again after such a big trip."

Her gaze looks past me, going hollow with old memories. The wrapper crinkles as I throw it away. I want to be as far away from Aunt Agathe and her memories as possible.

The living room lies still in the moonlight slipping in past thin curtains. Stepping onto the metal stair, Grandma startles me. "Come here, Soph."

Hand pressed against the rock growing in my chest, I turn around. Sitting in an antique rocking chair in the corner, she could easily be mistaken for a ghost.

She smiles, teeth gleaming in the faint light. "Your mother has talked to you about the pain of love, but she only knows what I've told her."

I sigh. Everyone has some kind of lecture for me today.

"Love is what makes life worth living," she whispers. "Without it, you'll be just as empty as the rest of us. Beautiful shells without the passion to be anything more. Give yourself a chance, darling. Make the choice to break this curse and learn how to live."

The idea of love has flitted across my mind many times throughout my life, but it's never seemed important. Not for me at least. But is Grandma right? Have I been hiding from really living?

"I'll think about it Grandma," I say, already sprinting up the stairs.

CHAPTER THREE

Mom climbs into bed with me as soft morning light crests the windowsill, her warm soft presence jolting me from time traveling nightmares. Wrapping her arms around me, I nestle into her embrace.

"I'm not going to make this decision for you," she whispers into my hair. "You're almost a woman now, you can make this choice yourself."

"Is it really as dangerous as they say?"

She pulls me closer, my scalp moist under her breath. "I didn't live through it, but the terror of what my family went through all those years ago is something they still carry to this day. They constantly had to hide, to move around and pretend like they were something else just to avoid all those crazy witch hunters. They killed innocent people, can you imagine what they would have done with a real witch? Fear like that shouldn't be taken lightly."

"Neither should the ability to break a centuries old curse."

Mom sighs. "That's true."

I snuggle deeper into her, watching the pale blush of sunrise crawl across the room. "I don't know what to do."

"I don't know what to do either." She tucks the quilt over my shoulders. "Your aunts and Grandma want you to do it, but I'm not sure it's what's best for us."

"We do just fine without men," I grumble.

"They have their place."

"Far away from us."

For as long as I've been alive there's never been a man living in the house. Even when I was a baby and we didn't live in the big house, there wasn't anyone else around. We do just fine without them.

"Where's Aunt Agathe?" I ask, wishing for her comfort.

Mom hesitates.

"What happened?"

"She met up with that boy again last night and he . . ."

"Couldn't deal with the curse," I finish for her.

Mom's shoulder's droop. "She's been crying all morning."

The door to my room slams open, Aunt Tanis bursting through. "I think we're almost ready!" Her plump body quivers with excitement, a pale white cloth clenched in her tiny fist.

"*You* are ready, Tanis," Mom says, disentangling herself from the sheets.

Aunt Tanis waves her away, leaping onto the bed. She holds out the cloth, running a hand reverently over the material. "This shift would pass any inspection. I sewed it last night myself."

Tiny even stitches run down the dress, sleeves breaking up the plain material.

"What am I supposed to do with this?" I ask, not taking the shift even as she thrusts it at me.

"It's like your underwear," Aunt Tanis says, brown eyes sparkling. "You put this on and then petticoats go over it."

"That's not what she's asking, Tanis." Mom frowns as she pulls the shift out of Aunt Tanis's hands. "You're making assumptions about what she wants."

"Everyone is making assumptions about what I want, and I—"

Aunt Tanis grabs my face, my reflection small in her eyes. "You want to live. I know that. But I also know—"

"Stop, just stop," Mom says, breaking our connection before Aunt Tanis can use her powers to read my mind. "We don't use our gifts on each other."

Aunt Tanis scrambles off the bed, smoothing down her tank top where it's rolled up over her curves. "I'm helping her see what she wants."

"She can make up her mind without you reading it." Mom pushes Aunt Tanis out the door.

"And I can make up my mind without you telling me what it is!"

Throwing myself back under the covers, the door clicks into place, the mattress sinking under Mom's weight. She doesn't say anything, the chirping of birds disturbing our silence.

My body trembles, tears falling down my cheeks. "I have to go, don't I."

"I told you, I'll never make you do it," Mom says, resting a hand on my back.

"But they'll never forgive me if I don't."

Mom's silence speaks volumes.

"What do I need to know?" I sigh, thinking of Aunt Agathe as I pull the quilt away from my face.

⁓ഄഄ⁓

The next few hours are a flurry of documents, musty books, and dress fittings. Aunt Tanis's gift enhanced fingers sewed up an assortment of dresses, all looking like they came out of a pilgrim village. Shades of black, brown, and pale white lay spread across the bed, their rough material standing out against the soft pink quilt. Underneath the layers of fabric lies what feels like a million ancient maps, each one depicting the relative area where I'll be going. It's our hope that having some idea of the land will keep me from landing in the middle of the ocean.

"Remember," Aunt Agathe says for what seems like the millionth time already today. "They didn't say 'hello' or 'goodbye' or any of the lazy things we say now. Remember 'good morrow' and 'fare thee well.'" She wrings her hands together. "I wish there was more time to go over all of this, but we have to move fast in case the warlock changes his mind."

I nod even as her instructions go over my head. There's too much. Too much that they expect me to remember. I should have paid more attention in school.

"Do you have any questions?" Mom asks, face etched in concern.

"We've covered etiquette, dress, my position as a woman, what else could there be?" I ask with a wry smile. All the things they never bothered to teach me before. Why should they? I've never traveled back farther than a year or two. Maybe if they had started earlier, there'd be more chance of any of this sticking.

Her mouth pulls tighter. "This isn't a game, Sophronia."

"I know."

Laying on the bed, I pull up the thick stockings Aunt Tanis finished only minutes ago. Nothing like nylons, my feet begin to sweat in their wool prison. Wiggling my toes, I pretend I'm not being suffocated by period pieces.

"You're a smart girl," Mom says, gripping my hand like a vice. "But they'll be looking for you."

"For me?" I give a startled laugh.

She clenches my hand tighter, my fingertips turning purple. "Not you specifically, but witches like you."

"I won't be in any danger." My voice turns hard. "I only have one gift, remember?"

"One is more than enough. Plenty of people died having none at all."

The thought is sobering. We studied early American history in school, which included a brief mention of witch trials, but I didn't take it seriously. I never thought I'd be trying to go back that far. When my family found my gift, the first thing Grandma made me do was promise I would avoid early America. Why learn more about a time I'd never see? The layers of heavy material press against my chest, breathing becomes difficult as my mind conjures up old drawings of accused witches being pressed to death.

"I want you to promise me that you won't take any unnecessary risks." She tucks a strand of burnt gold hair behind my ear.

"Don't worry, I'm not going to risk my neck for some boy. I'm not doing this for me." I stare past Mom to where my aunts crowd in the doorway. Each face holds a hope in me that I'm not prepared for.

"Out of my way!" Grandma scatters them like a flock of birds.

Sinking into the bed next to me, she takes my other hand, a half-rolled stocking slipping down my leg. Her tear glossed eyes peer into my face, the wrinkles lining her forehead are deeper than I've ever seen them before.

"This is the right thing to do," she says in a soft whisper, leaning closer so our foreheads touch.

"Did Tanis dream it?" Mom bites out, staring at where she lingers in the hall.

"I don't need Tanis to dream it to know it's true," Grandma says.

"I'll get out at the first sign of trouble," I tell Mom, still looking at Grandma.

"Just don't forget to take that boy with you," Aunt Daphne calls out, earning a swift glare from Mom.

Grandma releases me and I pull my hand from Mom's grip to yank my stocking up. Standing, I smooth out the long length of material swirling around my legs. Mom grabs the laces of my petticoat, tugging them tight. My reflection in the mirror watches me as she accentuates my slim waist. Twisting my hair into a bun, she hides my gold locks under a plain white coif.

"You look perfect," Aunt Agathe breathes into the silence sitting heavy in the room.

"I look like a nun."

"I don't think nuns would appreciate that little thought," Aunt Daphne chides with a grin.

"I think it's a compliment," Aunt Agathe laughs.

"You look so . . ." Grandma flounders for the right word, waving her hands in the air as she thinks. "Greek."

I laugh. "I don't think there's much I can do about that, you know, considering my genes are almost entirely ancient Greek."

"Almost," Mom says, face closing in on itself. As the last of Grandma's children, she was born hundreds of years after them, her father less than ancient by their standards. Mine decidedly less so.

"So, you're going to find Matthew." Aunt Tanis steps over Aunt Daphne where she's sat her narrow frame inside the room. "Find him and don't let him drown, then we'll be free!"

"No pressure," I say with a strained laugh.

"You'll do fine." Grandma pats my knee with a firm hand.

The room is warmer with my whole family crowded inside it, even the pale yellow of my nightstand lightbulb feels cozier. Aunt Agathe leans against the bed frame with Aunt Tanis hovering beside her. They're my whole world.

"Do I have to go?" I know I sound like a child, but I feel a little like one.

Fear creeps in at the thought of leaving all of this behind. I've learned to leave love behind and focus on my family. It's been such a flip to take that back and say love is worth fighting for. Plus, my aunts aren't saying it, but there's true danger in going back. And that's if I can get there.

Aunt Agathe's eyes narrow in sympathy. "You'll be fine, and we'll be right here waiting for you."

"If everything goes well, it'll feel like you never left." Aunt Tanis smiles. "For us at least."

"Consider it your first adventure as a woman," Grandma says, her smooth cheeks rosy. "Enjoy being free of us, if only for a little bit."

"But I never wanted to be free of you," I whisper.

Mom scoops me up onto her lap, pressing my face to her chest. "See what you're doing to her? She doesn't want to go!"

"There are many things we have to do that we don't want to. This is just the first for her," Grandma scolds Mom with kindness in her voice. "Everybody out. Let her sleep before she leaves."

"Do I have to keep all this on?" I gesture at the get up they just finished putting on me.

"It'll be good for you." Grandma looks over me one last time. "It'll help get you used to wearing it all the time and then you'll be ready to go first thing in the morning."

Shuffling footsteps echo down the hallway before my door clicks closed. Mom breathes into my hair, running her hand up and down my back in gentle circles. Staying close to her, I feel like a child again. With what lies before me, I wish the feeling were true.

Kissing me on the temple, Mom lifts me off her lap and onto the bed. Standing, she takes a breath to steady herself. "I'll see you in the morning, okay? Don't run off before saying goodbye."

"I won't."

She leaves without looking back, and the room is cold with my family gone. Even with the layers of heavy wool, goosebumps break out across my arms. Legs tangling in my skirts, I scramble into bed and pull the quilt over me, turning off the light.

The moon is dark tonight, no stars keep me company. The dark stillness lies on my chest like a stone.

Laying on my back, staring at the dark outlines of cracks on the ceiling, I try not to think about where I'll be sleeping tomorrow night. Will I be back safe in my bed? Or will I be stuck helping some annoying boy who doesn't know enough to save his own life. Did he never learn to swim? I find that hard to believe. It doesn't matter what the rules are, boys always find ways to break them.

I read somewhere that if you lay without moving for fifteen minutes, you're guaranteed to fall asleep, but it feels like hours pass and I'm still wide awake. My heart beats quick in my chest, and I can count its pulses pressing against my temple.

My stomach sits like a stone when I get up to use the bathroom, something I haven't had to do in the middle of the night since I was a small child. A granola bar sits on my nightstand, probably one of my aunt's thoughtful gifts. My stomach rumbles but I know I can't eat right now. Instead, I grab it and shove it into the bag I'm going to take with me. Just in case.

The light in Grandma's room is still on, the line of bright light filling the cracks between the door and the frame. Whispers flit around the silence, and I sneak close to her door, making sure to avoid the wood board directly in front of her room, that one's had an awful squeak for as long as I can remember.

"—comes back," Mom's voice slips through the crack, and I freeze.

"That's not going to happen," Grandma snaps.

"You don't know that. You lived then, you told me you were too afraid to leave your home for years!"

"There's no other way," Grandma says. "And Soph's not strong enough to take anyone with her. She'll have to do this alone."

"I can't lose her." A sob rips from Mom's throat. "She's all I have to live for."

"Hush yourself," Grandma snaps. "It's another effect of this curse. When family is all you can love, you form unhealthy attachments. Let her go, just like I had to let you go."

"But I was never in any danger."

"Not that you could see."

Leaning forward, the board under my foot groans. The whispers stop, and my blood stills.

"She'll be okay," Grandma says, voice softer.

On light feet, I sprint back to my bed, bladder forgotten.

CHAPTER FOUR

ccleep

Aches from sleeping twisted up fill my body as I lean forward in bed. The ratty quilt falls from my shoulders, and the autumn chill seeps into my bones.

"Good morning, baby," Mom says, jolting me awake. Uncurling from the wooden rocker in the corner of my room, she slinks into the bed next to me. "Are you ready for today?"

The chill sinks deeper into me, goosebumps pricking up along my arm. Mom lifts the blanket up over my shoulders, rubbing my arms in brusque movements.

"How did you sleep? I was thinking I could make you up something for breakfast," she whispers in my ear, warm breath tickling my skin.

"I'm ready to go," I lie, pulling out of her arms, feet thumping to the floor.

"Oh good, you're up!" Aunt Tanis comes into the room with an armful of clothes. "I wanted to go over wardrobe one more time before you left. Just in case."

"In case of what?" Mom asks, a frown deepening the lines in her face.

Aunt Tanis shrugs as the rest of my family shuffles in, all of them looking about as well rested as I do. Grandma pulls on a robe as she yawns, eyes sparkling even as the bags under her eyes cry out for sleep. "Let's get moving, it's a big day!"

Whipping the blankets back, my stockings protect me from the worst of the frosty morning's bite. Aunt Tanis pulls me out of bed. Mom practically growls at her as she smooths down my shift and petticoat, plucking away the stray, long blonde strands of hair. Mom lets my hair down from the bun we put it in the night before, brushing it out with smooth strokes before pinning it back in place, tugging my coif back over my hair.

"You look beautiful," Grandma says, hands folded across her chest as she surveys her children's work.

"And she's done!" Aunt Tanis exclaims, eyes glazed.

"Say your goodbyes and get downstairs," Grandma says, stepping in before Mom's clenched fist can make contact with Aunt Tanis.

Engulfed in hugs, they whisper their encouragements to me. Aunt Agathe gives me one last squeeze, her eyes red rimmed as she follows her sisters through the hall. Their whispers drift into the room, ghosts of excitement staying with us.

"You too, Iole." Grandma's voice is quiet as Mom links her arm through mine. Her eyes plead with Grandma as tears fall down her cheeks, but Grandma shakes her head.

"I love you, baby girl," Mom whispers to me, body shaking as she holds me tight against her chest. "I will see you again."

"I love you too, Mom," I whisper back, body frozen in place as she follows her sisters out the door.

The floor creaks under Grandma's weight as she steps forward to embrace me, my body flinching at the unexpected noise. She scoops me in her arms, holding me like she hasn't since I was a small girl. My shoulders stay rigid, my body wound tight, ready to spring away. She lets her hand trail up and down my back, nails applying the faintest amount of pressure into my spine.

"You'll be fine," she says into my hair. "And when you come back, the world will be very different from what it is now."

"I doubt something as small as love will drastically change the world," I say with an uneasy laugh.

Grandma leans back, holding my face in her slim hand. "That's because you've never felt the power of true love."

Pulling back, I plaster on a fake smile, the one I usually use to placate my aunts when they tell me fairytales. "Any advice for me?"

"Don't use your power around anyone," she says, face sobering. "Not even that boy. Tell no one what you can do."

"I don't think that will be a problem," I tell her laughing even as my heart beats so hard I fear it might explode.

"I'm giving you the power of tongues."

"What on earth would I need that for? The majority of settlers that came to this area were *English*."

Grandma sighs. "Do you remember your Shakespeare unit?"

"What about it?"

"How good was your understanding?"

She knows very well I got a D on that paper.

"While they may not be talking exactly like in Shakespeare, Colonial English will be different. You should be prepared." She lifts her hands, green fire flickering between her fingers. "Stand still and say thank you."

Grandma raises her hands and her power drifts over me like a chill mist, seeping into my pores as I mumble a quiet, "thank you."

"It's time to go then." A small smile twitches at the corner of her lips. "Be brave, my love."

Nodding, I sling the bag Aunt Tanis threw my extra clothes in over my shoulder, and step away into the half circle of the bay window. Grandma smiles, giving me a nod.

Closing my eyes, I try to imagine where I'm going. 1640s New England. In theory, it won't be that different from where I live now. New England hasn't changed that much, right? It's still just trees and people that tend to be a little more closed off. Maybe just a little less people in the 1600s.

Breathing deep, numb fingers shaking, I dig deep into my mental power well. Darkness fills my mind. My body tenses, pressure flowing through me like water down the drain.

"I love you," Grandma whispers.

The door materializes and I hold my breath as my arms shake. Just a few days ago I couldn't even make it to 1950 and now I'm trying to travel hundreds of years further. What makes my family think I can do this?

Shoulders tense, I step through the door and it feels like my body condenses, folding into itself as I wink out of time. Opening my eyes, swirling cosmos fills my view. My body swirls through a twisting mass of violet stars as I'm dragged through pink and purple clouds. Pain blooms in my chest as my body picks up more speed.

Mom said he's in the Nantasket colony. The name repeats in my mind, over and over as my body twists and contorts through narrowing gaps between hardening mists. Flying through a spiral, I spin around and around until I have to close my eyes to keep from getting sick.

I close my eyes, cutting off the last of the light, and plunge into complete darkness. Squeezing even tighter, it's like I'm going through a narrowing funnel before finally popping out the other side.

My body slams into the ground, knocking the wind out of me. I roll over gasping. Cracking an eye open, the sky swirls around before me. Clouds mix in the light blue sky, framed by the rustling leaves in tall maple trees.

Rolling onto all fours, legs tangled in the long layers of my skirts, I dry heave into the grass. My stomach clenches. Dark spots pulse in and out of my vision until I give into the darkness, my head hitting the ground hard enough to finish what the time travel started.

~ell)))s~

Children yell back and forth to each other, the sound of their running feet pound into my head. Turning over, I half expect to be staring at the same rusty swing set I traveled to before.

A group of boys stand several yards away, their knee length pants and short jackets over lace collared blouses giving me a good clue I'm not in the 2000s anymore. They laugh amongst themselves, backs turned towards me. I crawl for the tree line, my fingers digging deep in the soil to drag myself out of immediate view. I have no idea what these people would do to me if they found me here, and I have zero interest in finding out.

Beads of sweat grow along my temples. I've gone back pretty far. Not as far as I need to be based on the boy's clothes, but still farther than I've ever been before. Excitement and fear war inside me. Gripping my knees to my chest, my knuckles go white. I can't believe I'm really doing this. It's really and truly happening. If only the coven could see me now.

Closing my eyes, I focus on breathing. In and out. In and out. Everything's going to be okay. I'm just lost in another time without any of my family. Not a big deal, not a big deal.

I focus on my power stores, drawing on the well deep within my core. It fizzles with my attention. Without the power to leave, I don't know what I'm going to do.

Closing my eyes, I focus harder, pressing against the walls of my magic until something starts to trickle in. It's nothing much now, but with a little rest it could become enough to keep jumping back.

Blocking out the mental images of my family waiting for me, their excited voices discussing what they'll do when the curse is broken, I dig around in my spare clothes bag. Surely one of them planned for the possibility of me not ending up in the right "when." Someone must have doubted my abilities.

My fingers flick against the plastic casing of a cheese stick. Sighing, I pull it free from the bag, ripping open the plastic. I don't even bother pulling the strings off, taking big bites out of it and leaving tooth impressions in the soft cheese.

Shoulders drooping, I finish my snack and check my power stores again. Eating something should have helped replenish the amount of gift I already used. My little trickle of magic grows into more of a river, filling in my core.

Biting my lip, I clamp down on the scream that threatens to explode out of me. The amount of magic it took to get here leaves no mystery to how much more I'll need to make it back.

Rest. I just need rest. Maybe a good nap will be enough. Tears burn in my eyes, but I refuse to let them fall. Only having one gift has made me stronger, at least emotionally. At least that's what I tell myself.

Curling in a ball, my clothing tangling in the tree roots and dead leaves, I clench my eyes closed and breathe. Fear makes a tight knot in my throat as I consider the possibility that I could really be stuck here. I'm not prepared for that scenario, not that I'm particularly prepared for any of it. I didn't really think it would work. But here I am, lost in time with a magic reserve that doesn't feel like enough.

A leather ball rolls across the lawn, thudding against my sprawled leg. With wide eyes, I watch the boys run after it. They stumble into each other. A chill runs down my spine. There's no way they won't spot me.

It doesn't matter what condition I'm in, I don't have time to rest. I have to get out of here. Now.

Concentration fragmented, the door I conjured flickers in and out of existence. It's weak, but I'm just glad it came at all after my last big trip.

With clammy hands, I grip the knob before it can flicker out again and tumble through it into the cosmos. Stars pass by me, flashing in and out as I spin through the tunnel. Blinking at the endless tunnel, everything goes black.

～⁂～

I tumble through memories like Alice falling into Wonderland. Darkness surrounds me with glimpses into my life on either side.

On the right I lean against the door to Mom's room, listening to her sob on the other side. The floorboards creak behind me, and I glance back to see Aunt Tanis standing in the shadows. She gives me a sad smile and mouths "the curse" at me. Glancing to the left as I continue to fall, I watch myself sitting on the faded front room couch. Aunt Daphne plods up the front steps, shoulders drooping as a blue Honda Civic pulls out of the driveway. Her lips quirk in a weak smile as I catch her gaze, her chin quivering.

"Don't worry, dear, just another failed date."

My body spins and I can't get a good look at any of the memories I pass. Even so, they fill the space around me, spiraling upwards into nothing. Suppressed sobs, gasping cries, and full-on yelling suffocate me as I fall further into memories. Centuries of failed relationships coming to a head as I attempt to travel into the past.

Fisted hands clench my ears as I squeeze my eyes shut. I don't need to see this anymore.

Tears run down my cheeks. The light behind my eyes fade and the voices go silent. Consciousness dims, my thoughts jumbling together. But I have one clear thought before it all goes black.

I will break this curse.

⁓ℰℰℰ⁓

"Hello?"

The deep voice echoes in the aching hollow of my head. I groan as I blink awake. Turning to the side, shiny black shoes gleam up at me.

"Ma'am?"

"What year is it?" I gasp, pressing the heel of my hand to my forehead as I sit up.

"The year of our Lord 1640."

"Oh, thank goodness." My stomach heaves and I turn, throwing up in the grass.

The shoes back away in quick steps, staying on the edge of my vision as I wipe my mouth on the back of my hand and try to stand. I've landed in a small clearing. The tree line begins only a few feet from where I stand. Oak and maple trees are lush and green despite the coming fall. Leaning against the trunk of the closest tree, I turn to face the man with me.

He wears short black pants, ending at the knee where his woolen socks meet. A long cream linen shirt is tucked into his pants, a wide brim hat shading his eyes. His broad shoulders shift as I stare at him. "Are you ill?"

I laugh, the puddle of vomit at my feet should be answer enough. "I'll be okay."

"You are a long way from home." He turns to stare into the woods behind me. "It is far from the settlement for a woman."

"Of course, that's all that would matter," I mutter. "Too far away for a woman."

"Pardon me?" he asks, taking off his hat. Blue eyes sparkle in the strong afternoon light, a line of brown stubble coats his jaw. He peers down at me.

"Could you take me to Nantasket?"

He frowns.

"I'm supposed to be meeting someone there." Never mind the fact that he doesn't know to be expecting me at all.

"Nantasket is just over the hill through the woods here. Who are you looking for?"

"Matthew?" I ask with a wince, realizing I never learned his last name.

He rubs his square jaw, fingers scrapping through stubble. His concentration on my face never wavers. With a wave, he gestures for me to follow him, his long steps making me hustle to keep up.

The thin line of a trail winds through the trees, more an animal path than a human one. We walk for a good ten minutes in silence, only the movement of chipmunks through the ground cover breaking up the sound of our footsteps.

"Why were you in the woods?" I ask, realizing just how far away from the settlement I ended up.

He glances back at me with narrowed eyes, shoulders tense through the thin material of his shirt. "I like to come out here to think."

"Oh." I roll my eyes and purse my lips. It's not like he was looking at me anyway.

"This is not even close to the paths to other settlements," he says without inflection.

My knees go weak. "I got a bit turned around. I've never been this way before."

"Few have." His voice is quiet as he pushes aside a low hanging maple branch.

"It's lucky for me that you showed up," I tell him, fluttering my lashes when he turns to look at me. My inner self dies a little at the obvious flirting, but I need this guy distracted from my less than orthodox arrival before we get to Nantasket. "I could have died out here."

"Probably." He walks faster now.

So much for my womanly wiles. Hiking up my dress, I pick up the pace, the leather soles of my laced-up boots not meant for climbing over roots and uneven ground. Stumbling, I breath out a curse as my knees hit the rocky earth. His footsteps clomp over to me, a calloused hand outstretched to help me off the ground.

"I have never heard a woman talk like that before." His head tilts to the side as he hefts me up.

"I'm probably not like any other woman you've met before."

His eyes peer into mine, and I straighten my shoulders in his reflection. "I think you are right about that."

"Who are you?" I ask when he doesn't let go of my hand. His brow furrows, creases lining his youthful face. Thrusting my hand away, he continues his march through the trees.

"Thomas Bradley."

The name is mildly recognizable. I think it was on the list of original settlers, but I didn't pay enough attention for any new name to stick. Matthew's is the only name I need to care about.

A line of sweat drips down my spine, the many layers Aunt Tanis insisted on making me overheat. Puffing, I'm sure my face is red from what shouldn't even be considered exertion. The toe of my boot catches on another root, and the palms of my hands scrap against the rough ground as I attempt to keep my face from slamming into the dirt.

"Do you need assistance?" Thomas asks, lips twisted.

"No, thank you." My red, smarting palms sting as I shove them behind me, rubbing them against my apron.

His blue eyes narrow as he stares at me. Reaching out, my breath stills in my chest as he grabs my earlobe, squeezing it between his thumb and forefinger.

"Where have you come from?" he asks, pressing his finger against the back of my stud earring.

A million curse words fly around my brain. Of course, no one thought to check if my jewelry was time appropriate. I've been wearing the same pair of silver studs for months, and never would've thought twice about them if not for Thomas.

"England?" I gasp.

"Where in England?"

The mental cursing intensifies. I don't know anything about England, aside from it being where many of our colonists came from. Of course Thomas would know about England, he's probably from there.

"Just a small town, I'm sure you've never heard of it."

"You might be surprised." He gives me a feline smile. My stomach drops. He's the cat and I'm the mouse.

My jaw hangs open as my mind works, wondering if I should lie. "Thomas?"

He whips around to the newcomer, my heart beating a mile a minute as my breath slowly returns.

"I didn't realize you'd gone out." The woman steps around Thomas, eyes taking me in as she turns back to him. The laces of her dress strain under her plump curves, her fingers curled around a wooden spoon.

"I went for a walk." Thomas keeps his voice low as he stares at the ground.

"You cannot leave without telling anyone. It's not safe out here." She's unrelenting, even as she has to tilt her head up to see his face.

He straightens up. "That's why I leave, to make sure we are safe."

"Is that necessary considering-"

"We have a new guest for our settlement." Thomas grabs me by the arm and shoves me toward her, cutting off whatever this woman was going to say.

"Good marrow?" That's what I'm supposed to say, right? I give an awkward wave as her gaze sweeps me up and down.

"This needs to be discussed," she says to Thomas, ignoring me completely.

Pushing me forward, he guides us around her bulk and back onto the trail. "This is not the right time, sister. I have to get this woman to Matthew."

Glancing around Thomas, I catch the end of the dagger eyes she sends at him before turning around to face the path again. The heat of her anger almost makes me miss being alone with Thomas, as fun as that was.

"Matthew said nothing about a guest coming when we saw him at church," she calls behind us.

"Maybe he was embarrassed." Thomas shrugs, his lips quirking as he looks at me.

"It's a surprise." I decide to tell the truth, as much as they need to know of it. They'll see him shocked at my arrival anyway.

Thomas's sister is quiet, her heavy steps plodding along at an even pace. His fingers grip my arm tight, even the thick wool of my shift not enough padding to protect me from the bruising pressure. His eyes sweep the forest in front of us as it thins. Wooden houses come into view, their plain walls broken up by evenly spaced openings where windows should be. They sit opposite each other in a long row and at the end create a circle looking like a modern-day cul-de-sac. Wisps of smoke come out of the sturdy chimneys as the sun tilts closer to night, sending the smell of burning wood into every pore. It's like I've found myself wandering through the Plymouth village in Massachusetts, everything rustic and serving a purpose.

A few men are still out, their wide brim hats shading their faces in the fading light as they bring in supplies through the open doorways full of warm light.

All of these people are dead already. It's a heady thing to be wandering through the ghosts of the past, but even stranger to see how much love is already here despite their conditions as women call out for dinner to the last stragglers still outside.

"Welcome to Nantasket," Thomas whispers in my ear, fingers digging tighter into the meat of my arm. "Let us find Matthew, shall we?"

"You better hurry home." Thomas's sister waves her spoon at him with a frown before stepping into the small home closest to our path.

He stares after her, even after the door is closed, mouth pulling into a thin line. A slow smile spreads across my face. He's going to be in for it when he gets home.

With a sigh, he pushes me forward again. Walking to the hard-packed ground of the center square, a few people outside turning to gawk at me.

"If I spend more time in the woods will the Lord provide a woman for me too?" one man leers as he leans against the wood beam fence running beside his house.

"This one isn't mine," Thomas says with a hard jaw. "I'm delivering her to Matthew."

"To Matthew?" The man frowns. "He knows nothing about having a woman, let alone that skinny thing you're dragging around."

Thomas forces a laugh and I clench my hands into fists. Focusing on slowing my breathing back to normal, I brush off his comment. It's a different time. I have to remember that. It's a different time.

We pass several houses, all of them smaller and more modest than any of the surviving structures I've seen in my time. He stops in front of a building off to the side of the main road that I had assumed was a shed. Its wood slat walls slid into each other, the steep roof missing more than a few wood shingles.

Thomas raps on the door, the sound echoing through the house and out through the roof. He mutters under his breath. "Matthew is never home when he should be."

There's an undercurrent in his voice when he says Matthew's name that makes me wonder what else has been going on. The tension there is much older than my appearance. I just hope it doesn't make my mission any harder.

Maintaining his firm grip, he drags me down the front step and around the side of the house. A fenced off section, looking just as sad as the house, sags toward the ground. A lonely goat bleats at us from behind the fence, but there's no one else around.

"Looks like you're not the only one who likes to disappear," I tease.

Thomas's frown deepens. "Matthew doesn't usually go very far."

With my free hand, I adjust the ties on my coif, ignoring Thomas as he continues his muttering. He lets go of me and slams his hand against the tilting wood post of the fence. The whole thing rattles and the goat scampers away from us with a bleat. Pulling off his felt hat, he scratches at his head, scalp dark from brown hair mixed with sweat.

"Do you need help, brother?" A slender man steps out of the protection of the trees, hat clenched in white knuckled hands.

"Matthew." Thomas sighs. "I have need of you."

Thomas pins the man under his gaze, and Matthew visibly shakes. "Whatever for, Thomas?"

"Something came for you today." Thomas shoves me toward Matthew.

His brown eyes go wide, swallowing his face as he stares at me.

"Sorry I didn't tell you I was coming. I wanted it to be a surprise." I give him a lopsided grin. "Good morrow!"

Matthew peers around me to Thomas. "I know nothing of this girl, I promise you."

"She says she is here for you."

"I did not send for anyone, I swear it." Matthew's face grows blotchy as he twists his hat between his hands.

"You have two more days, then you're out of here. Remember our bargain." Thomas points at him, face stern, before turning his back on both of us and walking toward the square.

Matthew's gaze follows Thomas, ignoring me until he's out of sight.

"So, two days, huh?" I ask, a stupid smile still painting my face.

Matthew frowns, smacking into my shoulder as he brushes past me. He continues into the shed, slamming the door behind him. Despite the nervous flutters dancing around my stomach, I follow him inside. There's no way I'm staying out here by myself.

I give a quick knock on the thin wood of the door. There's no sound from inside, but I know he's there and he can't hide from me. Lifting the rough wooden stick functioning as a door handle, I let myself in.

He leans over a small table filling the center of the room. His shed looks more like a studio apartment than a house, the table and a small bed with a red quilt spread over it on the side wall the only real furniture besides a trunk sitting under a greased paper window.

"Who are you?" He reaches for my arm.

I twist out of his reach. "Soph."

"Soph," he tries out, the name sounding awkward coming out of his mouth.

"Why have you come?" he asks, shoulders sinking.

I think over the quick plan Grandma gave me. I'm from England. I've been sent to help him. It's obvious he needs it based on his house and the way Thomas talked to him. Maybe if I can give him a hand, he won't have to leave in two days and he'll be saved from going down with the ship.

Easy peasy.

"I'm here to help you."

He turns to face me, his face backlit in the darkness. The longer he looks at me, the more his body straightens out. "I did not send for a girl."

"I didn't come because you sent for me." I shrug.

"I have no interest in a wife," he says, standing a foot taller than me.

"Good, because I'm not willing to be one."

He runs a hand down his face. "Then why are you here? Why else would you come to Nantasket?"

The truth grinds against my mind, but Grandma's warning keeps my lips sealed tight.

"Like I said, I came to help you out."

Matthew turns towards the window, light glancing off his profile and highlighting his straight nose. "I do not know who you are but getting on Thomas's bad side will not be helpful in whatever your purpose is."

"What makes you think he's on my bad side?"

"The look in his eye as he handed you over to me."

"Who cares what he thinks?" I don't care about Thomas at all now that he's delivered me to where I needed to go.

Matthew drags his hands down his brown pants, worn short like Thomas's. "He is the reason I must leave. He is our constable. You cannot take his attention lightly."

"What did you do?"

"It is of no consequence." He shifts so his face is in darkness again. "I'll be gone soon enough."

I file away that little clue about what's going on. Something really did happen between him and Thomas. The question is what?

"To where?"

Matthew paces to the chest. "Home."

Matthew opens the chest, smoothing out his hat and placing it inside. He closes the lid and sits on it. Staring at me, he rubs his hands over his face.

"You cannot stay here."

"I wasn't planning on staying here." The weight of my spare bag is heavy against my shoulder.

"You cannot go anywhere today, darkness is coming on and the next settlement is days away on foot. You must know that." He leans on his knees, dark eyes gleaming in the washed-out light.

"You don't have to worry about that. If you don't want my help, I just have to tell you something." I stop to bite my lip before plunging in. "You can't get on that boat."

He blinks at me.

"I'm serious. Do not get on the boat you've been planning on for your trip home."

Cocking his head, he raises a brow at me. "How would you recommend I get home then, fly?"

"Maybe you can fix things with Thomas, or you can get on another boat, just don't get on this one."

Matthew leans back against the wall, chest creaking under his weight. "Who has sent you?"

"My aunt."

He sighs. "I am to leave in two days. There is no other choice, even if I did believe you."

Twisting my hands around in my apron, my heart sinks. "I know there's no reason for you to believe me, but I pray you will."

"What shall I do with you in the meantime?" He stands to pace by the window, his shadow trailing across the floor. "You cannot stay here."

"I trust you not to touch me."

He barks out a dark laugh. "It matters not if you trust me. Your reputation will be ruined, you will be a ruined woman. I could not in good conscience do that to any woman, no matter how little I knew her."

"You don't need to worry about me."

Shrugging, he grabs me by the shoulder and opens the door. The sky ripples with red light as the sun dances against the treetops. Thomas leans against a trough set up in the center of the square, watching Matthew's house as he chews on a loaf of bread.

"Finished with her already?" Thomas pushes off the trough, walking toward us.

"She is in need of somewhere to stay tonight."

"There is nowhere she can go. There is no inn around here, Matthew, just honest men trying to build their homesteads."

Glancing at Matthew, his eyes narrow as he stares at Thomas. "Maybe she can stay with you then. Mercy would not mind helping out a fellow woman."

Thomas grinds his teeth. "We have no space for another in our home, let alone a stranger."

I open my mouth to once again say I don't mind staying with Matthew, but he gives me a sharp look that has my words dying on my tongue.

"Have you forgotten why we came here? Have you forgotten your Lord? *And if thy brother be waxen poor and fallen in decay with thee; then thou shalt relieve him: yea, though he be a stranger, or a sojourner; that he may live with thee.*"

"I am well aware of what the Lord has asked of us." Thomas's voice is like a growl. "I will take her in this night but know that I do not believe that she fits what the Lord would describe as a need."

I rub the snub away by telling myself Thomas's behavior has little to do with me and everything to do with Matthew. I'm sure if someone else showed up and needed a place to stay that Thomas wouldn't talk about them like they were some leper.

"Sometimes we are blessed with more than what we need, who are we to decide she is not deserving of that?"

Thomas throws the rest of his bread to the side, the hard crust cracking as it hits the ground. "Come girl."

Matthew releases me and turns toward his house without once looking back. My heartbeat pounds in my ears. Thomas's nostrils flare as he takes me in.

"I'm sorry to be such an inconvenience," I whisper, gluing my gaze on the ground to keep from looking at him. "I didn't realize how much trouble I would be to you."

"Why is that not a surprise?" he asks, crossing back through the clearing to his house.

His sister stands with her back to us, beating the dirt out of a rug. Her shoulders straining, body shaking with each swing of her arm.

"Sister!" Thomas calls, slowing so we walk in step with each other. "We have a guest."

She turns, her eyes narrowing, but she doesn't say anything as Thomas leads me into their house.

The wood floor creaks under my feet as we walk in. The front room is small, two carved chairs sitting across from each other in the bare space. The back wall has two closed doors, which I can only assume are their bedrooms.

The lock snaps into place as Thomas closes the door behind us. Turning on feet like cement, I meet his gaze as he takes off his hat.

"I do not trust you," he says, open voice bellying the narrowing of his eyes. "No woman should be out in the woods alone. It is a place for witches and the devil's work."

I lick my lips before I speak, my clammy hands clenched in my skirt. "I swear to you sir that I wasn't doing the devil's work in the woods. I was just looking for Matthew."

"A lady wouldn't swear." He prowls toward me on near silent feet.

Light from the open window flashes in his eyes as he gets closer, the hair on my neck rising. Standing so close to me that I have to tilt my head to see his face, he breathes heavy, warm breath caressing my face.

"Thomas?" his sister calls, banging on the locked door. "Let me in! What are you doing in there?"

With a withering glare in my direction, he strides over and opens the door for her. Her face is red blotched as she pulls the rug back into the room, warming an otherwise spartan room. Thomas sinks into a chair, his eyes never leaving my face.

"Thank you for your hospitality." I move to help straighten out the rug as she struggles to get all the wrinkles out.

"No need to thank me." She brushes back a loose strand of pale blonde hair that's escaped her coif. "We are all here to do the Lord's work, and sometimes that means taking in His children. I'm Mercy."

"Soph." I keep my hands at my side as she did.

"Soph?" Thomas asks as he pulls out a pipe.

"Short for Sophronia." I wince at my full name.

The chair creaks as he leans back. "You are not English then?"

"My mother favored the Greeks."

Why couldn't I have just picked a fake name? Suspicion gleams in his eyes as he lights his pipe.

"We cannot be held accountable for the sins of our mothers." Mercy takes out a pot to set on a hook hanging from the narrow fireplace behind the chairs. "I still think I was named as an attempt to even out my brother, much good it did."

Thomas snorts. Mercy strokes up the embers in the bottom of the fireplace, adding a few small branches and logs as it builds back up.

"You came for Matthew then?" she asks, voice muffled.

"Yes."

"But he knows nothing of her," Thomas says to Mercy over my head.

She chuckles. "You are not one he would take into his confidence if he did know. You just have to look at the man the wrong way and he'll surely wet his pants."

"What do you have against Matthew?" I ask, settling into the other chair.

"Thomas just does not like any sign of weakness around here, believes it will bring the whole settlement down."

I quirk a brow at him and Thomas holds my gaze. "Winter will be hard enough without anyone who is unable to pull their own weight."

"So you've condemned him without giving him a chance? That doesn't sound very Christian."

Thomas glowers. "I have the welfare of everyone in this settlement to think about, we cannot afford any weakness. Look at his house! You think that will last the winter? Not even the first week!"

"That can't be all though. You can't send a man away just because you don't like his house." And it's obvious he doesn't like Matthew either.

Mercy moves around her pot, mouth tight. "They had an encounter last week that made Thomas decide this punishment."

"So it *is* a punishment then. What could he have possibly done that would warrant this?"

Thomas frowns. "Nothing I would share with a stranger."

"He was suspected of making an unholy deal." Mercy supplies.

"What do you mean?"

"Thomas does not know where Matthew's goat came from."

That seems stupid, but I keep my mouth shut to avoid them turning their attention too closely to how I came to be here. If a goat appearing was suspicious, what would they do with me?

"How long have you been here then?" I watch Mercy scoop out food from her pot into small clay bowls.

"This will be our second winter here," she says, handing me a bowl. "But we have been on the continent for two years living farther south near Boston."

She gives me a carved wooden spoon as I stare into the shallow depths of the bowl. Something akin to oatmeal's cousin lies in the bottom, and not very much of it either. Thomas lays his pipe aside to dig in, not adding any sugar or milk.

With a small smile to encourage myself, I take a small bite and try to swallow. The bland mixture sticks to my mouth like putty, my body rejecting it before it even has a chance to go down.

"Sorry we don't have more to offer you. Everything gets rationed this time of year," Mercy says, watching my smile turn to a grimace.

I swallow the thick lump. "Oh no, this is great. Thank you for sharing with me."

She gives me a warm smile, dimples forming in her cheeks. "We do not have a lot, but we are always ready to help others. Even Matthew," she says with a look in Thomas's direction.

"Not that you'll need to." Thomas goes back to his pipe. "He will not be with us much longer."

Mercy's mouth pulls to the side, but she doesn't say anything. Finishing her bowl, Mercy gets up and pulls a rough piece of burlap over the window, blocking out the fading light.

"She can have my bed," Thomas says to his sister, blowing smoke in a long trail. "I shall stay out here tonight."

"You don't have to do that—"

"No woman is going to sleep on the floor in my home. And I would not ask you to stay with Mercy, she snores."

"What?" she protests with a laugh. "So do you."

Thomas opens the door to the left, showing me a bed covered in a thick plaid blanket. "It should be warm enough. Let me know if it is not, it has been getting chillier of late."

His hand lingers on my arm as I pass by him to get inside, warm sparks shoot through my skin. "I'm sure I'll be fine."

"Of course you will," Mercy says, handing her brother a bundle of blankets. "And so will he."

Thomas closes the door behind me, sending me into instant darkness. Their murmured voices continue in the other room as I tug at the ties holding me prisoner in my costume. The slim knots slip through my fingers, Aunt Tanis tied them too tight for me to undo them by myself, let alone in the dark. So, for the second night in a row, I climb into bed in my clothes, ignoring the way the dirt and sweat caked fabric rubs against my skin.

The rasping of straw scrapping against itself fills the room as I attempt to get into bed. Despite knowing that I couldn't expect much, the straw mattress sinks my dampening mood. Tears burn in my eyes as I sit on the bed, which isn't much better than the floor. My arms lay heavy in my lap, my chin sinking into my chest.

"Tomorrow," I whisper with a thick voice. Tomorrow I'll get out of here. All I need is a promise from Matthew that he won't get on that ship and then I can go.

CHAPTER FIVE

Knocking echoes through the room as a heavy fist pounds on the thin door. "Wake up!"

Untangling myself from the blanket becomes harder than I would've thought, the materials mixing with my dress until I'm not sure which is which. "Just a second."

Grabbing my now less than white coif from where I tossed it last night, I fling the door open. Thomas leans against the wall, looking even better for his night on the floor, his not quite shoulder length hair escaping the ponytail attempting to tame it. He gives me a grim smile. "Sleep all right?"

"Like a baby," I say, then cover my mouth with a hand. My breath must reek.

"What is it?" His already serious face morphs into a frown.

Whipping my hand away, I try to look more normal. They wouldn't care about my breath. "Nothing."

He shakes his head, footsteps heavy as he grabs a metal cup off a narrow table set up by the fireplace. Groaning in satisfaction, he drains its contents. "I will take you back to Matthew this morning. Let us hope he is awake."

"Where's Mercy?" Looking around I don't see her larger frame hiding in the small room. "I'd like to thank her for her hospitality."

"Already out with the cow, you'll just have to thank me instead," he says, uncomfortably close once again, his breath tinged with the smell of rich rosehip tea as it brushes against my cheek.

I step away, my back hitting the wall behind me. "Thank you."

He nods, gaze lingering on my lips. My breath catches in my throat. "I am always glad to come to the aid of a lady."

Thomas gives me a short bow, then walks out the front door, leaving it open for me to follow.

The crisp morning air chills my lungs as I step out into the clearing. Around me, the sounds of men talking drifts through the air. Despite the early hour, the sun not yet completely up, there's almost twenty men out working. Even a few women are there, their deft hands milking cows in sheds behind their homes and handing out more bowls of mush.

"Matthew!" Thomas calls, the frost along the ground crunching under his feet.

His door opens on weak hinges as he pulls his hat on. "Yes?"

"I brought your bride back."

"She is not my bride," Matthew says, teeth clenched as he watches me approach. "I already told you, I have no idea who she is."

Rubbing my shoe against the back of my leg, stockings bunching around my ankles, I try to look inconspicuous. Thomas gives me a wicked smile and claps me on the back before leaving us alone.

"I was hoping you would disappear overnight." He stares at the ground between us.

"No such luck." I cross my arms over my chest. "Will you promise me you won't get on that boat now?"

He pulls a thin, navy blue vest on over his shirt. "You still have not given me any reason why I should not and I am not in the habit of listening to stranger's advice, especially not strangers who appear out of nowhere."

Matthew raises a brow and my lips thin in irritation. "I'm trying to save your life."

"Looks like you'll have to try a little harder." A side smile perks his lips before he turns away from me.

He tromps behind his house, picking a piece of long grass to slash the side of his failing fence. The goat gives him a morose bleat.

"You should go back to wherever you came from," he says, climbing over the fence to join the goat.

Picking up a bucket, his quick fingers express milk from the animal. Matthew slides to the side as the goat throws out a kick, all while watching me through pale chocolate eyes. "Why are you still there?"

"I have nowhere else to go until you agree to my demands, which are perfectly reasonable. I'm not saying you can never go home."

"You just expect me to come up with new funds for a different trip."

"Can't you just get a refund?" I lean against a fence post that buckles under my weight.

In a smooth movement he stands and grabs his pail. Approaching with narrowed eyes, he peers into my face. "What do you mean? I cannot get money back after it's already been paid."

"They do it where I come from," I say, looking toward the goat as it moves closer.

He chuckles. "Alright, what if I believe you? What would you have me do now?"

"Maybe you leave early, you know, catch a boat leaving sooner?"

"Where are you from?" he asks, voice tinged with astonishment. "There is not a line of endless boats making their way to England."

He climbs over the fence, taking the bucket with him back into the house. Darkness closes in as he sets it on the table, pouring himself a cup. A pale white dribble of milk runs down his chin as he takes huge gulps, brushing it away with the back of his hand.

"I don't know what the solution will be, I just beg you to listen to me."

Light from the open door catches his eyes, softening the edges of his face. "For the time being, we shall pretend that I am listening to you."

His words give me no relief. I can't go home if he won't change his mind.

"Thank you," I tell him even as my heart sinks.

"Does that mean you will go home now?"

"I'm afraid to travel alone again. I'll have to wait and go with you" The lie forms in my mind as I speak.

He frowns. "You shall have to stay with Thomas again."

"I still don't get why I can't stay here. I promise you, I'm in no fear of a ruined reputation." I dread the thought of another interaction with Thomas. My arm still aches from where he gripped it yesterday.

"Maybe I do not care about your reputation anymore, maybe I am too worried about my own," he says with a smirk. Matthew gives me a wink, and I find myself smiling in return.

"I'd hate to ruin your precious innocence."

"I would hate for anyone to think of me as a ruined man." He presses a hand to his chest in mock horror.

I grab the door latch. "I guess we'd better leave this open then."

"It would definitely preserve my nerves." He grins at me. "Want some?"

He tilts his empty cup at me, the edges blue with a lace pattern. A drip of white milk swings toward the bottom as he shakes it. "No thanks."

Warm milk wouldn't sound appetizing at the best of times, let alone fresh from the teat and completely unpasteurized.

"This is my most valuable possession." He stares into the half full bucket. "Without it they would think of me as a beggar."

"Are you? A beggar, I mean," I clarify as he glances up at me.

He picks the bucket up and pours it into a clay pitcher. "I work as hard as any man. I cannot be blamed for my poorly producing garden."

"And now they're making you abandon everything."

Putting the bucket down, he runs a hand along his stubble-lined jaw. "I will have to take whatever I can fit in the trunk."

"So you're leaving the goat? Your most prized possession?"

"Someone else will take her in, I am sure." He shrugs. "She will survive."

"As will you," I say as his shoulders droop.

He gives me a tight smile, accentuating his square jaw. "I shall have to, now that we are stuck together."

"It's not all that bad." I straighten my shoulders. "Now you have two more hands to help you get ready. What can I do?"

He looks at my outstretched arms and laughs. "Laundry?"

Laughing harder as he watches my face fall, I try to be open to his request. I know how to do laundry in a machine, but somehow I don't think that's an option here. Plus, I'm not sure how close I want to be to Matthew's dirty clothes. "Do you think Mercy would help me?"

"I am sure she would not mind the extra help." He hands me a sack full of clothes. "If you move quick you might catch her before she leaves."

Adjusting my dress with one hand, the heavy bag in the other, I scurry out the door. Mercy stands in the clearing with a couple other women, all toting bags almost identical to mine. She smiles and gives me a friendly wave as I approach.

"Tired of Matthew already?" she asks, the other women laughing delicately.

"Just thought I'd help him out a bit with the laundry. I'm not too late, am I?"

"It is almost impossible to be too late," one of the other women says with a chuckle. "We spend more time on laundry than anything else."

Mercy puts a hand on her hip. "What do you expect when the men are working so hard for us?"

"You are far better than me," the woman says, adjusting her pale blue dress. "I do not know that I could have left everything behind to help my brother."

"Can you imagine Thomas trying to take on everything by himself?" Mercy asks. "Could any of them?"

Maybe that's why Matthew struggles so much. I can't imagine taking on "the new world" by myself. These people have more courage than I would have believed. Most of my history lessons about them have talked about their suffering and their desire for a place of their own, but never about how brave they were or how hard they were willing to work to make their dream come true.

"Do you miss your home?" I ask Mercy.

I don't know what her life was like before this, but I'm sure she had more options than she has here.

Her eyes grow dull. "There is nothing there for me. Thomas is all I have."

Taking her statement as a cue, the group walks out of the village, venturing onto a well-worn path. The smell of salt tingles my nose, growing in intensity the farther we walk.

"Are we by the ocean?" I ask Mercy as we lag farther behind the other women.

She gives me a sidelong glance. "Of course. How would the ships have reached Nantasket to form our settlement?"

"I guess I didn't think about it that way," I tell her, my face heating. I really should have done more research before leaving. The number of times I've shown my own ignorance is astonishing.

"We like to wash the clothes just before the river meets the ocean. It keeps the water pure," she says, plodding along.

"That's smart." The mention of water has my throat burning. How long has it been since I had a drink? That night in the kitchen already feels like a million years ago.

The path opens, trees growing thinner. I gasp at the sight of the river meeting the ocean. Rippling waves spread out in an arrow, plunging into the sea. The women turn in, following the irregular riverbank up from the beach. I stumble more times than I can count, my shoes slipping in the moist, rocky earth, causing several almost twisted ankles.

"Are you okay, Soph?" Mercy asks, giving me a sidelong glance.

"Fine." Grunting I heave the bag of laundry onto my other hip as I nearly topple over, hitting a very well camouflaged rock.

"You haven't been on the continent long, have you?" Her tone has the slightest inflection of a question, but her knowing eyes tell me I don't have to answer.

I shrug. "I'm only here for Matthew."

"Very romantic," the woman in front of us sighs. "I wish my John were worth crossing the ocean for."

The women laugh, Mercy excluded. Her eyes narrow in sympathy. "He was not what you were expecting?"

"He definitely wasn't what I was expecting, but that's fine. I'm not here to marry him."

Mercy bites her lip as she stops to really look at me. "If you have not come here to marry him, then why have you come?"

Gaping at her like a goldfish, no easy lie comes to my lips. She tilts her head, mouth twisting to the side. "Get here and change your mind, did you?"

"Yes," I sigh, relief bubbling up in my chest at her welcome explanation. "Now I'm just here to make sure he goes home."

"Well, that will be an easy task," she says with a laugh. "Thomas will be more than happy to help you."

Distracted by Mercy, I almost trip over the other women as they stop to set up their washing station. Setting down my laundry, I clamber around them and upstream just a little farther. My knees press into the soft earth around the riverbank. Scooping a handful of river water into my mouth, the clean icy taste has me groaning in satisfaction. My head lolls back against my shoulders, hands limp in my lap as I sit with the bright morning sunlight on my face and the refreshing chill of the water in my belly.

"Soph?" Mercy asks, her head poking up from the crowd of women as she stands up to look for me. "What are you doing?"

"Sorry." I clamber to my feet. "I just needed a drink."

She gasps. "Soph you cannot drink the water!" Climbing over the women between us, she grabs my face in her hands, staring into my eyes.

"What's wrong?" I garble around her tightening grip.

"Out here we must always boil the water first." She presses the back of her hand to my forehead.

Pushing out of her hands, I back up a few steps. "Are you saying I'm going to get sick?"

"We have lost many settlers that way." She grips me by the hand and leads me to the group. "Pray pardon me, I must take this one back."

They give me smiles that don't reach their eyes as she drags me away, laundry bags forgotten.

◦◦◦

"Thomas?" Mercy's cry echoes through the empty walls of their house as she sweeps through, urging me back onto Thomas's bed. "Are you here?"

Ordinarily, I'd laugh and tell her probably not. There aren't many places to hide in their small home. However, during the short walk back to the settlement, my brain had begun to go fuzzy. My vision fills with black spots as the room spins around me. Stomach seizing, I let Mercy lay me back on the bed, covering my shoulders with the red plaid blanket.

"Just rest here a moment," Mercy breathes, eyes wide. "Thomas will know what to do."

I couldn't move if I wanted to. Chills flow down my body, and the chattering of my teeth fills the room. "Mom?" I croak, a tear running down my face and disappearing into the pillow.

Heavy stomping streaks across the floor, Thomas's boots filling what's left of my vision. "Not Mom."

The pain in my stomach intensifies, my body curling itself in the fetal position in response. "I'm dying," I gasp.

"Not today." He bends over so I can see the frown cutting deep lines across his forehead. "Did no one tell you not to drink the water? Probably not, they probably thought you had some thread of common sense."

"This really isn't the time for berating the poor girl," Mercy says, skirts whispering against the floor as she holds out an empty bucket. "You will need this."

Thomas takes if from her and flips it over, sitting on it to get a better look at my face. "She is not sweating. It is possible she'll be fine."

"But the symptoms came on so fast." Mercy wrings her hands together. "Should we tell Matthew?"

He gives her a sharp look, blue eyes cold as his shakes his head. "Matthew doesn't need to know about this. As far as he is concerned, she has a headache and had to lay down. Go grab some prepared water, she will need it."

"Doctor?" I gasp, almost biting my tongue as my teeth chatter.

Thomas turns his glacier gaze to me. "There is none. You shall have to make do with me."

Preparing to ask for someone else, I sit up a little. A bubbling feeling travels up my stomach, my chest clenching against what my body knows is coming. Thomas moves fast, flipping the bucket over as a nauseated grunt pushes past my lips. Body seizing, the meager meal of pottage I had last night erupts into the bucket. My shoulders shake as I wipe my mouth off with the back of my hand.

"Mercy?" Thomas calls, not even glancing at me as he grips the bucket and slides it out the door for her.

He takes a cloth out of the pocket of his earth brown pants and wipes it against my mouth. Leaning into the soft material, I don't even care that he's treating me like a baby. Pulse pounding in my temples, the room swirls when I open my eyes.

"You'll be fine," he whispers, large hands gentle as they encourage me to lay down.

"Here you go." Mercy pushes the bucket back in the room. "Is there anything else you need?"

"Maybe some pottage," Thomas tells her, my stomach clenching at the thought.

"Please no." My protest is weak and immediately ignored.

"Of course," Mercy says, closing the door behind her.

If my head weren't pounding so hard, the irony of being left alone with Thomas would have me laughing. I only manage a weak smile, a line of cold sweat forming across my forehead.

"You're going to need a lot more liquid. You will overcome this." He leans over with a clay cup in his hand.

"What a relief." Even though my words are quiet, barely leaking past my drying lips, Thomas laughs.

"You are an interesting woman, Soph," he says as he tilts the cup against my mouth, warm streams of water spilling down the side of my face.

My swollen throat burns as the water runs down. Choking and gagging, I lift a hand to wave Thomas's efforts away.

"You must finish it." His voice is stern as he presses my hand back onto the bed.

I don't want to admit it and wouldn't find the strength for it even if I could, but he's right. The warm water sits well in my stomach, easing some of the chills. When I open my eyes again, the room stays solid, Thomas's clean-shaven face filling my view. His brows draw together as his shoulders stoop over me. Breath warm in my hair, he presses a smooth cheek against my forehead. Flutters rise through my chest, and I lick my dry lips as he lingers by my face.

"It is not a bad fever." He settles back on the bucket. "That is the quickest recovery time I have ever heard of."

"Lucky me," I whisper, bringing a smile to his face.

"Yes," he says, lips pressed flat as he crosses his arms. He watches me from under his drawn eyebrows.

With the pain in my stomach ebbing away, drowsiness takes its place. My eyelids droop, and I open them once before they close again, falling asleep with the image of Thomas imprinted on my mind.

Hushed whispers fill the voids of my mind. My name repeats over and over, swirling around until I'm like Alice falling into Wonderland.

"Soph?" a hard male voice asks, rough hands shaking my shoulders until I blink blearily awake. "Soph? I think you're having a nightmare."

As clarity returns, I find myself staring at Thomas. Flushing, I try to pull up my blankets, but they're tangled in my legs, skirts holding them captive. Someone's taken off my petticoat, leaving me in my shift. Thomas leans over, chest hanging parallel over mine.

"Are you feeling well?" His forehead wrinkles as his gaze travels over my face.

"F-fine,"

His blue eyes are pale in the dim light, like a calm summer sky.

Thomas jumps off me, bucket rattling as he sits down. "You were calling out in your sleep. I worried you were distressed."

Worried? The word creates a shifting in my chest I've never felt before, my cheeks flushing under his gaze. "Well, I'm fine now."

"Yes," he coughs. "You look better than you did last night."

"Is it already morning?" The room is so dark without a window. I'll never be able to accurately tell time in here.

He nods. "Yes, although it is still early enough. Mercy is not yet up."

"Poor Mercy," I groan. "I forgot all about the laundry I was supposed to do yesterday."

He waves away my worrying with a large hand. "She washed and thought nothing of it. We are here to serve each other after all."

"What caused your change of heart?" I ask with a laugh. I can't imagine the man so irritated by my presence just two nights ago now being completely fine with his sister laboring over his enemy's laundry.

"A heart can change many times. It doesn't always need a reason."

Sure, because people can just change their personality without thinking about it all the time. Oh well, it doesn't matter why he changed, as long as he can be nice for one more day.

"Here." He gives me a cup of water, letting me sit up and hold it myself.

The water is warm and soothing, filling a thirst I didn't realize I had. From the floor next to him, Thomas picks up a bowl, holding it out for me to take. Our hands brush as I put the cup down and grab the bowl, stomach flipping as he quickly yanks his hand away.

"You should eat. This will be the quickest way to help you recover, Lord willing," he says, standing and heading out the door.

Eating the pottage in silence, I try to think about what I'm going to do with Matthew, but my thoughts drift back to Thomas. Did he stay with me all night? I can't believe such a hard constable would care so much about what happens to me, and yet the evidence points in that direction.

A soft knock taps against the door.

"Hello?" My voice is raspy after the rough night, but it's already stronger than it was when I talked with Thomas.

Mercy's round figure pushes open the door. "How do you fare?"

Leaning back against the pillow, I breathe a sigh. "Much better."

"Good." She grabs the empty cup and bowl. "I'm glad to see your appetite back."

"Thank you."

Her mouth pulls into a tight smile, hand resting against the door-frame. "Of course."

Tucking the blanket up to my chin, I run my hand down the inside of the blanket. My body sinks into the straw mattress. Light peeks through the open door as the sun comes up in the glass window. Thomas probably left to take care of his real work, done babysitting a sick girl.

For some reason, the thought of him not coming back has my chest tightening. It shouldn't matter. I shouldn't care what he does. I've never cared about anyone like this before.

"Mercy?" Thomas's deep voice calls from the front door and my pulse skyrockets.

"Yes, brother?"

"Matthew is thinking about leaving today. Will Soph be up for the trip?" his monotone voice betrays no emotion, creating a disappointment I don't understand.

Mercy answers him in a whisper, Thomas responding to her the same way. Irritation prickles my scalp and I sit up, letting the blanket fall from my shoulders.

With only my shift for modesty, the material covering more than I'm used to but still thin and foreign enough to make me squirm, I stand and make the bed. My eyes travel around the room, but there's no sign of my black petticoat. Mouth twisting to the side, I debate my options. Going out there like this would embarrass everyone, myself included. Staying in here means I won't find out what's happening with Thomas . . . and Matthew.

Ripping the blanket off the bed, I wrap it around my shoulders for some meager modesty before stepping out the open door. "Mercy?"

She stands in the front doorway, arms crossed over her chest as she watches something in the front yard. My bare feet pad silently across the floor. Standing next to her, she glances at me with wide eyes. "Soph? What are you doing out of bed?"

"What's going on?" I ignore her question.

She sighs. "There has been evidence found of a witch."

"A witch?" My breakfast sits in my stomach like a rock.

Mercy nods. "There was something found in the woods. Thomas had to go investigate."

"Did he say what it was?"

She turns to face me. "Something about an unnatural circle in the woods. I think he said even the tree branches had been broken in the same circle."

I don't know whether I should be relieved or worried. I don't remember what the area I landed in looked like. Was it a circle? Or did someone else create it and I'm overreacting? Probably that last one, and even if it isn't, I'll have to pretend it even as my heart beats hard against my chest.

"What will Thomas do?" A tremor runs through my voice.

"He'll have to observe all the evidence and decide who it was. It is an oddity. There has never been a witch in Nantasket before." She tightens her arms against her chest.

"Yeah," I breathe, stepping away from the door. "Could you tell me where my petticoat went?"

Mercy follows me into the house, her eyes still staring out the front door. "I cannot remember. It was I who helped you, but it was a stressful night."

I rush back to the bedroom, chest heaving as I realize how long I was in my "undressed" state and who probably saw me. Running a cold hand over my face, I lean against the hard plank wall of my room. I can't believe he allowed that.

Despite the fact that I'm still more dressed than many of the girls at school, in this time period it would be unheard of for a man to be around an undressed woman he wasn't married to. Unless she was a prostitute. Thomas doesn't think of me that way, does he?

Fingers digging into my hair, I pull at my scalp. My breath hitches and I will myself to breathe. Shoulders shaking, I sink to the floor.

Forcing down a hiccupping sob, I stare at the floor and count to ten. And then I see it. There, tucked far back under the bed is a blotch of black that's deeper than the other shadows. Crouching onto all fours, I stretch out an arm under the bed. My fingernails scrap against rough floorboards as I snag my petticoat and rip it out.

It sits in my lap like a limp rag as I dig my fingers into the thick fabric. Pressing the petticoat into my face, I breathe deep. The smell of Aunt Tanis's sandalwood perfume wafts in the air. Tears press against my eyes. I've never gone this long without my family before. I've never had to try and make relationships with other people besides them, and I'm obviously not very good at it.

Mercy bustles around me while I sit in her hard chair, staring out into the wavy glass pane's distorted world.

"Did Matthew end up leaving?" I watch a man in a wide brim hat drag a pig across the square by a rope.

Mercy shakes her head and settles into the chair opposite me, handing me a teacup. Looking up at her with wide eyes, Mercy's cheeks redden. "There are not many occasions to pull these out. We have not had any visitors."

"It's beautiful." I watch as her face looks more and more like a tomato. The cup is delicate, the handle twisting into an elaborate curl where it meets the cup itself. Taking a sip of tea, the trail of steam coming from the warm drink tickles my nose.

"So, what happened to Matthew?"

Mercy leans back in her chair, nose buried in her own cup. "What do you mean?"

"Why didn't he leave today if that's what he was planning? Didn't Thomas want him to leave?"

"Thomas thought it impossible for you to handle a trip yet, plus some other reasons." She sighs, letting the cup rest in her lap. "Thomas took Matthew with him to investigate the witch's mark he found."

For a man he seems to hate, Thomas spends a lot of time keeping tabs on Matthew. Not that I'd mention that to Mercy. I don't have any siblings to compare, but even so their relationship seems too tight for me to openly question Thomas's decisions with her.

"Do you think I'll be ready to go by tomorrow? I know that's when Matthew is supposed to leave."

Mercy smiles broad enough to show her yellowing teeth. "Excited to leave with him?"

"What? No! Not like that," I protest as she gives me a knowing grin.

"I have seen plenty of women about to be wed, and they usually go in one of two directions. Scared out of their minds or more eager than maiden virtue should allow."

"Well, as you can see, reason hasn't left me." I scowl. "Plus, like I've said before, I'm not here to marry him."

Quirking her brows at me as she tilts her head to the side, Mercy continues undaunted. "If you are unsure, but interested in marriage, I can give you a wide selection just from our humble settlement."

"I swear to you, I'm not—"

"I mean, even Thomas himself has not yet had time to gain a wife. You can see what a great husband he would make. Just look at the fine house he built." She leans forward conspiratorially. "I will wager none of the other houses in the settlement are built half so well as mine. I would not even consider Matthew's creation a house."

"It does the job well enough," I say, feeling the need to protect Matthew from the opinions of the others in the settlement. "But like I said, I didn't come here for a husband, just to make sure Matthew comes home."

"Next time your father should send a man then," she says, eyes twinkling as she sips from her cup.

Cheeks burning, I don't try to keep the conversation going. I have no interest in marrying her brother. I have no interest in marrying anyone, no matter if I break the curse or not. I'm only here for my family. I might have to repeat that a few more times to get it to stick. *I'm only here for my family. I'm only here for my family.*

"Mercy, have you—Oh! Soph, you are awake," Thomas stutters halfway through as he takes in my small form wrapped in one of Mercy's knitted blankets.

Mercy sets her cup down on the table. "What did you need?"

"It is nothing." He sits in her vacated chair.

"Were you successful?" Mercy asks. "Did you find the witch?"

Thomas shakes his head, taking off his brown wide brim hat. "Nothing. It is as though the witch dropped out of thin air."

My breath stills, and Thomas glances at me.

"Are you feeling better?"

I try to look normal, forcing air in and out of my constricted chest. "Yes, much better. I'm sure I'll be recovered enough by tomorrow to accompany Matthew home."

"Oh, yes," Thomas says, eyes narrowing. "It is not necessary for you to go with him. If you found the idea tolerable, we could find a place for you here."

Over his shoulder, Mercy leans forward with a broad smile. I'm surprised she doesn't topple over with her heavy chest.

"No, thank you. It's time for me to leave. I've inconvenienced you enough already."

"There has been no inconvenience." A little smile pulling at the side of Thomas's mouth. "We have enjoyed helping you, as we enjoy helping all God's creatures."

His gaze meets mine, and I shudder under his stare. His blue eyes darken, promising a storm.

"Are you hungry?" Mercy steps between us and frees me from his attention.

"I would take some bread if you have some."

Mercy pats my shoulder as she goes back to the table. "You know I always make sure to have bread for you, brother."

"Should I find Matthew? Talk to him about our plans for tomorrow?" I tilt my head towards Mercy.

Thomas leans forward, resting his forearms on the bark brown pants covering his thighs. "There is no reason to seek him out."

"Leave her alone," Mercy says, returning with a hunk of flat bread. "You know Matthew is far too nervous to come here on his own."

"You should have seen how nervous he was to be out in the woods with me today." Thomas grins. "I thought he would wet himself."

"He probably thought you'd taken him out there to kill him." My voice is dry as Thomas whips his head toward me.

He frowns. "Why would he think that?"

"You're obviously eager to get rid of him," I say, my hands gripping my petticoat with white knuckles.

"You misunderstand me." He leans back in the chair, smoothing out his cream shirt, the sleeves rolled halfway up his arm. "It is not that I want to get rid of Matthew, it is that the settlement is not set up to support people that are unwilling to help themselves."

Breathing in the smell of smoky embers still glowing in the fireplace, I calm my trembling chin. "It seems like he's been trying hard to support himself. Just because he's not as handy as you doesn't mean—"

"He has not been asked to leave due to lack of handiness," Thomas interrupts. "We have offered him help time and again so that he would be set up for winter, and every time he has turned us down. You see that shack he lives in? He could have let us help him and had a decent house. As it stands now, we will have to tear it down once he leaves so we can salvage the wood. The house itself is unlivable."

"Wanting to do things on his own should have endeared him to you. It doesn't sound like he's looking to get help this winter," I point out as Thomas stares through the wall in the direction of Matthew's house.

He glances back at me. "I refuse to have his death on my hands." He stands, moving for the door on heavy feet. "I need to check on the animals."

Mercy's eyes go wide but she glances at the floor before he can notice. She chews her top lip as she approaches Thomas. "Would you be interested in supper? It has been a long day, let yourself relax."

Thomas gives her a tired smile. "If you prepare a plate for me, I would much appreciate it when I come back."

His pride itches against my skin as he pulls on his boots. Only a man would think someone else's behavior was something they could take responsibility for. The idea that Matthew's potential death would be on his hands still has my mind spinning. What would make him think that?

He opens the door, prepared to move outside when I'm on my feet. "I'm coming with you."

I don't know why I say it. I know it won't be well received. But before he can tell me no, I'm out the door and into the night.

$$\sim\!\ell\!\ell\,\ell\!\ell\!\sim$$

Thomas follows after me, a sneer on his face. "Night is no place for a woman."

"Too bad I can't escape it. If you haven't noticed, night comes even inside your house."

He sighs, walking along the edge of the sun-bleached wood beams of the perfect fence holding two goats and a few chickens. There are a few houses like his with fences, but many seem to have no animals at all. It's about the only distinction I can make when every house looks almost exactly the same. Without the luxury of siding or paint, every house is the same shade of brown, many of them with windows in the exact same spot. It's like living in an ancient twilight zone as I stare around the square. The only real difference is in the larger building seated in the middle of the rounded row. This one looks big enough to hold all the members of the town with some room to spare.

Thomas walks toward the building, his hand trailing the fence. "I would prefer my solitude."

"Surely if there's work to be done, it'd be better to have help."

He lifts his wide-brim hat to run a hand through his sweat drenched hair, no place safe from the rising New England humidity. "It is not work that drives me away."

Why does that sound like something his modern-day counterpart might say? Then he'd proceed to complain about the pressures imposed upon him from his wife at home.

"Then what is it?"

He places the hat carefully back on his head, staring around the simple homes with softening eyes. "As constable I have many pressures. Sometimes I need to retire to the woods to have some peace."

"Is that why you were out there the night I showed up?"

He nods, jaw tight.

"I'm sorry I ruined the only place you had to find peace."

"It would be a lie to call it my only place of peace." His gaze drifts towards the large building. "I often find respite when I attend our church sessions on Sunday."

"Sessions?"

"We got to church twice on Sunday."

I can't imagine the torture of marathon church. You'd have to really believe in it to want to dedicate so much time. But I guess that was what these people wanted. They came to America for their religion, so I guess it makes sense that they'd want to make the most of it.

"Good thing you find it to be relaxing then."

His eyes narrow as he gives me a sidelong glance. I'm sure I've said something wrong. Again. I'm not sure I'll ever figure out the right thing to say out here.

"Indeed."

He leaves the fence, moving farther towards the woods. I follow behind him, the only sound our footprints through drying leaves. Breathing in the smell of wood smoke from the homes around us, I can almost believe that if I closed my eyes, I'd be in my hometown. So much is different here, but the glimpses of how we're the same tickle my mind.

"Why did you want to follow me?"

I blink against the abrupt nature of his words. "It was better than sitting in a chair waiting to go to bed."

He nods, turning his attention back to the trees. With only the barest of glances in my direction, he heads into the woods, leaving the minor comforts of their little town behind.

A hesitation I don't understand makes my feet go still. I have to physically push myself past a barrier I can't see to move and follow after him. But even with a clear warning in my heart, I do it anyway.

Low-hanging branches pull against my dress, ripping my coif from my hair and choking me with its ties until I can pull the stupid thing free. Thomas moves with a surety that speaks of a well-traveled path, even if I can't see it yet. I stumble after him, keeping up with a pace that feels brutal on my tortured feet.

"Where are we going?"

He says nothing but looks at me with the barest hint of a smile on his face. My heart picks up its beating, resuming where it left off before.

We tear through the underbrush, moving faster and faster, that light smile all I needed to get moving. I'm so caught up in following him that I miss the signs of the forest pulling away. Instead, I'm thrust into a star filled meadow, the shock tripping me up and sending me sprawling through the thick grass.

Thomas chuckles, extending a hand toward me. My face burns, smears of dirt coating the front of my dress. His hand is warm and strong as he pulls me to my feet. My breath catches and I rip my hand away from his. Thomas seems not to notice, his attention on the field before us.

"Where are we?"

Thomas raises a finger to his lips, and I clamp my jaw closed. The burning in my face flaring up again. He sits in the grass, motioning for me to sit beside him. I oblige even as my body protests. I've had enough embarrassment for one day, but I can't help but sign up for more.

The sky is dark around us, the last of the sun dipping behind the trees during our walk here. He opens a small pouch tied to the waist of his pants, pulling out what looks unmistakably like a cake. Not anything like I'd find in modern day stores, but the outer texture certainly isn't bread. He breaks off a piece and hands it to me. It's moist in my hand and I know it has to be cake.

Thomas doesn't watch me as I eat, his gaze traveling over the meadow. I'm grateful for the moment of reprieve as I nearly swoon at the taste of something actually sweet on my tongue.

He leans back next to me, body relaxing in a way I haven't seen once since being here. Removing his hat, he lays it in the grass swaying in the cool evening breeze and runs a hand through his sweat-stained hair. My mouth moves to say something and stops, remembering him telling me to be quiet. Why I need to be quiet, I feel like I'll never know. But I guess that doesn't matter. It's not like he wanted to bring me here. I forced him to take me.

The last of the sun fades out of the sky as Thomas wipes his crummy hands off in the grass. He gives me a sidelong glance, mouth curled in a small smile.

"What are we doing—"

Thomas clamps a hand on my mouth, the other pointing across the meadow. Thousands of tiny bright lights flair up through the long grass, blinking in and out in lazy succession. My words trail off in a gasp as the world around me comes alive.

Thomas's hand drifts away from my mouth, landing on my arm. He leans into me until our shoulders touch as we watch the fireflies. A sweet peace steals into my heart, slowing my breathing and letting me relax against Thomas despite the voice in my head telling me not to.

I don't know how long the world passes us by as we sit against each other, Thomas's hand heavy on my upper arm. A tingle runs through my spine. Tilting my head away from the fireflies, I find Thomas staring at me.

"What?"

I jerk out of our almost embrace. His hand around my arm grips tighter and pulls me back in.

"I have never come here with another before." His voice is a low whisper, caressing my face.

"I . . ." I don't know what to say, what to think. Is this his version of a date? Of a make-out point? Because that's not what I want. Then why does it feel like the fireflies have taken up residence in my gut?

His grip on my arm loosens as his other hand reaches up to trail along my face. His blue eyes never leave mine as he leans closer. I should move away, I know I should, but I'm frozen, held captive by an untellable feeling in my chest.

"I want to express my sincerest apologies for how I acted before. It was an unconscionable way to treat a woman. I hope you can forgive me."

"I—of course," my voice is high and breathy, something I don't recognize in myself.

His head dips closer to mine. "I have not had the good fortune to meet a woman as beautiful and charming as yourself in a very long time."

"I'm not sure that charming is the most accurate description of me." Neither is beautiful but I'll focus on one problem for now.

"You are nothing like the other women. There is a fire in you that has not been dulled by time or fear. You are a truly an incredible woman."

His words are heady and intoxicating. My breathing stills as we move closer together. I tell myself I don't know what's going to happen, even though I've watched enough TV to know.

His head tilts, his proximity alarming, my body warm and on complete alert. "I never should have thought you a danger to our community. Sometimes it is difficult for me to stop being the constable."

My eyes have been half closing, waiting for whatever is sure to come next when his words hit me like a bucket of water. Jerking back, I clamber to my feet. Thomas sits in the grass, gaping at me as I send fireflies scurrying.

"I am sorry if I was too forward." His eyes are wide, fists tight as he slams his hat back on.

"That's not it." I shake my head for emphasis but don't move back to him.

I hate the distance that's been put between us. My heart twists as he stands and moves farther away from me. But I couldn't continue. Not with the reminder of who he is and what I'm here for. Thomas is a constable, charged with removing threats, and I am a witch on a mission to save his next target. How could I have ever forgotten that? What could have possibly made me almost . . . I can't even think the word.

Thomas moves through the forest, leading me back in complete silence. Shaking my head to remove the last tendrils of whatever intoxicating moment I let myself fall into, my legs are weak as I follow him.

There's a weight in my chest as we enter the village again that I don't understand. Something has happened to me here, something I'm not ready to acknowledge just yet.

We're a silent pair as we file back into Thomas's house. Mercy glances once at us before busying herself with dinner. Whatever she found on our faces must have been enough to answer any questions she might have had.

I sink into the hard, wood chair by the table, wishing I could wash the last hour from my mind. Thomas stands by the window, his shoulders tight as he carefully avoids looking at me.

Mercy is dishing out boiled potatoes when a soft knock taps at the front door. Her hand freezes midair as she stares at Thomas. His eyes narrow to almost imperceptible slits, his hand curled in a fist. My heart beats fast in my chest, any hint of the peace from earlier completely obliviated now. The room is silent as he lifts the latch of the door, opening it to find Matthew hunched over on the other side.

"Thomas." He straightens so they almost stand eye to eye. "I have come to talk to the girl."

"The girl?" Thomas sneers. "Do you not know her name or do you expect me to provide one for you?"

"Sa-So-Soph!" Matthew stutters, shoulders back despite Thomas's glare.

"Yes?" I ask over Thomas's shoulder. He whips around to give me the same glare, but it has no power over me. I can't let him affect me anymore. It's far too dangerous.

Slipping around his broad shoulders, I step out into the night.

CHAPTER SIX

"Thank you," Matthew whispers, his shoulders slumping as we walk away.

Thomas stands in the open doorway behind us, his gaze boring into my back. Grinding my teeth, I try not to look back at him and see the hurt I know will be lingering there. But I can't help it, I look back anyway. Thomas's frown is twisted, most likely because of his warning emotions of anger and betrayal. But this is why I came here. I have to focus on Matthew, no matter what else has happened with Thomas. A chill breeze blows across the square sending ribbons of goosebumps up my arms.

"What did you want from me?"

"I assumed you would want to know what my plans were for tomorrow. Although, with you disappearing all day today and yesterday, I had begun to suspect you were not so interested in coming at all."

"I've been ill." I don't care what lie Thomas and Mercy gave everyone, all I have is the truth. "That's why you didn't see me."

He gives me a sidelong glance. Peering at him, the top of my head barely comes to his shoulder. He sighs, heading over to his front step and collapsing onto it, gesturing for me to do the same. "I am not sure how well prepared you are for this journey. Are you sure you would not be more comfortable here? Thomas and Mercy seem very fond of you."

"I'm here for you, so I'll be leaving with you." Crossing my arms, I narrow my brows.

"That is not to say you are not strong or clever enough," he says, though his brown eyes tell a different story. "But I do not think it safe nor appropriate for you to be traveling alone with me."

"But I shouldn't be traveling alone." I don't understand the rules here and I doubt I ever will.

"Well no, that's true. However, I do worry about how it will affect your standing—"

"That's a decision for me to make. What time do we leave?" I tug at my collar as it starts to itch. Three days in the same outfit and my dress can practically stand on its own.

He sighs, running a hand through his unkempt hair. "I shall come for you at first light. We have a long way to go."

"Perfect!" I clap his thigh and stand to head back.

"Wait." Matthew reaches out and grabs my swinging hand, halting my steps. "You do not have to do this."

I wrench my hand out of his grip. "You've made that abundantly clear, but you don't know what I have to do. I'll be coming with you to make sure you don't get on that boat."

I stomp away, his hand still outstretched.

~✤~

Thomas's home is almost unbearably warm after being outside in the early fall chill. Sweat drips down my neck in fat drops, mixing with my limp and greasy hair.

"Is it all right if I go to bed?" I ask my hosts as they sit hunched together in their chairs, whatever conversation they'd been having hushed by my presence.

"Of course." Mercy clambers to her feet to follow me to Thomas's room. She closes the door behind us, the room lit by the warm glow of the single tallow candle she brought in.

I tug at the ties trapping me in my petticoat. "I want to make sure I get enough sleep tonight. We'll be leaving pretty early."

She nods. "I shall be sorry to see you go."

Her deft fingers pluck at the knots in my petticoat, the material falling away without protest.

"I'll miss you too."

"And I know I am not the only one who will miss you."

I can't look at Mercy, not knowing who she's talking about. "I'll miss him too."

And I hate how true that is. This isn't supposed to happen. I've never cared about anyone before, so why now?

Swallowing me in a hug, Mercy pulls me tight so my head is almost laying on top of hers. I've never let someone touch me like this, but I miss my family so much that my hands wrap around her back. Tears prick at my eyes as I press my face into the rough material of her simple dress. Pushing her away, I wipe my face with the back of my hand before she can see them in the dim light.

"Write to us when you are safely docked in England," Mercy says with a watery smile. "We will be so much more at ease once we know of your condition."

Not trusting myself to lie, I nod vigorously, wishing it were true as my chest tightens. Maybe I was never intended to live in the modern day. I've never connected with anyone the way I have in the few days I've been in Nantasket.

"I took the liberty of grabbing your pack from Matthew's house earlier today, so you will have something fresh for your journey." She points to the slumped bag lying in the corner of the room. "Let me know if you need any assistance."

"Thank you, Mercy . . . for everything."

With a last tight smile, she leaves the room, handing me the candle before she goes. The light flickers in the faint breeze as the door closes. Strange shadows shift along the wall as I put the candle down on the floor and sit on the bed.

Scratching at my back, lines of sweat now dried into my shift, I debate taking it off. The sad lump of my bag of extra clothes mocks me. I didn't think I'd ever need them. But I also don't want to get into fresh clothes with my sticky body. New clothes will just have to wait until I've been able to take a bath.

The bed creaks as I get in, straw shifting under my weight. I stare at the corner of the room where Thomas sat with me last night in the fading light. My body relaxes into the blankets, cheeks warming at the idea of Thomas keeping watch over me. What would Mom say about how much time I've spent thinking about Thomas versus actively working to save Matthew's life? At the very least my aunts would be disappointed. Shame burns my cheeks, but I can't help it. Despite everything, I fall asleep thinking of Thomas's smile.

"Soph?"

Jolting upright, I'm startled out of a dream revolving around ice blue eyes to Thomas's voice on the other side of the door. The candle on the floor is burnt out, lumps of wax crusted to the wood floorboards. Light filters in under the door, the long shadows of Thomas's legs making my heart beat quick.

"Yes?" my voice scratches out, the long night taking its toll.

There's a small thump from the other room, and I imagine Thomas leaning his head against the door. "I was hoping we could talk before you left today."

Throwing the blankets off, I scramble for my petticoat. The chill air makes my fingers clumsy as I try to put it on, the knots impossible. I throw open the door, my petticoat on but just barely.

He blinks at me for a moment then recovers. "Oh good. So, we can talk?"

"About what?" I cross my arms and lean against the doorframe.

"I wanted to tell you that—" he stops, coughing hard. "Would you like to come out? Maybe have something to drink?"

"Sure." I'm not sure what to think as he shuffles over to the teapot hanging over the small fire and pours me some in one of Mercy's teacups, all while avoiding my gaze. "Is everything okay?"

He stumbles against the chair while putting the cup on the table. "Fine, yes, all is fine."

A rooster crows outside as I sink into a wood chair highlighted by the orange haze of the rising sun. "That's good." He sits opposite me, legs restless. "Has Matthew been by yet?"

Thomas presses his palms into his thighs, eyes dark. "No, not yet."

"I hope everything's okay. I thought he wanted to get an early start." I take a sip of the warm beverage, almost burning my tongue in the process. It immediately makes me miss Mercy's attention.

"Matthew would not know how to get an early start if it—I apologize, that is not what I wanted to talk to you about." He sighs. "I know Mercy talked to you a little, but I thought I should be the one to make any official offers."

"Offers?" My blood runs cold.

He runs a hand down his jaw. "Well I guess not offers per say, but I thought you should know that in the last few days I have . . ."

"You've?"

"I do not know what I am doing. I should not have woken you." His mouth twists as he gets up and paces in front of the window. "All you need to know is that it is not necessary to go with him if you do not want to, you will always have a home here if you want it."

"I don't understand." But I do understand and that's what's so terrible.

The feelings of the night we shared in the meadow come rushing back, leaving my chest full to bursting as I stare into Thomas's blue eyes.

Reaching out to me, he holds my hand tight in his. "I am asking if you would consider being my wife."

"I . . ."

"There is no rush to answer now. I thought you should know that Matthew is not your only option."

He sinks to his knees, our blue eyes meeting. He moves closer, his breath tickles my eyelids as I close my eyes and lean forward. Close enough that I can practically hear his heart beating, he startles back. "Forgive me."

"What?" My eyes fly open to see him scrambling onto his feet. "You're sorry?"

"This never happened." He doesn't meet my eyes. "Grab your things and meet Matthew. He has been waiting for you outside."

"He's been—" I don't even let myself finish, springing back into my room for the wilted bag still sitting in the corner.

"Fare thee well, Soph," Thomas says as my hand rests on the front door latch. His blue eyes are watered down in the pale light coming from the window, jaw clenched tight.

I'm out the door before I can think better about it, before I can think about what just happened. "Goodbye, Thomas."

~eℓℓﬗﬗ~

Matthew kicks at a clump of dirt just outside the front step and my heart beats erratically at the sight. "Oh good," I breathe. "I didn't think you'd still be here."

I can't believe Thomas knew Matthew was waiting for me that whole time and lied to me about it. If he hadn't come to his senses, Matthew would've been long gone and I don't know what I would've done. Gone home and left Matthew to die?

"You certainly took long enough." Matthew's brows are furrowed as he takes in my rumpled appearance.

I push my linen bag farther up my shoulder. "I'm sorry, I didn't realize you were here until just now."

"For someone who has insisted so ardently that you were coming, I expected a little more timeliness."

My mouth opens to defend myself, but Matthew isn't looking at me, probably hasn't been looking at me since I walked out. His gaze travels over the small town, eyes lingering on the small shack that was his home, the goat tied out in front. He sniffs, wiping his nose with the back of his hand. "Let us away."

Our pace is slow, but even so the forest soon swallows up all signs of the settlement behind us. Matthew doesn't say anything, and I find my throat going scratchy at the thought of never entering Nantasket again.

The road out of the settlement is narrow, the roots of the large trees around us breaking through the cleared path despite the hack marks through them from men trying to keep nature at bay. Birds twitter in the trees above us, and somehow I manage not to trip.

Still, our departure has left a pall. The farther from Nantasket we get, the more Matthew's shoulders droop. A broken man fleeing a broken dream.

"So, what adventures are waiting for you in England?" I ask when I can't bear the silence anymore. "Will you be meeting up with your family?"

"My family is dead." His voice is cold as he tromps down the road with a small pack similar to mine slung across his back.

The silence stretches out between us again as I try to think of something to say. "Have you thought about staying in the colonies then? There are other places you could live other than Nantasket."

"I was not made for city life."

Daylight spreads across the road like butter as the sun arcs through the sky. My throat dries out as we walk, the parched pain making me long for the tea I left behind with Thomas. Matthew pulls out an oiled skin flask, water dripping down his chin as he takes a long swallow. My throat swallows with him, miming its deepest desire.

He gives me a small smile as he puts the flask away, effectively drying up any potential for asking for some. Pride surrounds me like a cloak. Squaring my shoulders, I walk with renewed purpose, ignoring the flaring pain in my throat.

"We still have a long way to go," Matthew says as I shoulder past him. "I would not advise using all your energy just yet."

"I'll have you know I'm very fit," I lie through my teeth as a cramp works its way up my leg. "And this journey should be next to nothing."

I can feel the evil in his grin as I maintain my place in front of him. "You may not feel that way tomorrow."

The word sinks in my heart like a stone. He told me it was a long way, but I never thought about it as a journey of days. I don't think I've ever traveled for days on any trip, not even the one time Mom took me to Florida. My feet slow their angered pace until Matthew and I are walking side by side, my face burning.

"I believe you are very strong," he says, voice softer this time. "We shall make it together and then you can watch me get on that boat."

"If you get on that boat, I'll have to come with you." I grind my teeth together.

He shrugs. "If that's what you feel you must do."

"That wouldn't bother you at all?"

Matthew glances at me, his dark eyes fathomless. "Why should it bother me if you travel to England? Where you go is really none of my concern."

It hits me once again how alone I am here. I've never been anywhere without someone who cared about my welfare on some level. My heart beats hollowly in my chest, echoing every footstep as my foot hits the packed earth. I could die here and no one would think twice about it. This must be how Matthew feels every day.

Where is his warlock father in all this? Where is the man who when spurned put a curse on a woman that would impact every generation of her family? He's never sounded like one who would leave those he loved alone. Maybe I'm biased.

"So your father isn't in England?" I probe, keeping my gaze on the rocks beneath my feet.

"I told you, my family is dead."

His tone tells me to leave it alone, but knowing what I know, I just can't do that. "Surely not all your family is dead."

"Do you need me to go into detail?" he asks, turning burning eyes on me. "I have no family there."

"What about your father?" Does he know I've come back to break the curse? How much can he care for the life of his son when his son won't even acknowledge his existence?

"I have no father and my mother is dead," he says, anger rippling through the air like a heat wave. "She died of smallpox five years ago."

"I'm so sorry." My quiet voice does nothing to dispel the emotion I've brought out.

He steps in front of me, making me stop and look at him. His shoulders shake and his lips have thinned. "You are sorry? You have pressed and pressed until I have to say it out loud and now you are sorry?!"

Instinctively, my shoulders bow in before I can give it any other commands. My head ducks down under Matthew's palpable wrath.

"I—" he stops, hands dropping to his sides. "I apologize. I should never have talked to you like that. It was not appropriate of me."

"I should've left you alone." I'm ashamed as fat tears bubble out and drip down my nose.

He clears his throat and keeps walking. Rubbing at my face with my hands, I try to get rid of the evidence of my overreaction. I've never backed down like that before, never cried when someone yelled at me either. What's wrong with me? The longer I'm here, the less like myself I feel.

Stumbling after Matthew's long stride, he slows enough for me to keep up. We don't talk and I don't try to find conversation for us. I've done enough damage for one day.

CHAPTER SEVEN

Matthew finds a little indent on the side of the road for us to stop when the sun starts to dip too low behind the trees for us to continue without me twisting an ankle. I'm grateful for the break, my body so sore I don't know how much more I could have gone on.

Trees surround us, filling the world around me like a blanket. Matthew starts a fire in the remains of someone else's embers.

"Is this a common stop on the way to Nantasket?" These are the first words spoken since our fight earlier.

He glances at me from his crouch by the small flame he's created. "I would assume so. I know this was my stop when I came earlier this year."

"This could be a good place for an inn maybe," I comment, mostly to myself. I'm still not confident enough to engage in a full conversation with him.

"Maybe, but Nantasket would have to be a profitable settlement to warrant enough traffic between it and other cities before you could have any halfway stops made."

Matthew pulls the wide brim of his brown hat down. I can't see his eyes through the deep shadows. "Are you saying that Nantasket isn't a profitable settlement?"

"If it were do you think they would be so worried about getting rid of me?" His lips twist into a wry smile.

"I guess not."

From what I know of early American history, lots of people died in the early settlements. Not enough food, too harsh winters, and illnesses ran rampant. Maybe Thomas was right in trying to make sure his people survived by cutting any obvious weaknesses loose. He wanted to make sure they made it, and history would prove him right to worry because Nantasket didn't make it.

The hard ground beneath me grows chill as the shadows of the trees lengthen across our campsite. Matthew finds a few larger logs left on the side of the cleared land. Dragging one into the fire, it sends up a spray of sparks. An ember drifts onto my petticoat. I pat it out with my hand, heart beating quick in my ears. Mom always said it was normal for a witch to be afraid of fire.

Matthew takes off his hat, eyes narrowed as he watches me. The small scorch mark leaves a ring in my petticoat, and my hand burns from where it touched the ember.

I'm not sure I can handle his full attention, so I do my best to brush it away. "I'm fine."

When he doesn't look away, I give up on waiting and look at my palm. A shiny red burn mars my hand, looking more like a fresh shiny callous than an actual burn. Still, stretching out my hand stings so I curl it into a fist and bury it into my skirts.

"If you have hurt yourself, it is better to take care of it right away."

Darkness surrounds us, Matthew looking like the lanky spirit of a tree as he stands across from me, only the top half of his long body visible through the murky black of night. His eyes glow in the light of the flames as he watches me.

"I'm fine, I swear."

Shrugging, he collapses on the ground and pulls out a blanket and crusty roll from his bag. Slinging the blanket around his shoulders, he digs into his small supper, the sound of his chewing echoing through the camp.

Reaching for my bag, I know there won't be anything inside but feel the need to make a pretense anyway. If I have to go two days of travel without any food, this journey might just kill me. Sticking my hand inside, I find the folds of my clean clothes and something else.

My fingertip glides against the smooth skin of an apple before landing on the crusty outer shell of bread.

A moan of relief bursts from my lips as I dig into the bread. Mercy must have packed this last night. If I'd changed my clothes like she'd suggested, then I would've known to say thank you. My heart wrenches, eyes watering. Her generosity towards me doesn't make any sense. I'm no one to her. Yet, she cared enough to make sure I'd be fed through my journey.

Curious, I pull out the material on top that I assumed was just my change of clothes. The plaid blanket I've snuggled in the last couple of days lands in my lap. Sighing, I pull it over my shoulders and lean back against a large rock. I won't be near as comfortable as I was last night, but this is so much better than the other option: freezing on the hard ground.

Despite the frigid air infecting the earth, sleep comes easy to me. Leaning my head against the rock, I'm warmed by the memories of Mercy's generosity and Thomas's bright eyes.

To my immense relief, when I wake up Matthew is still snoring against the ground. As much as I like sleeping, I'd hate to have him wake me up every day. I want to look just as interested in this journey as he is, if only to stop him.

Why won't he just agree to taking a different boat?

With his eyes closed, he looks older. The stress of this trip is obvious in the lines of his face, something he must hide when he's awake. A dark curl falls over his eyes and my fingers twitch to brush it back. Yet the memory of his anger yesterday keeps my hands stiff in my lap.

Adjusting the blanket around my shoulders, I grab the apple I left the night before and chomp down, making sure to be as loud as possible as the sweet, juicy flesh rips under my teeth. Matthew blinks at me, eyes bleary as he adjusts to the morning light.

"Good morning, sunshine," I say with a teasing smile. "Good of you to join us."

Sitting up, he stretches out his back with a groan. "You are awfully chipper this morning."

"I'm just excited to get going. We should make it to the next town today, right?"

He grimaces. "In theory. We have to cross a river today. I do not know how long it will take for me to fashion a float now that I am traveling with a—" he stops short, eyes wide as he stares at me.

"Traveling with a what?" I rest a fist on my hip.

He shrugs in helplessness. "Traveling with a woman."

"Why would you need a float because you're traveling with a woman?" I ask, a hard edge taking over my voice.

"The river is deep," he says, rubbing the back of his neck with an open hand. "Too deep to walk across."

"So what? We'll just swim."

He gapes at me with wide eyes. "You can swim?"

"Of course." I don't understand why this should be a big deal. It's not like I'm a child.

"I have never had the fortune of meeting a woman who could swim before." His voice is filled with awe even as his eyes narrow.

Oh crap. I forgot about the ridiculous restrictions on the opposite sex during this time. "Oh, well, my father thought it would be a good idea to be ready for any situation."

At least that's what the dads I see on tv would be interested in. Surely not much has changed in the last three hundred years. Dads still want the best for their daughters, right?

"He did not consider it to be . . . inappropriate?" Matthew asks with a wince.

"Inappropriate or not, it will help you make better time today, right?" I wish we'd never gotten into this and shove my borrowed blanket back into my bag.

Matthew follows my example, his movements hesitant. "I suppose. I worry what people would think if anyone saw you."

"Aren't you people?" My tone is light as I try to beat the seriousness out of him. "And you'll be fine with it, right?"

"I am not sure fine is the right way to describe my feelings."

Sighing, I kick dirt into the embers left from last night's fire. It looks pretty dead, not even a hint of red showing anymore, but I'd hate to be responsible for creating a wildfire and changing history.

My bag bites into my shoulders today, the skin sore from its abuse yesterday. Biting my bottom lip, I keep my complaints at bay as Matthew leads us back onto the road.

His back is straight, shoulders thrown back as a smile grows across his face. I wish I could share his enthusiasm, but I'm not on the road five steps before I've already tripped. I'd kill for my sneakers right about now.

Matthew whistles with the birds as we march through the forest path. His tune sounds like something I might hear in a church, which it probably is. It's not like they had a radio to teach them anything else. The more I think about it, the happier I am that I have a modern house to go home to.

"So, you said yesterday that you're not made for the city. Is there a reason behind that or are you trying to be mysterious?" I ask, knocking my shoulder into his side with a playful smile.

He grins, revealing surprisingly straight teeth. "A bit of both I suppose. It is not often I have a pretty girl to impress."

Heat floods my cheeks, confusing and embarrassing me. I've never acted like this when boys at school gave me their lines, and it's not like the lines have improved any in the last few hundred years. Yet, this strange feeling keeps happening to me.

"So." I cough. "What's the logical reason you can't stay?"

"I like more space, and to be alone sometimes. You never get that in the city, even behind the closed door of your home, someone is always close enough to know what you are doing." His eyes darken, the smile sliding off his face.

"*Wow,*" I mouth, looking back at the ground instead of Matthew. Talk about your issues. The cities he would have to complain about here would still be so small compared to anything he left back home. I would have thought that could have made the experience feel fresh, even if just because it was all new people. I guess not.

"So, you must want to settle in the country when you get back to England," I say, still watching the road.

"Most likely, if I end up settling there at all. There are other places to explore."

If he only knew. I could probably list about fifty different places he's never even dreamed of, still waiting for their eventual populating. Glancing at him sidelong, he ambles forward. The spring in his step from earlier is gone thanks to my prodding. My body grows heavy at the thought, making it easy for me to miss the small rock protruding from the road.

"Holy crap!" I bite back the real curse just barely as my body flings forward and I summersault against the ground for a few feet.

My body stops rolling, although my head feels like it's still turning, and I attempt to disentangle myself from my many folds of fabric. But my skirts have gone everywhere, twisting through my arms and legs until I'm sure I look like a pretzel. Breathing heavy, I stop moving altogether. A low rumble of laughter takes the place of my struggling. Looking through a gap between my arm and some fabric, Matthew doubles over in almost silent laughter. His body shakes, eyes screwed tight as a few tears leak out and the low quiet laughing continues.

"Are you—" he pauses, gasping for breath as he wipes the tears away. "Are you hurt?"

I wave one of my captured arms at him with a scowl.

Matthew climbs to his feet and steps closer, examining the Chinese puzzle box arrangement of my limbs. "This is a mess."

"You think?"

He ignores my biting tone, coming closer to untangle my skirts. His dark eyes soften as he works, hands gentle as he pulls one of my arms free. "Just a few more."

Matthew makes quick work of the other knots until I'm sitting wide legged on the ground, my shift and petticoat spread around me in a sweaty circle. He settles in front of me, eyes searching my face.

"Do you mind if I?" He scoots closer without waiting for my answer. His light fingers pick through the dank strands of hair until his fingertips slide against my scalp.

"What are you doing?" I try to sound mad, but the breath has left me.

He shows me a finger, the tip dark and shining with blood. "Making sure your head is going to be okay."

The sight of blood effectively shuts me up, and I sit with hands folded in my lap waiting for him to finish. He spends a few more minutes finger combing my hair before sitting down in front of me.

"Well?" I ask as he wipes the bloody finger against the dark brown of his pants.

"I think you shall be fine. No amputations today!" He grins.

Indignant, I grab a handful of dry leaves from the side of the road and throw it at his face, catching him in the mouth. Sputtering, he pulls a long oak leaf out of his mouth, eyes wide as he stares at me.

Laughing, I point at his face, where my toss has given him a dark circle of dirt around his mouth.

"You've asked for it now." His eyes narrow while the grin grows bigger and he surges from the ground.

Shrieking, I look frantically for somewhere to hide. Ducking behind one of the trees lining the road, I press my back into the rough bark.

The forest around me goes still, the air heavy as my heart beats loudly in my ears. Minutes pass, and the excited fear drains out of me. "Matthew?" I peer around the tree and back toward the road.

"Ha!" he cries, jumping in front of me and shoving a dirt clod into my face. Sighing, a puff of dust blows out of my mouth and into his. He chokes on it, and I start laughing again even as I rub off the biggest pieces of dirt.

"Truce!" I cry as he reaches toward the ground again.

He holds his large dirty palms up in mock surrender. "Truce."

Lifting the black material of my petticoat to my face, I do my best to rub away the dirt. "We're going to look like a mess when we get to the city."

"Worry not, they will assume we ran into Indians."

"Does that happen a lot?"

He shrugs, dislodging a few brown leaves still clinging to his shoulder as we continue down the path. "Enough that it would not be questioned too much, if they even bother talking to us at all."

The path in front of us grows wider, the trees becoming less dense. The sound of moving water slapping against rocks has me picking up my pace. Matthew scrambles to keep up with me as I practically sprint around the bend in the path.

The road stops abruptly, leaving me scrambling as I teeter on the edge of the bank, my arms swinging back to keep my balance. The toe of my shoe edges off the bank, a bead of sweat forming along my brow. Below me, the deep blue water rushes by, breaking against the side of the bank before continuing on.

Losing the fight, I slip towards the water, feet clambering for purchase against the mossy bank. Shrieking, my toes dip in before a large rough hand grabs me on the arm and hauls me back up the bank. The wind knocks out of me as I fall on his chest. His muscles are firm under my back as I lay gasping, staring up at a few wispy clouds drifting across the blue sky.

Matthew groans, and with my breath restored, I scramble off him. I crouch on hands and knees while next to me Matthew sits up and rubs the back of his head. His brown curls spiral off in all directions as he pats more dirt out of them. He glances at me through errant curls.

Caught staring, my cheeks flare up. Hiding my reddening face, I stand and brush my skirts out. They've definitely seen better days. Holes dot the front of the material, and there are several stains I doubt will ever come out. I hope my aunt can forgive me. But if I break this curse, she'll have nothing to complain about.

"Yeah, sorry about that."

He stands, stretching out his back. "I should have warned you the road stopped so abruptly, but never in my life did I think you would take off like that."

"Sorry." I look at the trees, the blush on my cheeks threatening to never fade. "I was excited to see the water."

"Are you sure you don't want to walk farther down the river and maybe find a float? Or at least an area that is a bit narrower?" he asks, smacking the dirt off his pants.

"No!" I say a bit too quickly. "This is fine."

He gives me a wry smile, but I don't explain. He doesn't need to know how long it's been since I've had a good bath. This could be my only opportunity for the rest of the time I'm stuck in the past, I'm not going to give it up for some girlish hesitation.

"Well, let us go then."

Without waiting for me to answer, he pulls off his shoes, the buckles on the front winking in the afternoon light, and socks. I pull off my shoes but stop short as Matthew unbuttons his shirt and slings it over his shoulder. I can't stop staring at the hard muscles of his stomach. Years of doing manual labor has been good to him and his muscles flex as he turns towards the river.

He slides down the bank, bag held high as he climbs into the river. It only comes up to his waist, but he keeps his possessions resting on his head as he navigates the fast current.

I'm not even tempted to follow his half nude example, my clothes too nasty to warrant saving. Instead, I slip my socks off and follow him into the water. Almost instantly I lose feeling in my toes, the water colder than I expected. My teeth chatter as I slowly submerge myself, body stiff as I let the water hit my waist.

"Come!" Matthew waves me over with a long arm. "You are almost there."

Despite the chill, and knowing it's a bit silly, I let myself completely submerge for a moment, sinking down until only my hands holding my bag stay above the water. My loosely tied coif floats free as my hair waves through the frigid current. Holding my bag with just one hand, I reach out to grab the strings of my hat before it can completely drift away.

"Lose your balance?" Matthew asks as I rise, blowing water from my open mouth.

"Just needed a little refresher."

"Refresher?" he asks, nose wrinkling.

"You know." I climb onto the bank. "When you're dirty and you just want to feel a little cleaner?"

His lips screw to the side as he shakes his head. "I do not think I know what that feels like."

Setting my bag down, I finger comb my hair back into its bun, sticking my soggy coif on top. "Good enough for the city?"

"I have no idea what they will make of you" He gives a wry smile at my sodden appearance.

Walking becomes more of a chore than before, my dress dragging me back to the earth with a vengeance. I almost wish I had followed Matthew's example, but the thought of being half naked with him has me quickly changing my mind.

"Just a few more miles." His voice is soft as we walk beneath the trees.

He was talking to himself more than to me, but I take comfort from them anyway. This walk has hurt more than I'd like to admit. Already, my feet are crying. The blisters from the unfamiliar shoes pressing against my calves and heel with every step.

The longer we walk, the more my wet dress presses against my body, sending chills down my spine. The day refuses to get hot enough to dry it, the material too thick for the weak beginning of fall rays to penetrate. I hope Matthew has somewhere for us to sleep tonight, because if not, I'll get sick. I can feel it.

I almost liked being sick when I was at home. There was always someone around ready and willing to take care of me. Bowls of steaming homemade soup brought to me in bed while I laid almost completely buried under the mounds of blankets they'd bring up. An ache spreads across my chest as I think of home, of the women I love and who love me. They're the only ones I could love, and this is the longest I've ever been away from them. If this is how my aunts have felt, how the curse has made them feel, I can't blame them for wanting to change it. Already it's only been a few days and if I could I'd be running back home and into Mom's warm embrace.

"Everything all right?" Matthew asks.

"Just missing home."

He rubs the back of his neck with a broad hand. "It is hard to be away from family. I miss my home too."

"What was your mother like?" I ask, already wincing as I prepare for the backlash asking about his family usually brings.

"Warm." His brown eyes are far away. "She had a smile that could light the whole world and hands that knew exactly how to bring relief from every little injury a boy could inflict upon himself." He laughs, glancing over at me. "I came here hoping to make a new life where I did not miss her every day, but she followed me just the same."

"The people you love never truly leave you," I say, remembering a card I saw at the supermarket once.

Matthew gives me a little smile. "This is true. No matter where I go, I will always miss her."

"I really am sorry for your loss."

"I know."

The road before us starts to broaden, the forest more clearly beaten back and grooves in the road depicting its usual travelers. The thick rut of wagons and the small prints of feet fill the packed earth as we trod along. "We must be getting close."

"Yes. There was a small fork back there, but you probably did not notice. This has turned into the main route for more than just our little settlement now." He sighs, eyes still far away.

"You'll be all right," I tell him with a smile, though the fakeness of it hurts my cheeks.

"I am just sorry it had to end this way."

Stepping in front of him, I stop and make him look at me. "Who says this has to be the end? Why can't you just try again somewhere else?"

"You would not understand," he says, still looking over my head. "Besides, it is too late in the season for me to start over now. I would have nothing."

"Wishing you hadn't left the goat behind now, aren't you?" I grin.

He looks down, his brown eyes meeting my grey ones. "She is probably better off where she is. They can really use her."

"I hope you're right. It'd be pretty sad if they just ended up eating her now that you're gone," I tease.

"This is what has to be. I never fit in in Nantasket. I knew that and Thomas made it very apparent. As far as the goat goes . . ." Matthew gives me a small shove on the shoulder, just enough to make me move out of the way. "We shall see."

The mood lighter, the heaviness of my wet dress doesn't seem as bad as before. We're getting closer to the city, and closer to each other, something I know will help me in my task later. He's much more likely to believe me if he likes me. Right?

I try summoning a door, just to see if we can get out of here before ever making it to the boat. My hands shimmer with purple light before fading out again. So much for that. I guess I'm going to have to wait a little longer for my reserves to build up enough for such a big trip.

The smell of the city greets us before we can actually see it. Rancid waste permeates the air. "Good grief that's bad," I squeak, covering my face with the sleeve of my petticoat. "Why don't they take care of that?"

"This is them taking care of it," Matthew says, his nose screwed up. "They do not have anywhere to take it. This is normal for a city."

If Matthew had said he didn't want to live in the city because of the smell, I would've completely agreed with him. That alone would keep me as far away as possible.

"This is not anything like being on the boat though, right?" he asks, his eyes narrowing as he glances down at me.

My breath slows but I try to keep my face blank. "Of course. I just hate it, is all. It's so gross. I'll spend the rest of my life trying to forget about it."

"Then you better not get back on the boat with me." Matthew smiles, eyes creasing with the size of his grin.

"Why don't you just wait to get on the boat? Hang around in this lovely fresh air with me for a few more days?"

"A few more days?" Matthew crosses his arms. "The next boat to England will not be leaving until spring. Everyone knows that."

I open and close my mouth a few times, but I'm not talking to Thomas. This is just Matthew. He's not scary. I don't have to worry so much about being caught out of place. "I just didn't realize there wouldn't be more people trying to leave before the Atlantic becomes uncrossable."

Not bad for coming up with something off the cuff. Maybe I should go into acting. Matthew shakes his head and keeps walking.

"Well, as far as I know, this is it. And I am not spending the winter in this foul cesspool of a city."

I'm primed to agree with him, but as we walk around the bend, the city in question comes into view. Crammed homes dot the landscape, their chimneys emitting dark smoke in the air. The smell of burning wood overtakes the smell of waste we've been walking in. The crooked lanes the houses lie on all curve toward the harbor where a few boats lie waiting. Only one of them is of any remarkable size—it's mast taller than most of the trees we've been walking under. Still, this "city" would probably be considered only a large town in my time.

"There it is." Matthew's voice is dark. "I am already ready to get out of here."

"It can't be that bad," I counter, watching the faraway shapes of people moving between the buildings, heads covered in white coifs and dark, wide-brimmed hats.

He cocks his head to the side. "Every city is the same, and none are worth spending any time in."

I bark out an awkward laugh which he doesn't reciprocate. The light mood from earlier has dissipated, our uncertain future lying starkly before us. I'd really hoped we wouldn't have made it to this point. I don't have a good plan for what to do next. Nothing I thought of ever had me actually getting on a boat with him.

The city grows bigger and bigger as we walk closer. The cramped homes look even smaller, the space between them almost nonexistent, their dark wood walls streaked with soot. As we enter the city, the people around us scurry past without a word. They barely acknowledge our existence, although one shrewd-faced woman in a brown petticoat gives me a dirty look when I accidentally block her path.

"Friendly bunch," I mutter.

He grips my upper arm, his tense hand betraying his discomfort. "They are not very trusting of strangers."

And neither are their descendants, I can't help but think with a laugh. New Englanders are known for being cold to outsiders. If you're not from there, you're from away. It's just how life is.

Matthew's tight grip leads me through the twisting roads of the city, helping me to narrowly avoid several catastrophes including almost being run over by a cart. My eyes practically pop out of my head as I continue to take in the old city.

The salty tang of the ocean grows in the air the farther in he takes me. "Are you going right to the dock?"

"I have to make sure they still know I am coming." His gaze is trained on the last line of homes as warehouses take their place. "I do not want them to leave without me."

Because that would be a tragedy. I roll my eyes. "I'm sure they're not going to leave without you." That would just be too easy.

"It's happened before."

Just one more thing to be grateful to my modern age for. If they left without me after I'd paid, I could sue. Simple.

The dock isn't much to boast of. I've seen boardwalks built better. The rough wide planks extend out into the water from the beach, looking like one good wave will knock the whole thing over. Matthew leaves me on the beach, his long legs making short work of the dock as he makes his way to a small rowboat with a few men sitting in it. He leans on the post the boat is tied around and talks to the men. They peer at him, their sea worn faces are grim. They shake their heads in unison and Matthew waves his hands to emphasize a point I can't hear.

The dock shakes under his feet as he stomps back to me.

"Everything okay?" I ask, not bothering to hide my grin.

He gives me a devilish smile. "It took a bit of convincing, but I was persuasive enough to get them agree to take you on too."

"Take me too?" The smile slips off my face.

"You said if I was going, you were going. I figured that was still the case, right?"

I straighten my shoulders, unwilling to be undone in front of him. "Yes, that's the case."

"Good, you will have to pay him before we leave tomorrow morning."

Money wasn't something Aunt Tanis thought to prepare me with. My empty pockets are a testament to my inability to pay for a trip I don't want to take. I'll have to figure it out though. Matthew can't get on that ship without me.

◦◦◦

Matthew leads me from the beach to a seedy looking building with a sign on the front proclaiming it to be an inn. The walls lean into each other, the roof looking worse for wear even though it can't be more than a few years old.

"Have you stayed here before?"

He swings the door open, the hinges creaking ominously. "Just once. It is pretty much the only place to stay."

Lovely.

The front door opens into a narrow hallway, the walls leaning in over me—streaked with greased palm prints, representing the bodies, large and small, that have passed through before me. We walk a few feet in before it opens into a side room with a narrow plain wood desk. A man sits behind it, looking more like a crypt keeper than an innkeeper. The skin on his face pulls in like a raisin, wrinkled and puckered where it meets thin lips parted in a toothless smile.

"How can I help?" he asks, his words sounding like wind escaping a cave.

"Two rooms," Matthew says, digging through his pack and pulling out a small bag of coins.

The decrepit man smiles wider. "We only have one available, sir."

Matthew glances sharply at me, brows drawn tight. "Fine."

"You shall be in room four . . ." The man hands him a key.

Matthew doesn't even look at me as he brushes past into the cramped hallway. Adjusting my bag over my shoulder, I turn my back on the innkeeper, hoping to never see him again.

Matthew's footsteps pound the hardwood floors to the left, and I follow them to find a spindly staircase reaching to the second story. "Wait for me!"

He gives me a sidelong glance but keeps going, the steps shuddering. I go as quickly as I dare, worried that the wrong step will have me plunging through the floor and into whatever creepy little room that man has created here.

A threadbare rug reaches through the hall, its once bright red pattern reduced to a faded mess. Matthew stands before the first door on the right, muttering under his breath. Clutching the knob in a white knuckled grip, I worry for a second that he'll rip the knob out of the door instead of just opening it. When he flings it open, it smacks against the wall, sending down a shower of dust from the exposed rafters.

Coughing, I follow Matthew into the dark room, brushing the offensive material off my dress. He flings the curtains open, letting in the dim light penetrating through the filmy, oil paper window. The one bed sits between us as I close the door behind me.

He thumps his bag onto the floor and sits in the lone wooden chair pushed up against the corner. Leaning back against the wall, he draws in a deep breath.

"Is the city everything you thought it would be?" he asks, eyes closed. "Ready to move in yet?"

"You know I wouldn't stay here if you didn't insist on getting on that boat." Crossing my arms over my chest, I give him the dirtiest look I can manage, one that even at the best of times would pale in comparison to the filth of this room. "What are your plans for the rest of the day?"

He gestures at the room. "This."

"As thrilling as that is, don't you want to actually get out? See the city? Watch the sunset? Something?" I set my bag down, not wanting to get any closer to anything else in the room.

"I would prefer to stay inside, out of trouble, and get ready for tomorrow." He closes his eyes again.

"One last meal perhaps?"

He peeks at me with one eye. "I don't have to rush eating right now. I do not suffer from seasickness."

"Well, I might." Walking on tiptoe, I dare to get further in the room. Grabbing him by the arm, I tug, trying to get him to stand. "Please? Just an hour out in the city?"

"Fine." He grabs his hat and jams it on his head. "But we need to get back early. We should be well rested before trying to take on the ocean."

I don't doubt that. I just have no intention of getting on that boat.

Chapter Eight

Rattling the house as Matthew tumbles down the stairs after me, I sprint past the check-in room. The air outside the inn is fresher, making me breathe deep despite the mix of manure, smoke, and sea.

"Don't you just feel more alive out here?" I release his arm to spin in a circle, my skirt forming a bell as it catches the cool breeze blowing in off the ocean.

He gives me a crooked smile. "Maybe."

"Maybe? This is a great opportunity. Don't waste it in that stuffy inn that's just waiting to fall apart while we're sleeping. Aren't you hungry for a real meal?" My stomach rumbles, loud in the quiet streets. Two days of stale bread has left me famished.

"Come on," he sighs, looping his arm through mine as we head further into the city.

The homes around us grow dark as the sun sets, their blank windows watching our slow progress. There's not another soul on the street for a few blocks, adding the ghostly feel of the city.

"Where did everyone go?" I ask Matthew in a hushed tone.

"Home?"

Shivering, I lean into his shoulder. He picks up the pace, shaking me loose as he lets go of my arm. Speeding to walk with him, I actually sigh in relief when I see another person.

"What ho!" Matthew calls to him. "Is there somewhere we can eat?"

"Take a right at the next fork, you cannot miss it," he says in a gravelly voice, not looking at Matthew.

"Rude."

Matthew shrugs. "This is city life, nothing personal."

I wish I could feel as confident.

The building housing the tavern looks as nondescript as the others, its brown walls dark in the receding light. Light flickers from its two front windows as bodies move past it, their hands full of drink.

"This is not the right place to bring you." Matthew's mouth is drawn.

"I think worrying about my reputation should be the last thing on your mind." Still, my body pulls away from the door he holds open to me.

For what it lacks on the outside, it more than makes up for on the inside. A large fire roars from a fireplace big enough to hold a man, the wood plank floor is full of carefully carved tables and benches filled with the hard backs of men. A few women flit between the tables. They smile and laugh, their faces lined with youth's receding traces.

I smile at Matthew as he directs us to a table close to the door. "See, there are other women here," I say, taking a seat.

"If you are like those women then I have been spending my time all wrong," Matthew says with a wry twist of his lips as he sits across from me.

My cheeks flush, but thankfully he doesn't notice when he turns to address the woman passing us. I take his distraction as a moment to calm myself. Hands pressed to my thin cheeks, I will the color to go down, will my heart to steady itself. When his attention slides back to me, I put my hands under the table, wringing my skirt between tense fingers.

He leans over the table toward me. "You look a little sick."

"I'm fine." I resist the urge to chew my bottom lip.

A chorus of song starts up farther down the table and Matthew grins. "I have forgotten how nice it is to be surrounded by people who do not see me because they are too busy and don't know me, instead of people who know me and avoid me anyway."

"Was it always like that?"

His face shadows a little. "Not always, just when I did not want their help."

"I still don't understand why that would be something they hated you for."

"Thomas does not care for anything he does not feel in control of," Matthew says with an uncharacteristic sneer. "Having people indebted to you makes them easier to control."

"So what, you refusing help was refusing to be put in his pocket?" That just doesn't seem like Thomas to me. Matthew's explanation is nothing like the Thomas I know. The Thomas I know wanted everyone to be able to fend for themselves, not to be leeching onto him. That's why he sent Matthew away in the first place. He had a hard shell and a soft interior. Surely I couldn't be the only one who had seen that.

"The Thomas you know does not exist." Matthew buries his face behind the large cup the waitress sets down before us.

Palming the cup between my hands, the warmth seeps into my bones. "I guess I don't understand."

"And you probably never will." Matthew sets his cup on the table. "Why are you really here?"

Sighing, I release the cup and slip my hands back under the table. "I told you. I'm here to make sure you don't get on that boat."

"So what is your plan then? I'm getting on that boat and going back to England. I'm assuming this means you're going with me. What will you do when we get there? Do you have family?" He leans over the table, dark eyes flashing in the firelight.

Sitting back, I chew my lip and look away from his searing gaze. Relief floods my system as the waitress comes back with two steaming bowls of rich stew. Lifting the spoon, I shovel the stew in my mouth, ignoring my taste buds burning at the too hot broth.

Matthew settles back into his chair. "So, no real plan then. What I still do not understand though is how you found me. There is no way you found me all the way in Nantasket without someone guiding you there."

"Nantasket did you say?" a man asks, leaning over from the table next to us. "I heard you have a witch up there. Is that why you two left?"

"No," I say through gritted teeth.

The man barely looks at me.

"There was a hunt for a witch going on when we left, but nothing had come of it," Matthew says.

"Pity." The other man takes a sloppy drink out of his tankard. "Nothing I love more than a good witch hunt. We don't need no devil spawn in these parts."

"Of course." Matthew slaps the man on his scrawny back as he turns back around.

Lifting my spoon, I glance at Matthew with narrowed eyes. "What did you and Thomas see when you searched for the witch?"

"Thomas only took me with him because he was so sure the witch was me, stupid man," Matthew says through a mouth of stew. "I know about as much as you do. There was a circular spot in the woods that had been cleared out of all debris with no evidence to incriminate anyone."

Only Thomas knows where I landed that first day in Nantasket. Has he thought of our first encounter while standing in those woods? I'm fairly sure the marks were left by me, even though I've never left something like that behind before. But it's truly ironic considering I'm the only witch any of these men will ever meet. Not that they'd know that. I'm safe in the city from Thomas's search for answers.

"That must have made Thomas pretty upset."

Matthew glances at me with a tilted head, his mouth still full.

"That he couldn't pin you as a witch."

Matthew nods and swallows. "He was getting rid of me either way, but I imagine having me accused of witchcraft would have been more fun for him."

"Have you ever seen a witch trial? What do you think they would have done to you?"

Matthew shrugs his narrow shoulders. "I've seen a few. I suspect they would have gone with burning. Much more fun to draw it out, and definitely more dramatic."

"They'd really do that?"

"I'm sure he already has before. He came to Nantasket straight from England you know. Witch hunts have become the latest form of religious justice over there."

An image of Thomas, slumped over in his chair giving me an easy smile, his freckles standing out in the weak light from the window comes to my mind. I just can't combine this man with the one Matthew knows. My Thomas isn't a mindless killer.

"Thomas wouldn't do that."

Matthew gives me a sad smile. "He already has. Everyone loves watching a witch burn." His gaze is on the fire as he takes a long drink from his cup.

"Not me."

Matthew glances at me, eyes narrowed. "Not you," he repeats.

Shifting under his gaze, I go back to eating. Anything to avoid his dark gaze.

"There's something different about you," Matthew says under his breath. "I think Thomas saw that too, didn't he?"

I shrug, but he doesn't need my answer as his eyes bore through me.

"What did he offer you? I am positive he hated seeing you leave with me. Women are scarce enough as it is, and you chose to leave with me, the unwanted instead of staying with him." A smile grows across his face. "That must have torn him up inside."

My lips press into a thin line, and Matthew's smile grows.

✦

Matthew whistles all the way back to our shabby inn. My lack of rebuttal put him in a great mood, one that grates against me. I shouldn't care. Thomas means nothing to me. Matthew means nothing to me. This is just a brief weird moment in the past. No one here should mean anything, especially not enough to make me so irritated.

"Would you just shut up?" I demand when he closes the door to our room behind us.

He blinks at me. "That is not very lady-like behavior."

"I've never been described as a lady before," I practically growl at him and thump down on the sagging straw mattress.

Matthew chuckles, the sound dark. "Missing him, are you? Cannot handle anyone being happy with his annoyance?"

"This has nothing to do with Thomas and everything to do with how much you personally irritate me." Taking off a shoe, I throw it at his head. He moves easily out of the way and the shoe hits the wall before falling harmlessly to the floor.

"That was not very nice," Matthew says as he sinks into the chair. "Especially considering I just paid for your dinner."

I stick my tongue out and go back to pulling off my stockings and tugging uselessly at my petticoat ties. Matthew coughs and looks away, a rosy splotch growing under the scruff of his growing beard.

"What?" I bite at him, feeling once again thwarted by my own clothes.

He coughs again, his hesitation making me look up to glare at him. His eyes are pointed anywhere but at me. The blush spreads across his face until it reaches his hairline.

He stares at the ceiling. "Besides the fact that I've never been in the presence of a woman undressing herself, it looks like you need help."

Laughing, I realize I let my anger get in the way of propriety. Of course he would be embarrassed by my behavior, he didn't even want to share a room with me! Did he expect me to sleep fully dressed then? That was not going to happen.

"I could really use help." I turn so I'm facing the wall. "Would you mind?" The floor creaks, as he takes hesitant steps forward.

His quick breaths warm my neck. There's a rasping sound as he wipes his hands off on his pants before attempting to untie my knots. His slim fingers make quick work of the knots without moving my petticoat at all. The tight material loosens around my chest as he goes from tie to tie, releasing me from my costume prison.

"Thank you." I turn around but find myself unable to look at Matthew's face.

He coughs again, stepping back and almost leaping into his chair. "You are most welcome."

With a sigh of relief, I tug the petticoat off, standing in only my shift. Trying to save him from further embarrassment, I climb into the bed and pull the heavy blankets up to my neck. Matthew tips his head back against the wall, staring at the ceiling for a moment before closing his eyes.

"Are you not coming to bed?" my soft voice carries in the stillness of the room and I know Matthew had to have heard me.

He doesn't respond. The silence stretches between us, making me wonder if he'll ever answer me. His voice is quiet and overly controlled when he finally speaks. "I would not feel right climbing into bed with you."

His eyes crack open, giving a slight gleam as the light coming in from under the door hits them. My chest warms under his gaze. It doesn't feel right to let him sleep in a hard chair all night just because of his old-fashioned sensibilities. "You can sleep here. I know you won't touch me."

"That's just the thing," he says with a laugh. "You knowing it and me knowing it won't change what *everyone else* thinks."

"But isn't the damage already done? We're staying in the same room together. So, they already think we're doing . . . whatever."

The chair squeaks in protest as he leans forward. "I suppose you are right. But I cannot ease my conscience."

"If you don't tell anyone, I won't either." I hide my face in the blanket. It smells heavily like sheep, and I pray it's been washed between customers.

He sighs and gives me a pained smile. "It is like sharing a room with the devil himself."

Rolling on my side, I give Matthew space as he takes off his shoes, their heavy soles thumping against the floor. He sits down on the bed with another sigh. When he doesn't move again, I turn my head to see him. In the pale light, I can make out his deft fingers as they unbutton his shirt before flinging it against the floor. His firm chest fills with shadows, but I can see enough for my insides to turn warm. With a sharp movement, I turn, blocking my view of Matthew's surprisingly nice body he hides under those ill-fitting pilgrim clothes.

Matthew breathes a prayer into the heavy silence of the room, the sound comforting even if I don't believe in it. I say a mental prayer of my own, sending it out into the cosmos I'm more comfortable with.

The bed is small, probably even for these times. We lay on our backs, our shoulders touching. My skin burns at his touch, every nerve ending coming alive and living for this small sensation. I lay wide awake staring at the ceiling, listening to Matthew's heavy breathing.

I should move away, roll on my side and give him room, but I can't bring myself to do it. I'm frozen next to him. He swallows, the sound pressing into my ears in the silent room.

Matthew rolls over, disconnecting our burning touch. I should be relieved, but I'm not. Heaving a heavy sigh, I press my lips tight. Despite the whisper in my mind that tells me not to, I roll over too, towards him. Expecting to face his back, a gasp bubbles out of my lips at the shine of light hitting his open eyes. Watching me.

"Apologies," he whispers, our faces close enough for his breath to caress my face. "I did not mean to scare you. I can move."

"No!" I blurt. "I mean, that's okay. You don't have to move."

He smiles, face soft in the darkness. "Let me know if I make you uncomfortable."

"Okay," I whisper, hands fisted in the blanket by my chest.

His eyes travel up and down my face. I don't know what he could possibly see, with the door behind me I should just be a backlit shadow. Still, he finds something that catches his interest. He stares at my parted lips. My breath stills in my chest.

He leans forward, head almost sliding off the pillow. "Forgive me."

"For what?" The slowly building burn between us instantly extinguished when he rolls onto his back.

"Never mind," he whispers, voice filled with longing.

Watching his chest rise and fall, I try to make sense of his apology. Was he apologizing for sharing the bed with me?

His eyes close, his breaths becoming even. Timing my breathing to his makes my body feel heavy and I don't even mind the sheep smell anymore.

CHAPTER NINE

My eyes fly open. Muted light filters into the room. A heavy weight presses on my chest. I stare down at Matthew's hand laying on my chest. Hesitantly, I reach out, letting my fingers run over his. Adrenaline rushes through me like lightning, wiping out all traces of sleep.

The sun has come up, light filling the room through the thread-bare brown curtains. Swallowing hard, I glance down. Matthew's bare arm reaches across my chest. Following the curve of naked flesh, his head is pressed into my shoulder while he breathes heavy.

I reach out, my hand hovering over his face—battling my desire to touch him. The stubble lining his strong jaw makes him seem so much more of a man than that first day in Nantasket. My fingers itch to touch his cheek, to follow the line of his jaw and scratch his stubble. Common sense leaves me suspended, halfway towards what I want to do and halfway to what I should do.

I can't understand this attraction between us. But I feel it there. Simmering in my chest. Despite our limited time together. But the side he's shown me on our journey has changed everything. We have spent barely any time together, and what time we have has been a mess of sarcasm and sass. It's not possible for me to care about him but there's something that's seeped through all our rough moments together that makes me want to draw him closer.

He groans, the arm around me squeezing. My side presses against his bare chest, his head digging further into my shoulder.

My heart beats fast as his arm rises and lowers with my stunted and shallow breaths. Someone pounds on the door. Matthew's eyes shoot open.

"Get up!" A man yells through the door.

Matthew rips his arm away from me and surges up, cold air taking the place of his body against my side. "We have to go."

I watch him pull his shirt on, his back muscles flexing. Red splotches crawl up his neck.

Reluctantly, I get out of bed. My dunk in the river yesterday washed off enough grime that I no longer look like a mole person, but it still doesn't feel great as I get moving and grab my bag. "Turn around, I'm changing," I tell Matthew needlessly as I drag out a new shift and petticoat.

The creaking of the floor stops, and I tug off my shift before I can lose my nerve. Naked, I bend over to hide myself as much as possible. My clean shift slides over my hunched body, my breathing rushed. Silence settles over the room. I could probably hear a pin drop. My body twists as I tie my petticoat, I fan my flushed face before facing Matthew again.

"You can turn around now."

Matthew starts to turn, then stops. Body frozen.

"Did you hear me? It's safe to look now."

He still doesn't move. With a sigh of irritation, I march over to him but stop as I realize I can see myself in the shard of glass not covered by the curtain.

"You could see me?!" I squeak, covering my now dressed body with my hands.

"I did not ask you to undress." His voice is strangled as he turns to look at me.

"I didn't know you could see me!"

He doesn't look at my face, staring at my feet with a bright red face. "I should have said something."

"Darn right you should have! I can't believe you!"

All his talk of dignity and protecting my reputation and he's going to just stand there and stare at me?

He grabs his bag and moves past me toward the door, his face becoming more like a stone. "Forgive me, but we have a boat to catch."

Shoving my dirty clothes into my bag, I scramble down the stairs after him. He doesn't slow down, even as I move like a rhino through the shuddering house trying to keep up.

Biting back a sharp remark, I rush out the door.

The boat looms dark in the water in front of us, framed by puffy white clouds crowding the blue horizon. Men shout back and forth to each other, the smell of old fish and briny ocean overwhelming. Matthew's nose crinkles but he doesn't comment on the smell.

My heart thunders in my chest. I never got the money for my passage. I'm going to get left behind after all. Maybe I'll have to go back in time again, kidnap him, and wait for the boat to leave before letting him go. Gosh dang, it would've been so much easier to just do that in the first place.

Panic feels my chest and I know I have to do something. Calling on my magic again, I take the risk no matter who could be watching. What will it matter if someone sees if I can get us out of here?

Flashes of purple grow across my hands. Closing my eyes, I strain to create the door. My body sways as the magic leaves me and I open my eyes. The dock is embarrassingly empty. The faint outlines of a door shimmer through the air before dissolving in a salty breeze.

My heart falls as Matthew dances across the rickety planks of the dock to the large ship. He hands his bag over to the men waiting for him, their faces dark in the early morning light.

"Goodman, Goodwife," a sailor with missing teeth greets us as he leans against the side of the boat.

I brush off his odd choice of words, attributing them to gaps in Grandma's spell.

Matthew glances back at me, hand stretched out. "Well?" he asks, his head tilted to the side.

"I just—I didn't," I trip over my words.

A grin spreads across Matthew's face. "All of that and you are not coming with me after all?"

I flounder, hands moving weakly against my legs. "I forgot about the price and got so distracted last night and I just—"

"Calm yourself," Matthew says with a lopsided grin. "It is taken care of."

"You—you paid?" My mouth drops open.

His eyes rove over my face. "I assumed you would not have much money on hand, so I paid for it yesterday."

"Wow," I breathe. "I mean, you really didn't have to do that."

He shrugs, holding me by the arm to help me into the rowboat that will take us to the ship. "I know."

Those two words rattle around in my head as the men begin rowing us farther out to sea. I guess this is really happening now. The odds of having to use my magic in front of Matthew has grown exponentially just by getting into this rickety rowboat. I close my eyes and breathe in and out focusing on the well of magic that lives in my core. Despite the flickering door earlier, there's still quite a bit of magic there. I focus on building my stores up, making the trickle of magic enlarge into a river. At least now I should be able to move quickly if I need to.

He takes my hand to help get settled in the boat, his fingers lingering in mine. My breath catches and I glance into his dark eyes. Maybe his generosity wasn't about believing me after all.

I brush off the thought as soon as it comes. That's ridiculous.

A wave pushes against the boat, water sloshing over the side. The frigid water seeps into my shoes, turning each toe it touches into an ice cube. Teeth chattering, I glance over at Matthew. He's watching me too, his eyes soft around the edges.

"It will be better on the ship," he says, digging around in his bag.

I stare across the choppy expanse of water. The grey sky overhead mirrors the coming storm in my mind. A weight falls against my shoulders. I turn as Matthew secures his grey coat around my shoulders. He shrugs. "You looked cold."

My heart warms as I tug the coat closed, feeling warmer than the material should warrant. I give Matthew a small smile and push my hands into the deep pockets. He smiles then turns and focuses on the growing ship ahead.

The sailors grunt as their oars slice through the water. The little rowboat makes slow progress toward the ship. Once we're past the waves, we move quicker, the salty sea air breezing cold against my face.

My heart falls with every stroke. Even Matthew is looking uncomfortable, his brows drawn together as he fidgets in the narrow wooden seat.

How am I supposed to save us?

"I am not looking forward to this," he says with a sigh, trailing his hand through the icy water. "I had hoped to never cross this ocean again."

"You don't have to you know." I nudge him with a shoulder.

"I told you, Soph." He flicks some water at me. "It's not an option." He smiles, but I can still see the worry in his eyes.

Wiping the water off my face, I give him a sardonic smile. "Only because you're too pig-headed to try and make it work in another colony. One you can start over in."

"Let us not fight about this again."

One of the men in front of us leans back towards Matthew, his face marred by a puckered scar that stretches across his cheek. "You're going to let your woman talk to you like that?"

Matthew opens his mouth to respond, but the other sailor cuts him off. "You're not one for giving advice. You couldn't get a woman to marry you if you begged, Leo."

"Not true!" Leo protests, his scar twisting as he shoves the other man.

"Is too true! There's a reason why the women run when they see you coming and its only partially because of your face," the sailor says with a broad grin.

Leo throws a punch, but Matthew reaches forward to block it. "Not in front of the lady, boys."

"Sorry if I offended you and your woman," Leo says with a shrug, muscles straining as he rows.

"No offense taken." Matthew sits back, leaning against the side of the boat.

His gaze roams around the boat, never landing on me. My gut twists.

"What's wrong? What are they talking about?" I ask, my jaw tensing.

Matthew grimaces, taking a pained breath. "I shall tell you more when we get settled."

My brows slam down over my eyes. "I think you'd better tell me now."

"Later," he says pointing his head at the backs of the sailors. They don't even pretend to not be eavesdropping.

"Fine," I bite out, sliding as far from Matthew as I can get on the narrow bench. But there's nowhere to go and our thighs brush against each other despite my irritation.

Digging my hands further into the coat, I turn my body so I don't have to see him. I don't know what those men were talking about, but I'm not his woman.

~ee℘℘~

The rowboat bumps against the side of the ship, and I tumble to my knees. The sailors laugh as a rope ladder is flung over the side. Matthew reaches to help me, but I brush him off. With a shrug, he grabs his bag, and his lanky body makes little work of the short climb.

"You next," Leo says smiling, mouth revealing at least three missing teeth.

Swaying from side to side, I struggle to stand in the small boat. My bag swings against my back, not helping as I reach out for the rope.

"Go on, we don't have all day," the empty-mouthed sailor says, scratching at his chest with a hairy hand.

"I can do this," I whisper under my breath.

Holding the rope ladder with both hands, I slide my foot onto the bottom rung. The big ship isn't as rocky as the rowboat, but the ladder is less than stable as I climb it. The tendons on my neck stand out, beating a pulse that I'm sure can be seen from land.

"Come on!" Matthew hangs over the side of the boat. "Just a little farther and I will help you."

"What a gentleman," I mutter as I climb up the rungs, frozen hands stiff.

I'm almost there when my foot slips. The lack of feeling in my toes is my downfall. Reaching for the next rung, I hang suspended from one hand—my feet swaying against the boat.

"Help," I gasp, my hand flailing through the air.

Matthew turns toward me, face going pale. "Hold on!"

He leans over, but I'm still too far down for him to reach. My ocean wet fingers start to slip and I scream again.

"I'm coming, just hold on!" he yells.

My bag slips off my shoulder. Reaching for it, my fingers slip further. It falls down and down, missing the rowboat and hitting the ocean with a splat. I hang frozen with my gaze glued to my bag, watching it sink into the water.

"You didn't want that did you?" Leo asks with a laugh.

Shaking off the shock, I swing my reaching arm back toward the ladder. I'm too slow and too late. My left hand loses its strength, my body not quick enough to swing my right hand back to the ladder. I slip off the ladder and for a moment I'm weightless. Time stills as I realize I'm falling. Falling towards a freezing ocean with fifty pounds of dress to drag me like an anchor down into its icy depths.

I barely have time to scream before my arm is being pulled out of its socket. I jerk my head up and come face to face with the shiny buckles of Matthew's shoes.

"Hold on," he grunts, breathing through pursed lips. He holds me by my wrists, his arm twisted through the ladder.

Swinging my other hand up, I grab onto his hands with a white-knuckle grip. His arms shake from the weight.

"Could you just," Matthew grunts. "Could you maybe grab onto the ladder?"

I stretch my feet toward the ladder. My body slams into the side of the boat, my feet tangling in the rope ladder. Pulse pounding, I release Matthew with one hand and grab at the ladder. It slips through my fingers the first time and I have to reach out farther, Matthew straining above me where he hangs over the side of the boat.

Matthew's arms curl up and he twists against the ladder, heaving me over the side of the boat. I hit the floor in a tangle of skirts and nerves, lean against the side of the boat, and take a few deep breaths.

Fingers digging into the rough floorboards, my pulse slows to a reasonable pace.

"You didn't want to leave her?" a sailor leaning against the side of the boat ahead of me asks Matthew. "Cut your losses and pick up someone new on the other side, eh?"

"I shall give thanks for what I have already been given," Matthew says without looking at him, pulling me up from under the arm.

Now that I'm standing on the deck, the boat looks much smaller than it did from the rowboat. It's not even forty yards wide, the flat space in front of me containing only a few barrels and a couple of sailors. To the back of the boat is a small platform set three steps above the rest of us where a large wheel stands unattended.

"So, what now?" I stare up at Matthew when he doesn't release my arm.

Face tense, he looks around the boat. His bag sits abandoned at his feet.

"Matthew?"

"Matthew?" the sailor mocks, dank dark hair hanging over his eyes.

Matthew shakes his head and looks at me. "Sorry, let us get settled below."

Hand digging into my skin, he leads me past the leering sailor and down a dark stairwell. I stumble down the stairs after him. Wooden boards line the hallway walls, throwing off the scent of an uncleaned shower, moldy and moist.

"How do you know where you're going?" I ask, gasping. I try not to breathe too deep.

"They are all about the same."

Somehow, I don't believe that at all. It's not like they all worked from blueprints, making sure each boat is exactly the same, like they do now. And weren't these ships all built individually? Whatever. It doesn't really matter anyway, I guess.

Matthew marches quickly down the hall, ignoring the many doors we pass until we get to one that looks just as nondescript as all the others. Without waiting to knock, he lifts the latch on the door and pushes his way inside.

I hesitate in the doorway.

Peering through the darkness inside, Peering through the darkness inside, I make out a narrow room with wooden, boarded walls, nooks created in the sides for two small beds on either side. Matthew shoves his bag onto one of the beds, stooping over to make it through the low ceiling.

"Are you coming in or not?" he asks with a frown, lighting a candle sticking out from a shelf halfway up the wall.

The floor creaks under my feet as I step inside and close the thin door. He glances at me and sits on the bed, pupils wide in the darkness.

"Why are you acting so weird?" I can't put my finger on it, but there's been something odd about him all morning.

Matthew sighs. "I am not trying to be so. I am just a little off. I hate these trips."

"Is that all?" I ask, sitting on the other bed. My feet swing, the bed too high for even my toes to touch the ground.

"Well . . ." he trails off, tucking his chin into his chest.

"What?" My stomach churns.

"I mean, I do hate these trips and it does make me uneasy to be back on a boat, but if I am going to be honest, that's not what the real issue is." He rubs his arm with a slender hand. Matthew looks up, brown eyes black in the candlelight. "I may have told them you were my wife to get you on the boat and to be sure no one messed with you."

My jaw hangs weak as I process his confession. "These men all think I'm your wife?"

"Truly." His eyes shine in the candlelight.

"But you don't think—"

"No, no, no!" Matthew says, trying to stand and hitting his head on the overhang.

Slipping my legs onto the bed, I lean forward to get a better look at him. "You promise this isn't a way for you to . . . you now."

"Of course not!" Matthew squeaks, rubbing his head where it hit the wood.

It's probably true. If he were going to try something, he could have tried it days ago. But then he was still worried about my reputation . . . now with that out of the way, there's nothing to keep him from . . .

"I only said you were my wife because they were not interested in taking a woman onboard and I knew they would be less likely to argue about a wife. Wives aren't as much temptation for the men, you see."

Yeah, because a ring on your finger suddenly changes how men look at you. That doesn't work in my time, and I doubt it would work now.

My back hits the wall as I scoot back from him. "I'm not looking to be temptation for you either."

My chest feels cold. It didn't seem that way when we woke up this morning. I don't know that I'll ever forget the feeling of his arm wrapped around me, my body pressed into his bare chest. Tingles spread down my arms as I think about it.

"It is a pity about your bag." Matthew stretches out on the small bed, his knees pressed into the ceiling.

"Yeah." Aunt Tanis won't be pleased to learn I lost the majority of her work to the ocean, but she'll have to deal. "I hope you'll be willing to share some of your clothes."

Matthew sits up so fast he hits his head on the ceiling again. "My clothes?"

"You don't expect me to wear this dress for the whole trip without washing it do you?" I ask, hand on hip. Even in the pale light, Matthew's raspberry blush is hard to miss. "What's wrong?"

He squeaks and buries his face under his pillow. I didn't think my request was that crazy. Although talking about changing clothes probably made him think about . . . My face warms and I resist the urge to cover up my already covered body. "Well, we'll work that out later."

Maybe we won't have to at all. I don't know when the boat is supposed to sink, but I hope it happens sooner rather than later. I just have to find a way to make sure Matthew survives. And me. I would also like to survive if that's not too much to ask. But maybe we'll get lucky and I'll feel that rush of magic that says I'm ready for our trip out of here before the boat goes down.

The boat rocks wildly underneath me, surging forward on a gust of ocean air.

"And we're off," Matthew mumbles from under the pillow.

"Should we go back up?" I unfold myself from the bunk's alcove.

Matthew shrugs, the pillow shifting over his face. "Why?"

"One last look at land? Aren't you going to miss it?"

He pulls the pillow down, resting it on his chest as he looks at me. "I will see land again."

"But not this land," I point out.

"I'll see it again." He stares into the wood plank ceiling.

The boat shifts in the water as we head into the open ocean. I've never been on a boat like this before, big shocker, and only now do I wonder if I'm going to end up seasick. At the very least it would be a good excuse to get Matthew back on deck so I can watch land falling away behind us.

"I think I'm going to be sick," I lie, pressing my hand into my stomach to seem convincing.

"You were just fine."

"I'm definitely going to be sick," I say, gagging.

"Fine." He clambers out of his bed, grabbing me by the arm to pull me back through the narrow hallway.

Matthew pushes me up the stairs and I take them two at a time. At the top I take a deep breath of fresh sea air. Running to the side of the boat, I rip my coif off. The salty tang in the air plays with my hair, pulling it out of my loose bun. Burnt blonde tendrils whip across my face. I watch the city growing smaller and smaller. Matthew leans next to me, face expressionless. Soon we get far enough away that I can't pick out the individual houses anymore.

This is it then. The only thing we have to do now is survive this trip. Survive the ship sinking and the curse will be broken.

I focus on my growing magic reserves. There's enough there for some sort of jump now. This could possibly work.

How bad could it be?

CHAPTER TEN

‿℮℮℮℮℮‿

We stand on the edge of the deck together until the sun burns high overhead. The coastline is long gone, only the sea keeps us company.

One of the sailors approaches us with half a loaf of bread wrapped in a cloth. He thrusts it at Matthew without even glancing at me.

Matthew hands me the bread, my stomach growling. The dirt crusting the cloth threatens to make my stomach turn, but the bread inside it is still warm. Delicately, I pull the cloth off, trying not to touch any of the questionable brown stains or let them touch the bread. I drop the offending material to the floor and bring the bread to my face, taking a deep breath. The rich smell of yeast is better than anything I've smelt all day. Even the cake we had yesterday can't quite compare.

The crust crunches in my hand as I rip off a piece and put it in my mouth. Matthew watches me with a side smile as I savor the bread with happy chews.

"You are easy to please," he says.

"I don't know that there's anything in this world that tastes better than warm fresh bread." Grinning, I tear off another piece.

His large hand brushes mine as he rips off a big piece of his own. Popping it into his mouth, he gives it a few slow chews. "I do not know what you are talking about. I can think of a hundred things that taste better than this bread."

"You just have no taste," I tease, taking a big bite out of the loaf.

Matthew shakes his head, leaning against the railing to see the boat instead of the lack of coast. There's even fewer crew members on deck than earlier, one at the helm and a few manning the sails.

"Where did everyone go?" I ask Matthew, his shoulders relaxed and face calmer than I've ever seen it.

"Resting probably. They do not all work at the same time," he says. "Otherwise we would be traveling with a lot of half-awake and very cranky men."

"Is there anyone else onboard?"

Matthew shakes his head, dark curls laying against his temples. "We are the only guests onboard."

"Guests?" I laugh. "That implies not having to pay an arm and a leg for this trip."

"An arm and a leg?" Matthew asks, forehead crinkled. "What does that mean?"

Brushing my hair back, I shove my coif back on to hide my slip up. "Oh nothing. Just that we had to pay a lot."

"*I* had to pay a lot," Matthew corrects me with a sly smile. "Is there any chance you might pay me back?"

"I would have paid for it myself if I could."

"Not likely," Matthew laughs.

"Ha ha, very funny." I cross my arms over my chest, ignoring the blush spreading across my cheeks.

He taps his feet against the deck with a hollow thud. "I did not think you would come with me to be honest. Especially after all that discussion of saving me from this trip."

"We probably shouldn't talk about this here," I say, watching the sailor closest to us twitch his head in our direction. Sailors are superstitious right? They probably wouldn't like hearing me say their ship is doomed to sink.

Matthew follows my gaze. "Ready to go back to our room now?"

"Are you planning on spending the whole trip down in that room?"

He shrugs and tilts his head. "If I can sleep through this adventure, I will."

"Going to go into hibernation, are you?"

His laugh is dark. "If only."

My chest tightens at the sound. I hate the disappointments tinging every facet of his life that have made him think this way.

"I don't know if I can do that." Sleeping for a month, no thank you.

"Sleep while you can," he says, already walking toward the stairs. "Later there shall be singing and games and all sorts of things to keep you awake."

I don't move to follow him right away. The idea of going back into that dank and musty air makes me think about setting up a tent right here. Some sailors used to do that didn't they? Maybe not tents, but hammocks, right? Maybe? Oh well. It doesn't matter what some men used to do, I doubt they'll let me do it.

Sighing, I follow Matthew back into the darkness.

Days pass in the same routine. We surface for meals, usually hardtack and salt beef, and go back to the cabin to sleep. The monotony grinds against me, and I would have lost my mind a long time ago if not for the small moments between Matthew and I. Often, when I look up, I'll find Matthew's dark gaze on me. It sends a warm blush across my cheeks, but he never says anything.

All I want is to go above deck and watch the ocean, but if I have to stay below, at least I have better company than I expected.

The air below deck is heavy and thick and I find myself unable to even sleep. Matthew's snores echo through the cabin while I count the ceiling boards for the fiftieth time.

"Are you awake?" I don't even have to roll over to know that Matthew is still fast asleep even as I desperately hope he's not.

He snorts, but his breathing grows shallower. "What?"

"Thank goodness, I thought I was going to lose my mind if I had to lay here for a moment longer." Twisting my head, I watch Matthew rub his eyes and wipe the drool from his chin.

"I'm sorry, what?" he asks through a yawn.

"All you do is sleep, how do you do it? I've spent the last two days just staring at this ceiling and waiting to die!"

He sits up and stretches. "That sounds a little melodramatic."

"Talk to me when you can't sleep, then we'll see how you feel," I grumble, climbing out of my bunk and into the small walkway between the two beds. "Please can we just go up and get a breath of fresh air at least?"

"You and your fresh air," he says with a side smile, slipping on his shoes and climbing out after me.

Standing together in the small space, our chests are barely an inch apart. My breath stills as he stares down into my face. I tilt my head up and wait, for what I'm not sure.

"We cannot get any fresh air if you will not move." Matthew's voice is low and deep as he points toward the door behind me.

Right.

"Oh, yes, of course," I stutter, my face red as a tomato.

Turning quick, I rush into the darkened hallway as Matthew blows out the lantern in our room.

◦⟋⟋⟍⟍◦

Matthew leans against the mast with a scowl on his face. His pinched lips make it no secret how much he doesn't want to be here. Trying not to let his attitude bother me, I stand by the railing and breathe in the fresh ocean air.

"Glad to see you finally surfacing," a man says, approaching without shoes. "We wondered what you could be doing down there that was so much more entertaining than being with the lowly crew." He waggles an eyebrow at me, and I turn away, ignoring the blush creeping up my cheeks.

"Matthew likes to get his rest." I refuse to call him my husband.

"I'm sure he does. With you around, I'd like to get my rest too." He gives a loud laugh.

Muscles tight and hands clammy, I take a few steps back. He closes the distance I build on silent feet, a leering smile spreading across his battered face.

"What's the matter? Afraid of your humble crew?" he asks.

My heartbeat races and I look for Matthew for help. Opening my mouth, words fail to follow.

"Cat got your tongue?" he asks, leaning down so that his rancid breath floods my nose.

He reaches out with a ship-calloused hand, just a hairsbreadth away from touching my face.

"Excuse me," Matthew says. Startled, the sailor's eyes go wide, and he almost falls over in his attempt to get away from me. "Can I help you, Goodman?" he asks, eyes glued to the wood planks.

Matthew pulls me close to his side, fingers digging into my flesh. "I would appreciate it if you could refrain from further discussions with my wife."

"Of course, sir, of course," the sailor says backing away on stumbling feet.

Matthew watches him slink down the stairs then turns flaming eyes on me. "What did you think you were doing?"

"What do you mean what was *I* doing?"

"Next time, stay below."

He pushes off the railing and strides down the stairs, back into the belly of the ship. Struggling to keep up with his long legs, I trip over my skirts until he's practically dragging me across the uneven floor. Shoulder screaming as he does a good impression of wanting to dislocate it with his yanking, he pulls us into our cabin and slams the latch door closed.

"I have not wanted you above deck for a reason, but you never want to listen, so you go up there and make a spectacle of yourself with the hired hand." He lets go and relights the lamp before pacing the two steps of walkway we have between the beds. Running a hand through his unruly hair, his eyes glow like embers in the weak light.

"I wasn't doing anything to draw attention to myself. I didn't ask him to come over or—"

"Do you not understand?" Matthew's voice is strangled. "There is nothing you need to do to ask for attention. Being the only woman on this boat is danger enough."

I press my back against the door to give him as much room as possible in our cramped quarters. "Being a woman isn't exactly something I can control."

Matthew grabs me by the shoulders. "I cannot fight off every man on this ship. I need you to help me."

"Do you expect me to stay locked in this room for months? Because I can't do it, I won't do it!" Just imagining being imprisoned here has me shaking my head, pushing against Matthew's chest. "I won't be a prisoner down here."

He releases me with a sigh. "You are not a prisoner. I consider you to be valuable cargo and want you to make it to England in the same condition you left the settlement in."

"If we even make it to England," I mutter before his words sink in. Valuable? The word makes my chest tight.

"But you came with me," he says, tilting his head as he stares at me.

"Yes." My chest flutters and I have to pause to breathe. "I did."

He reaches across the space between us, my chest tightening as he runs a warm hand down my cheek. "Why did you do that?"

"I made a promise—you will survive this journey." My voice goes up as he tilts my head toward him.

Letting go, he sits back against the wall, my cheek cold as he leaves me. "Who did you promise that to?"

With only the lantern, the room fills with dark shadows. Matthew's face is hidden in the darkness so I can only see the curve of his strong jaw.

"Myself."

He leans forward, eyes burning in the faint light. "I do not believe you."

"I don't know what you want me to say." The spreading warmth from his touch fades until my chest is a hollow shell.

"How about the truth?" Matthew asks, voice dark. "Who sent you to Nantasket for me? There is no way you could have found me there unless you were told where I was. And you would not have known I was taking this ship until long after you would have had to leave to meet me. You must see how strange this is."

"I don't see what's so strange about wanting to save a man's life." I avoid his question and wrap my knees into my chest.

He clasps his hands together. "How do you know I need saving?"

"I've been told this ship will sink. Wouldn't that imply you'll need saving?"

"Who told you it was going to go down?" he asks, knuckles turning white in his grip.

"My aunt."

"And your aunt has a vast knowledge of ships, does she?"

Sliding down the wall, my chest is so compressed I can barely breathe, let alone talk. "No."

"So, your aunt, with no knowledge of ships, said this boat would sink and you jumped at the chance to save a complete stranger from certain doom?" he snarls.

"I guess you could say that," I whisper, knees pressed into my lips.

"Tell me who really sent you."

"She is who sent me." It's not a full lie. *I* didn't talk to Matthew's father. *I* wasn't personally asked to go on this quest. Technically, it's Aunt Tanis's quest that she bequeathed me.

Matthew blows out in exasperation, slamming his back into the wall. "I do not believe you."

"I can't make you believe me."

"Obviously."

"So." I lie back on the bed, ignoring Matthew's dark eyes and the nervous rock in my stomach. "Did you at least bring a book or something?"

"I find no enjoyment in reading." Matthew crosses his arms over his chest.

"Is that a no then?"

Matthew laughs. "Yes, that would be a no."

I press as far away from our earlier conversation as I can. "You can't honestly just sleep the whole time."

He shrugs, picking his hat up off the end of his bed and twirling it around on an extended finger. "I do not always have to stay down here the whole time. Like I said, when we are farther underway there will be games and songs and such going on above deck."

"Will you let me out then? Or will I just have to hear other people having a good time from my dank prison?"

He catches my half smile and gives me a grin in return. "It is my prison as much as yours. According to you, it will even be my coffin." He pauses for a moment, his eyes on my face. "I am positive if you went up, you could make other men tempted to abandon ship too."

Sitting up too quickly, I bash my head against the overhang of ceiling above my head. "You're tempted to abandon ship?"

"Only to get away from you, my dear," he says, laughing as I rub the growing knot on my forehead.

"You really shouldn't tease me like that."

"How else should I be expected to spend my time?" He grins.

I give him a dirty look, lay back in the bed, and start counting planks again.

Chapter Eleven

Matthew stays below deck with me as the long days pass. We go up for meals, something I'm pretty sure he does for my benefit alone. If he asked, they would probably bring our food directly to us. I'm grateful he hasn't.

I spend my time below building up my magic. The well in my core is full now, even more so than when I left to come here. I don't know when I'll get the opportunity to get out of here, but at least I know I'm as ready as I could be.

We stand together on the deck sharing our breakfast of more hardtack. I like coming up here to stare out over the water. I especially like looking where the sea meets the horizon and finding the right angle to make them look seamless, the sky melting into the water. Twisting my head, there's no way to make them meld together today. The dark ocean water is too choppy to meet the still blue of the sky. Instead, I watch the giant pillowy clouds filling the sky above us as we struggle to stay upright.

Goosebumps break out across my arms. Shivering, I turn to Matthew's tight face. "Aren't you cold?"

"Not really, I've learned to adjust. Are you very sensitive to the weather?" Matthew asks, looking down at me with a smile. "Last night you were upset because it was too hot."

"It was crazy hot last night!" I couldn't sleep, the air in our cabin too heavy against my skin, the smell of unwashed men and stale water permeating every corner of my sleeping bunk.

"I am sure you shall be too hot again soon enough, just wait a second."

Huffing, I slouch onto a low barrel next to the railing. A delicate spiderweb stretches between two of the dark beams. Flecks of water sit like jewels suspended by the webbing. Watching the web, a fly lands in the middle, its struggles, sending the water flying. Curious, I wait for the spider to come and check the disturbance, but after a few minutes, the fly calms down and the spider never shows.

"Weird," I whisper to myself. It didn't look like an old web. "Hey Matthew, come and look at this."

"Not now." Matthew waves me away without even looking up.

I stand and look over to where Matthew is staring. A group of sailors are gathered around the helm, their backs making a solid wall around whatever they're looking at.

I rest my hand against his arm, and he glances down at my touch before looking back at the group. "Something is wrong," he whispers.

"Are you sure?" My heart pounds in my chest. "Why would you think that? Maybe they're just playing a game."

Is this the moment I've been waiting for? Animals are supposed to be able to sense a storm coming. Is that why the spider didn't show up for an easy meal?

Now that it could be here, I don't know if my nerves will let my magic work despite all the preparations I've done.

"They are far too quiet for it to be anything good," he says under his breath. "Maybe you should go back to our room."

I shake my head, the tie to my coif coming undone as the wind coming off the waves picks up, flinging water over the side of the boat and across the deck. "I'm not leaving without you."

"I need to find out what is happening, and I do not know how safe it is up here right now."

One of the men in the group turns, scanning the ocean and sky in front of us as the ship rocks to the side, his face is dark and lined with tension. Matthew pushes me toward the stairs.

"Are you sure it will be safe for you?" I dig my heels into the floor.

He gives me a tight smile. "I shall be just fine. Now you get out of here."

I pause. Unable to move. This could be it. The moment the ship goes down. Matthew hesitates beside me. His hand twitches, drawing my attention. He's moved closer. I stare up into his dark swirling eyes.

Breath stilling in my chest, he wraps an arm around my waist and pulls me flush against him. Matthew lowers his face to mine and all I can hear is the pounding echo of my heart.

"In case we do not make it after all," he whispers, so close I can feel his breath on my face.

He doesn't give me a chance to answer before he's pressing his lips against mine. Hand wrapped around the back of my neck, he pulls me closer as his lips move against mine. Our breathes mingle, the turbulent storm forgotten despite the water spraying off the deck and soaking my skirts. Pulling back, he slides his hand across my face, rubbing my cheek with the pad of his thumb.

Resting his forehead against mine, we stare into each other's eyes as reality slowly sets in. Stepping back, his eyes cloud and my heart beats quick in my chest.

"Get below," he says, not meeting my gaze as my lips tingle from his touch.

"Don't you understand? This is what I came for! You need to let me help you!" I have to yell to be heard above the impending storm and my pulse is going crazy either from what's about to happen or the memory of Matthew's kiss, I can't tell.

"I'm not going to let anything happen to you." Matthew's face is stern as he pushes me further down into the ship.

With a final shove, I tumble down a few steps as Matthew slams the door behind me. Thrust into the dark, I run my hand along the damp wood walls as I step down the last few steps. With careful steps I make my way down the hall. Tripping over something soft, a rat squeaks as it runs down the stairs and past me into the dark. Grunting in disgust, I move faster through the hallway toward our room.

Opening the latch door, the ship lurches to the side, throwing me into the room. My head hits the back wall of the room and the lantern falls off the shelf and hits me in the temple. It rolls towards the wall, and I run my fingers along the floor to grab it before I lose it in the dark completely. My hands find the edges of Matthew's bag, muscles burn as I push the surprisingly heavy bag out of the way.

Fingers curling around the lantern, I shove it back on the shelf and light it. The candle flickers, filling the room with the low amber light. Matthew's bag lays at my feet, partially open from my rough handling. With a sigh, I grab the bag to put it back against the wall but stop as I catch a glimpse of something through the open drawstring. Brows drawn, I reach into the bag.

In the pale light, the silver of a wrapper gleams. Slack jawed, it takes me a few moments to understand what I'm looking at. I lie it flat on the bed as my breath catches in my throat.

Before me is the unmistakable wrapper from my granola bar.

How did Matthew find this? My aunts were so worried about authenticity and look what I've done! But why didn't he say anything about it? Does he know I'm a witch?

My heart beats fast in my chest, my hands growing cold. I'm saved from my own reaction by the sound of someone coming down the stairs.

Thumping echoes down the hallway behind the closed door to our room, and I shove the wrapper under my pillow with shaking fingers. Kicking Matthew's bag back against the wall, I fling myself onto my bed just as the latch to the door opens.

Matthew's tousled head pokes through the door as he stumbles in, the ship tilting back the other way. Nervously, I glance at the lantern. If it takes a spill now, we'll all be in trouble. Thankfully, it stays in place.

"How did you fare?" Matthew sits on his bed and pulls off his shoes with a groan.

"F-fine." My voice shakes as I glance at my pillow and imagine the secret hiding underneath it. "Did you find out what was happening?"

"A storm is here," Matthew says, laying on his bed. "And it looks pretty bad."

"Well, how bad is pretty bad? Is there something we should be doing to get ready?" My legs shake as I stand.

"There is nothing they would let a woman help them with. Just lay back and ride it out." But he doesn't relax either, his body tight in the bunk.

The boat shifts again, throwing me into the closed door. "Are you sure that's all we should do?"

"Yes, just sleep."

I sit on the bed but can't get comfortable. My thoughts run around and around, chased by the wrapper and the pending storm.

"I don't think I can sleep," I whisper, feet flat against the wood floor.

Matthew sits up. "Should we stay up together then?"

"Are you not worried about the storm at all?"

He narrows his eyes. "You act like this is your first crossing. We shall go through more storms than just this one, I assure you."

My arms shake and I cross them to hide my obvious unease. "Of course I've been through other storms. I just don't like weather like this when it's on the ocean."

Matthew gives me a side grin and starts talking and I try to stay focused on his words to keep my breathing from becoming erratic. This could be it. This could be the moment I've been waiting for. I might have to save Matthew's life before the storm passes. My magic is ready, but am I?

I dig my sweaty hands into my armpits. "I'm sorry, what were you saying?"

"I said, nothing is going to go wrong and you shall be fine. I went through a storm similar to this one on my way over and the only lives lost were a few rats. We will survive."

My lip trembles. "Are you sure?"

"Here." He opens his arms to me. "Just bunk with me for a bit if you are scared."

Trying to be strong so that I can be ready for what comes next, I open my mouth to refuse when the boat tips again, dumping me into Matthew's lap.

"This is not what I had in mind." Matthew laughs as I scramble off him and onto the bed. "Although if you want to continue what we started earlier . . ."

"Don't flatter yourself."

A low rumble grows in the distance, building as it hits the ship. I stare wide-eyed at Matthew. "What was that?"

"The storm is coming."

I grip his sleeves with white knuckles. "You said this is normal, right? We'll be fine?"

"That is correct." His eyes stare vacantly, and my chest pinches.

"Do they have any life jackets on this ship?" I ask, gulping down deep breaths.

Matthew looks at me with a wrinkled brow. "Life jackets?"

Crap. "Never mind, I'm just being silly."

He tilts his head as he gives me a long look. Opening his mouth to say something, he stops as another rumble shakes the ship.

"That was louder than before," I whisper into his shoulder.

He slings his arm around my shoulders, rubbing my arm in quick strokes. "It is going to be a big one."

"But we'll be fine, right?" I know I keep asking the same question but I'm just hoping that at some point when he tells me it will that I'll actually believe it and I won't have to think about the trip through time I'm going to have to attempt with him if things go south.

"Of course," he says, but doesn't meet my eyes. "I should go see if I can be helpful."

I open my mouth to protest, but nothing comes out.

Letting go, he drifts out the door. I get up, legs shaking, and follow him. He didn't say I couldn't come and I'm not going to wait down here alone.

Water flows down the stairs from the open door. The ship tilts and I lose my balance on the wet floor, landing on my tailbone with a grunt. I grab the railing with both hands, keeping my balance as the floor tilts under me. Tripping over myself, I stumble onto the deck.

The men shout back and forth to each other over the roar of the wind and pounding rain while they roll up the sails. Fat raindrops pelt the deck, my dress instantly soaked as I stand clinging to the stair railing. I try to find Matthew in the chaos. Through the veil of rain, everything and everyone looks the same. The world is a blurry watery mass of moving shapes that lack meaning.

"Matthew!" I shout, my voice swallowed up in the fierce wind.

A large wave smacks against the side of the ship. Grabbing onto the handrail with white knuckles as the ship leans to the right, my eyes scan for Matthew even as my feet slip in the water pooling on the deck.

One of the sailors rushes past me in sodden shoes, a rope curled around his arm. "What are you doing up here? This is no place for a lady!"

"I'm looking for Matthew," I shout at his already retreating back.

The men have the same rope on them, some have it wrapped around their arms and others have it tied around their waist. Is Matthew with them?

I war with myself, wanting to make sure Matthew is okay and wanting to survive the storm. I slowly make my way back down the stairs. The thought of sitting alone in our cabin makes my blood run cold. I can't leave now, not when I'll have to save Matthew. There's no doubt in my mind that this is the storm. Now I just have to find him.

Another wave pushes against the deck and an anguished scream rings out above the noise of the storm. I race to see what happened, and more importantly, who it happened to.

One of the ropes lining the deck is pulled taught, with men gathered around where it dips over the side of the boat. My grip on the railing loosens as I lean toward the action. The men grunt and call over the side as they work to pull the rope back up. My breath stills as my body shakes in the storm's chill.

The frigid rain pounds against the deck as they work furiously to keep hold of the rope. They slip against the slick deck, their groans carrying over the sounds of the storm. After a few frantic minutes, the men in the front reach down and grab the waving hand of the downed man. They pull him over the side like they would a fishing net, and he flops over, arm wrapped around the waist where his rope is tied. His body is limp and the rain is so hard I can't tell if there's any blood.

"Get him below!" One of the men yells. Two men grab him under the arms and drag him across the deck toward the stairs where I stand frozen.

"Out of the way," a man grunts, shoving me aside. They drag the injured man below.

My heart pounds in my chest. I lean over, struggling to get a glimpse of the man's face. "Matthew?" My question is drowned out as a crack of lightening races across the sky with a boom of thunder.

"If you're going to keep stranding there, at least make yourself useful!" the other man yells, his soggy hat melded to his face.

The slapping of my boots through stagnant puddles echoes through the hallway as I follow after them. The first man shoulders open the first door on the right, wet hair flapping against his face as he maneuvers the injured man into the room.

"Get him on that table," he says and together they hoist the man onto the long wobbly table filling the room.

The man groans, face pale under a patchy beard. Definitely not Matthew.

"We'll have to get that rope off him," the first man says. He pulls a long knife from the belt around his waist and saws at the thick rope that's cutting into the man's stomach.

I linger in the doorway. Unable to turn away. The rope falls away revealing a torn slash in his shirt. They wrench his shirt off. A blotchy purple bruise spreads up his chest and down into the waistline of his pants.

"Is it bad?" he asks in a breathless whisper, eyes clenched tight while his hands make fists against his sides.

The man in the dripping hat turns to the other and whispers, "He's bleeding inside. The rope tried to tear him in half."

Running a hand through his hair, he gives the injured man a grim smile. "Not too bad, I'm sure you'll live another day to irritate us yet."

"But—" the floppy hat man says, cut off by his leader.

"It will be fine," he says through gritted teeth.

"Did you want me to do anything?" I nervously rub my shoe against the back of my leg.

The leader nods. "Stay with him." They push past me. "We have work to do above."

My stomach drops as I stare at the man lying on the table. What am I supposed to do now? I've never had to do even basic first aid before and no I've never been left with a man who's almost guaranteed to die whether the boat goes down or not.

"They left, didn't they," he says, eyes still closed.

Dragging a chair from the corner of the room to his side, I try to hide the panic in my voice. "Yeah, I guess the storm is going to be taking everyone's attention today."

"I've never seen a storm like this before," he says. "It came out of nowhere."

I sink into the chair, the wood protesting my weight. It didn't exactly come out of nowhere. I knew it was coming.

I take a deep breath of the cold sea air breezing through the hold and try not to look at the swelling in his stomach.

"I'm sure it will pass soon enough, all storms do." I reach out to take his hand, then stop. Should I take it? I don't know him. I have no idea what he would want.

"It'll pass and we'll be at the bottom of the ocean," he hisses, pressing his hand to his stomach.

"You can't really think that. I'm sure you've seen tons of storms before."

My stomach hardens into a rock. He cracks open an eye and stares at me. "This one was like the heavens themselves opened up and dropped on us. In all my years on the sea I've never seen the anger this storm possesses."

My leg bounces up and down, my body yearning to get out of this room. I don't know what do here. I don't know how to comfort a dying man. I want to run and find someone else to help him, but I know there's no one else. He gives a soft sob and I place my hand on his shoulder.

He grabs my hand, crushing it in his too strong grip. His eyes darken as his face grows red. "Don't leave me to die alone."

"You're not going to die." I let him wrench it closer. I've never seen someone die before and the dark pallor of death is here with us, beckoning him home. A chill runs down my back and I have to keep my feet still despite my overwhelming desire to run.

"I always knew I would die at sea." He lays back, tears streaming down his face. I squeeze his hand, trying to offer comfort.

"I was only ten when I made my first trip across the sea." He turns and looks at me out of haunted eyes.

"Really," I say, my voice hoarse. "Did you travel with your father?"

A ghost of a smile crosses his face. "Yes," he says barely a whisper. He winces as he shifts closer to me. Understanding, I lean in. "He . . . he . . ."

I pat his hand. "You don't have to talk . . ."

He falls back on the table with a groan, releasing me to clutch at his stomach.

"Can I look at it?" I don't know what else to do. Maybe getting a look at him will distract me from the overwhelming sense of doom crushing me.

He nods. My hands won't stop trembling. He looks away from me, staring at the ceiling and mouthing a silent prayer. Slowly, I reveal once more the spreading purple bruise. A thick line runs across his stomach. I run my finger along its length, the skin corded from the rope, until it wraps around his body and I can't feel it anymore. Staring at the damage, I'm surprised he didn't break his back. He would've had to be thrown with a lot of force for this kind of damage to occur.

He is hemorrhaging on the inside and there's nothing I can do.

Feebly, I elevate his long legs, the muscle in them drawing tight. It's about the only thing I remember from first aid classes I was required to take at school and I doubt it will be of much use at all. This and the fireman's carry. I'm about as useful as a tomato.

"Do you want to talk?" I ask, sitting back down.

His dark eyes bore into mine in the semidarkness, the sound of the crushing storm filling the room. "What should I talk about?"

"Your life maybe?" I chew on my bottom lip to hide my growing discomfort.

"My life?" he asks, staring at the ceiling again. "I doubt it would be of any interest."

I laugh. "I think you'd be surprised what I might be interested in."

"Well, then," he sighs. "My parents were merchants, surprising right? How disappointed they were in their sea-loving son. My father always wanted me to take over his shop and instead I chose a life of menial labor. I haven't talked to them since I left. Too afraid I guess."

I reach out and take him by the hand as he talks.

"I wonder what they're doing right now. I wish I had told my mom I loved her. She deserved at least that, deserved a better son than I made." A tear runs down his cheek. "Could you maybe look her up for me? When you get to England? Let her know her John loved her and thought about her in the end." He chokes and I squeeze his hand.

"Of course I will," I tell him, feeling the burn of the lie. I have no intention of making it all the way to England.

"We had a house right in town with real glass windows. My mom was so proud of those windows," he smiles, eyes glazing over. "I thought I might actually visit this time."

His voice trails off. I keep my hand in his, kneading the top of his hand with my thumb. The ship rocks back and forth, the lantern hung in the corner sending up slanting shadows with each movement.

Being down in the boat, it's easy to forget how terrifying it felt above deck. I almost forget how sure I was that this was the night I would have to save Matthew's life.

Matthew.

My spine straightens and I'm instantly on alert. I have to find him and make sure I haven't already failed in my task. I can just imagine the look on Aunt Tanis's face if I came home and told her I'd missed out on the one moment I came here for because I was too scared to stand on deck.

But I can't leave John to die alone.

Tightening my grip on his hand, I stand and twist to see into the hallway. Water pours down the stairs in buckets, pooling and sliding along the floor as the ship heaves back and forth. No one's coming for us.

"Hello?" I call up the stairs as loud as I dare. "Is anyone coming back?"

John turns unfocused eyes on me. "They're not going to come down for a girl and a dead man when they have a ship to save."

"You're not dead yet," I protest, realizing too late that I shouldn't have tacked on the 'yet' as his face falls.

"I know." He turns back to the ceiling. "I'm sure it won't be long."

He's not wrong and the thought makes me feel sick. Even without being close to his stomach, I can see his skin bulging with the blood filling his chest cavity. I don't even know if modern medicine could have saved him now.

"Do you need to make a confession or something?" I hide my face by staring up the damp stairs.

"I didn't realize you were a priest," John says with a laugh that turns into a cough. "Are you just curious about what a sailor can get up to in ten years?"

"Only ten years?" I ask with a jolt, glancing at John's wrinkled face.

He gives me a weak grin, running his hand over his weathered cheeks. "It doesn't take long for the sun to have its way with you when you're out on the ocean."

"I guess not," I say candidly. "I wouldn't have guessed you were so young."

"I'll just be forever young and beautiful right?" he asks with a smile.

I squeeze his hand again. He doesn't need me to remind him how the years of his life have left their mark on him, he knows. But if he's only been at sea for ten years, he could be as young as 22. It's just hard to fathom.

"Of course."

My eyes blur with tears as my simple agreement makes the lines of his body go soft and peace enters his face.

John exhales slowly, the breath rattling as it leaves his lungs. His smile goes slack and his eyes lose focus. Squeezing his hand, I wait for a response that doesn't come.

He's gone.

Chapter Twelve

I grab the handrail and take slow steps up the stairs. My limbs are weak and my heart is aching as tears slip down my cheeks.

The wind keeps the door from closing. Giving me a glimpse of the punishing storm outside. Maybe John was right. The storm will pass leaving the boat at the bottom of the sea.

Lightning streaks across the sky. Thunder booms so loud it sends me to my knees. Water seeps into my dress, weighing me down as I crawl the rest of the way up.

Once more I stand at the top of the stairs, staring out at the men trying to keep the ship in one piece. They rush back and forth over the deck through the thick currents of rain. Still I can't find Matthew.

Keeping a hand on the side of the ship, I crawl out of the stairwell, cold rain pelted down on my face, and move toward the helm. If anyone knows where Matthew is, it'll be the captain.

Another wave buffets the ship, the cold water making my muscles seize up. My fingernails dig into the floor as my body starts to slide. Visions of John being thrown from the deck flash through my mind and I dig in harder. But the ship keeps dipping.

Everything left loose on deck tumbles past me. Large wooden crates and round barrels roll off the ship and into the turbulent sea. The angle of the deck shifts past 75 degrees and I can't hold myself up anymore. Sliding across the deck, my dress pulls up, my legs biting into the rough boards. Splinters lodge into my bare flesh. I cry out. But nothing can stop my slid toward the edge. Salty rainwater fills my mouth and I panic.

"Soph?" A hand reaches out, grabbing me around the waist and stopping my fall with a jolt.

Clinging tight, I stare up into Matthew's dark eyes.

"You saved me," I breath out, relief filling me.

"I thought you were supposed to save me," he says, forcing a smile.

Rope is twisted around Matthew's arm. I can see the strain in his face as he tries to hold on. He breathes heavy on my temple, his hair plastered to his face as the rain continues to beat against us.

"What do we do now?" I yell, staring into his face.

He leans down, lips against my ear. "There is nothing for us to do, Soph, but hold on and wait for the storm to pass." His face is grim as he stares out at the darkened sky. He looks down at me. "We will have to save each other."

"I'm supposed to keep *you* safe," I mutter and he pulls back with a frown.

I don't know what to do. I don't think I can work my magic. Not here. Not buffeted by the storm. I won't be able to keep my concentration long enough to make a door, let alone go through it.

A barrel rolls toward us with a vengeance. Water sprays off its rims as it picks up speed. My already too-tense body shifts but there's nowhere to go.

"Move!" Matthew cries, twisting my body behind him.

Before I could clear the barrel's path, it clips me in the shoulder. Pain slices down my arm. Matthew pulls me close as I cry out.

"Are you okay?" he asks, his eyes searching me. I can make out each individual fleck in his brown eyes.

Trying to move my arm, I have to stop as my shoulder stabs with pain. I massage the damaged tissue with a cold numb hand. "I can't move my arm very well."

"I need to get you below." Matthew's grip tightens around my waist.

The rain shows no sign of letting up, the fat drops falling in thick sheets. The crew is gathered around the helm, wrestling the sails.

No one is going to save us now.

A monster wave approaches in the distance, its size already taller than the mast.

"M-m-Matthew!" I cry out

But it's too late.

The wave crashes against the ship, plowing through it like we were a pebble in its path.

A loud crack penetrates the roar of the wind.

I don't even have time to catch my breath as the ship is plunged into a wall of dark water.

Blind terror shoots through my limbs. I cling to Matthew in a desperate attempt to keep us together. We are sucked down into a vortex of cold water. Matthew's rope twists loosely around me as we spin through the water and his arm comes loose from my waist.

My lungs burn for air as I stare into an abyss of darkness. I've lost Matthew. I can't tell what's up and what's down as I stare through the dark water. Bubbles escape through my nose. My jaw clenches and I can't think straight. Lungs burning, I try to swim to the surface but I can't find it. Panic has me wanting to open my mouth to scream.

The rope around my body pulls tight, dragging me down, down, down. Clawing through the water, my efforts aren't enough to propel me forward.

Rough hands brush against my face. Eyes wide, I try to move my hair out of the way to see anything. Matthew's face swims into focus. Heart flopping against my chest, he pulls out a large knife from his pants. His chest is bare as he surges through the water toward me, the rope tugging me towards the ocean floor.

Knife gleaming in the murky light, Matthew attacks the rope around my waist. Bubbles escape from his parted lips as he furiously saws, their path to the surface marking our escape route. My body jolts as he tugs on the rope, the twisted knot pulling tighter. He glances at me with wide wild eyes, dark hair tangling around his face. Staring into his dilated pupils, he gestures for me to stay with a large hand.

He turns, bare feet kicking as he shoots to the surface. Despite his instruction, I try to go after him but I can't. The rope keeps pulling me down and there's no way I can hold my breath any longer.

My heart pounds in my ears as the water gets darker. I open my mouth as my body attempts to breathe but only salty water rushes in. I choke on it as my lungs fill, sealing my fate as my body tries to flail to the surface one more time.

CHAPTER THIRTEEN

Dark splotches play in my vision, mixing with the black water. My hands trail above me as I continue in my slow descent. My thoughts linger on John. He knew who he wanted to see and what he wanted to say at the end. Do I have anything like that? My thoughts trail off. It's so hard to think. Everything is fuzzy. I should be doing something but I can't remember what anymore.

A hand closes around mine. My head jerks up as Matthew uses my arm to pull himself down to my level through the water.

He came back for me.

The words echo around in my empty mind: he came back for me, he came back for me, he came back for me.

Matthew's eyes are narrowed as he draws his knife again. Floating limp, my body jerks back and forth in the dark water with his strokes as he works at the rope again.

Eyes slipping closed, Matthew holds the rope in front of me, but I can't focus on it.

We break the surface, lungs screaming as something thumps against my back. Breathing in reminds me of what a newborn must feel like as my lungs swell and I cry out.

"Oh, thank heavens," Matthew says.

I blink water out of my eyes. My body convulses, sending me into a coughing fit. Matthew thumps me on the back again. Water shoots up my throat and out my mouth. I shift, and my legs meet only water.

I lay over a wooden pole, my legs still dangling in the water. Matthew leans on the pole next to me. We ride our makeshift lifeboat up and down on the waves. "Where's the ship?" I cough out, chest still sore.

"Gone." He looks out over the water then back at me. "I was able to find part of the mast."

We're stranded. My chest tightens. I focus on my gift, relieved to find my magic intact and overflowing.

"Thank you for saving me."

He gives me a soggy grin. "We were connected, remember?"

"Oh right."

The sky above us is dark, veined with the faint streaks of lightening. Debris floats around us. Barrels and pieces of wood spread out on the choppy water. At least the rain has stopped.

"Are we the only survivors?" I ask, stomach falling.

"I have not seen anyone else since we came up." Matthew swings his leg over the pole, straddling it. "The water is so rough it is possible they floated further out and we can't see them."

The look on his face suggests he knows this isn't true.

My mouth goes slack and I rub at my eyes. Saltwater drips off my hand and into my eyes, spreading the burning sensation from my lungs to my head as I cry the water back out.

"What do we do now?"

Matthew leans closer to me, taking my hand in his. "You were right about the ship." With a bitter smile and a heavy sigh, he rubs the back of my hand with his thumb. "I should have waited. I should have listened when you said it was dangerous."

"I can't blame you for not believing a girl you just met." Or for not believing the mad ramblings of a crazy girl.

He winces, releasing my hand.

"Superstition is supposed to be strong with me, I mean it is for everyone else. Hearing you say the boat was going to go down so many times should have made me stop and listen. Instead, it just made me more determined to go. I brought you down with me."

I shrug, kicking my legs to try and get higher up on the pole. "I didn't have to go with you. I made that choice on my own."

"I helped though. You never would have been able to come if I had not paid for you, had not lied for you."

"Regretting making me your wife?" I ask with a wry smile.

He laughs. "Only because that lie is going to die with us. I cannot imagine how happy your parents will be when they find out you 'married' me."

The grin slides off my face. "I don't think you have to worry about that."

"Of course not," he says with a shrug. "I shall never have to face them."

"That's a great idea," I whisper, Matthew's brows narrowing.

"What do you mean?"

I don't have to die here. This doesn't have to be the end. All I have to do is use my gift. Now that the storm has passed it should be easy for me to focus enough to get us out of here.

"I think I know how to save us," I keep my words slow.

"You have another ship hidden in that petticoat or something?" Matthew asks. His tone is light, but I don't miss the undercurrent of despair.

I square my shoulders as best I can while slumped over the pole. "I haven't told you everything about me."

"I have not known you very long, I would assume you had not told me everything. Just enough, right?" He smiles but it doesn't reach his eyes.

"Just stop for a second." I hold my hand out to reinforce my point. "I need to tell you something, and it's going to be hard for you to believe."

"I doubt that," he says softly, a wave of water lapping at his legs.

"I'm not joking."

He raises a brow at me but doesn't respond, his gaze traveling over the still choppy water.

I start slowly. "I think you would've drown out here if I hadn't come with you."

"You think your presence alone will keep me from drowning now that our boat is gone?" he asks with a smirk that doesn't reach his eyes.

I try to lift myself higher on the mast, but end up flopping into the water again. "It's not my presence that's going to save us . . . it's my gift."

Matthew's eyes whip toward me, growing dark despite the rays of sunshine poking through the clouds.

"I couldn't use it before, but this might be our only option to survive," I continue before he can interrupt me. "And honestly I'd hate to die just because I was keeping you company."

"Your gift?" Matthew asks, brows tight over his narrowed eyes. He laughs, the sound a dark stain through the air between us. "You are a witch."

"A witch who'd like to save your life."

"Maybe I do not need the help of a witch." He looks down his nose at me and something deep in my chest feels like its breaking.

"Look around you." I gesture at the open ocean and broken debris around us. "I'm your only chance!"

I wait for him to shut me down, to rain his religious fury on my head even as we stare death in the face. But it doesn't come. Some of the darkness recedes from his eyes as he watches me with a tilted head.

"I should have known," he finally whispers. "All the signs were there, and I ignored them."

His fingers dig into the muscle in his legs, hair whipping back and forth in the last of the storm's breeze.

"I shall come with you," he says, not looking at me but back out at the ocean. "As long as it doesn't incur a life debt."

I laugh. "You're looking at the prospect of drowning and you're worried about owing me a *life debt*?"

"I can understand why that might sound funny to you, but I assure you, where I come from, life debts are very serious."

"Whatever." I fling his worry away, still thinking it's stupid. "You won't owe me a life debt. I just want to save your life."

He's silent for a moment then shrugs. His eyes sparkle as he stares at me, sending a shiver down my spine. "All right then, witch, show me your grand power that will transport us away from this mess."

"I've never been able to use it with another person before," I confess. "So, I'm not entirely sure how successful I'll be."

"Sounds like a promising way to start a journey."

"You can always back out, I don't have to take you with me," I grumble, conveniently forgetting that saving him right now is the only reason I'm here in the first place.

He holds up his hands in mock surrender. "Pardon my teasing. What do I need to do to help you?"

"Just take my hand and shut up." I don't even look at him as he places his hand in mine, sending a warm jolt up my arm.

Screwing my eyes tightly closed, I count down from ten in an attempt to relax. Maybe I should go back in time alone and try to convince him once again not to go. Or convince Thomas not to send him away. That's even assuming it will work at all this time.

Peeking at Matthew's calm face, I know this is what I have to do, have to try my hardest to do.

Warm threads of magic work their way up my arm, and Matthew's startled squeak is enough to tell me it's starting to work. Purple threads twist through the air around us, binding us in a tight ball. I have no door this time. I don't have the power to move us both through the door, but I might be able to do this.

The threads glow in the semidarkness, pulling tighter and tighter as I grab for more. I'll need every last scrap of magic in me to move us. Matthew's hand tightens around mine, his pulse easily felt where our hands connect.

The globe surrounding us begins to spin. Water whips up where my magic meets it.

I pull an image of the forest into my mind. Only for it to slip as Matthew grips my hand. "Stop!" I yell.

There's no time to explain to him what I'm doing, the vortex as already started to form. Where do we go? Should I travel back to my time? I should have had him describe his home in England. The only place I know in this time is the settlement. Before I know it, an image of Matthew's home crystalizes in my head.

Oh crap!

Squeezing Matthew's hand, I close my eyes and pray this won't end up biting me in the butt.

CHAPTER FOURTEEN

Without the door to walk through, we're whipped through the purple cosmos of stars and swirling clouds. Faster than I've ever traveled, I cling to Matthew's hand as my pulse races. Tears build in the corner of my eyes and tear across my face. Matthew's arm wraps around me and we curl into each other.

I pour my magic into the portal. My arms go limp first, the strength draining out of them. Matthew holds me up, my head buried in his chest. I taste the coppery tang of blood in the back of my mouth as I'm sucked dry. It's happening too fast, becoming something I can't control. My body goes dry, my limbs tightening as my life force begins leaving with my magic. My eyes burn and the pressure in my head builds until I want to scream.

All at once it stops. The purple threads of my magic fades away. Darkness engulfs us as we get to the end of the tunnel. Matthew's arms crush against my chest. His breath is ragged, blowing in my hair. My mind grows fuzzy as my limbs weaken. A thick, black blanket of magic wraps around us.

"Soph!" Matthew yells.

I fall, my body hitting hard against the earth, and pass out.

I wake up with a start. My arms reach, hands searching for Matthew in the darkness. But there's nothing there. Nothing, not even dirt comes back in my clenched fists.

Light blooms in the distance. Scrambling to my feet, I almost fall in my haste to run after it.

Barren landscape spreads on either side of me in the faint light. The only sound in the empty space is my heavy breathing. I run, faster and faster toward a light that never gets closer. Legs straining, I lean over, resting my hands on my thighs. Still the source of the light stays out of reach and I'm no closer to finding out where I am.

A groan crosses the distance to me in the darkness. I stop running, turning toward the sound. The darkness pulls past me, brushing my hair off my shoulders and down my back in the chill wind.

"Matthew?" I ask the dark outline standing in front of me.

The shape groans, the sound making my chest constrict.

"Who's there?" I try again.

The figure moves closer on silent feet. It towers over me by at least two feet, and I have to tilt my head to stare into the dark expanse where his head should be.

Shadow hands reach for me with long taloned fingers. Coldness floods my chest and adrenaline surges through my body as I shove away out of the reach of the shadow creature. Backing up, I run toward the light. The creature follows me, groaning as I get farther away.

With the light behind me, my view is shaded and dark. Still, the shadow creature stands out, a black blot against the landscape. The long body shrinks down to the size of a man as we get closer to the light.

"Soph?" it calls with a gash of a mouth, but the voice that comes from it is Thomas's.

I stop. Body still, the creature continues its slow approach until we're almost chest to chest. It bends over, face lit by the light behind us to reveal Matthew's grin. It laughs with Thomas's laugh, face still Matthew's, eyes flashing as it reaches out to me with its shadow hands and I sink into darkness.

"Soph?"

Gulping down breaths, I refuse to open my eyes, afraid of what I might see. Rough hands grab me by the shoulders, shaking me until my eyes flutter open.

Matthew sits in the grass in front of me. His shirt is still gone, ripples of water cascading down his bare chest from his wet hair. "Soph? Are you okay?"

Am I? I take stock of my own body. There's nothing but my damp petticoat in the spot where the demon touched me. I check my magic stores but it's almost empty again. I release a shaky breath as Matthew watches me with wide eyes.

"I got worried when you didn't wake up and I shook you but you still didn't wake up—"

"I'm fine." I sit up. And I will be. It was just a dream. "Where are we?"

Matthew laughs, running a hand through his hair and sending water flying. "It looks like we're back around Nantasket. I never thought I'd end up here again."

"Nantasket?" my stomach sinks as I remember my last thought before we traveled. Thomas. "Are you sure?"

He gestures to the small clearing around us. "This looks almost exactly like the same clearing where Thomas brought me to accuse me of witchcraft."

Of course it does. I've just brought us back to where I arrived when I traveled to this time.

I lay back in the grass, ignoring the rapid beating of my heart. "We should stay here for a bit. I don't know if we traveled back in time or simply to the same spot."

"You mean to say we traveled through time?"

"I did what I had to do to save us," I remind him while throwing an arm over my face, so I don't have to see him. "I can't help this is all I can do."

"This is all you can do? Truly?"

I peek at him from under my arm. "Yes. Why?"

He sighs, settling next to me in the grass. "You are not from this time at all are you?"

I give him an embarrassed grin. "I didn't really do my research before I left."

"And your aunt is the one who knew what would happen to me?"

I sigh, grateful he's going to ignore my rash actions. "She dreams true. She told me I had to save you. Your father told her to."

He doesn't need to know about the curse. Why does it matter that I came to save my family more than I did to save him?

He's quiet for a long time. Geese call through the air as they pass over us. A burnt orange leaf floats down in lazy circles.

He shifts in the grass. "This is very unexpected."

"I'm sure. Take your time."

Matthew leans forward on his knees as he takes a few shallow breaths. "Don't you think we should check out the settlement, maybe try to find out what time you brought us back to and how long we have to hide out here?"

"I suppose." Reluctantly I get up with him. He's been saved now, can't I just go?

The thought of home doesn't fill me with the same relief as before. Despite everything, I don't feel like running for home anymore.

I follow Matthew through the trees, chest empty. If I weren't so drained, I could just open a door now, walk through and leave Matthew to figure out when we are on his own. But a large part of me refuses that idea. Instead, it keeps me marching after Matthew with shaky steps.

He turns toward me with a barely perceptible sigh. "Fine."

He grabs my hand and pulls me along. His hands are large and rough, swallowing mine in a way that makes my mouth go dry.

"Do you do this often then?" Matthew asks, his head framed by fiery red leaves. "Travel through time to rescue people you don't know?"

"Who says I don't know you?" I tease.

His head tilts as he considers my words. "Do you know me?"

I shake my head. He gives me a small smile as he turns to face the narrow path in front of us. "I guess that is good," he says. "I like thinking we know the same amount. We can get to know each other together."

If I told him about the curse then maybe that would be true. I don't know what keeps me from saying anything. It's not like he could do anything about it. In fact, it could be broken by now for all I know. But I can't bear to see the look in his eyes as he realizes none of this was for him. I like him thinking of me as someone who is willing to risk my life to save someone else instead of someone who will risk their life for their own gain.

"I've gone back in time before, but never more than a few years. This is my first trip back like this," I tell him instead to ease the building ache in my chest.

"Really? If it were me, I would have seen everything there was to see." He looks over his shoulder at me. "But you came all this way for me after not risking it before . . . what made my life so important to save?"

My feet falter until I realize he's teasing me. His mouth pulls into a large side grin.

"I never felt powerful enough to do a big trip through time before. So, you're just lucky my aunt dreamed it. If she hadn't, I might be safe and warm at home right now, completely oblivious of you." Matthew gives me a look of mock horror and I stick my tongue out at him.

"Thank goodness for your aunt then."

I smile, pulling my dripping skirts wide, their heavy fabric pulling my body down.

"How far back do you think you took us?"

"I can't imagine it was very far," I say, water squishing between my toes as it slowly drains from my shoes. "To take both of us was more than I've ever done before. So, it could be as little as a few minutes or as much as a few hours. I can't imagine us being any farther than that."

We travel in silence, less worried about running into our past selves than I was before. Pebbles roll under my feet as we go. What will Thomas think of me coming back?

The thought stops me cold. Matthew keeps plodding along without me. I should not be thinking about Thomas, shouldn't care what he thinks about what I'm doing. A shiver runs down my back as I remember the shadow with Thomas's voice. I don't know what it means, but I'm pretty sure staying away from him would be for the best. I'm a witch and he's a witch hunter. Getting close to him is asking for trouble.

Dry leaves rustle under my feet as I catch up with Matthew, racing past my own confusing thoughts.

"Are you all right?" Matthew asks, turning to me.

"Just stopped to check out a pretty leaf," I tell him with a broad smile that shows almost all my teeth.

Soft voices from the not-so-distant settlement ripple through the trees. Matthew and I jerk our heads in its direction. There's danger there for both of us and I'd so much rather hide in the trees.

"We should stay together. Just in case." Matthew rubs a broad hand down his bare shoulder and I watch the goosebumps prickling along his arms.

"Cold?"

Matthew shrugs. "I will take this over the ocean any day, but I have been wishing I had not left my shirt and shoes behind."

"Your shoes?" I've been so distracted I didn't even notice he was barefoot. "Your feet must be killing you!"

"It is just as well," he says, letting his hand fall.

A grey squirrel climbs up the tree next to me, its little claws making scratching sounds against the bark. The soft pad of Matthew's feet against the trail makes my stomach twinge. He's been walking shoeless this whole time and all I could think of was myself. Matthew walks with confidence, keeping his eyes ahead and not on the ground in front of him like mine have been.

"I'm sorry I didn't notice." I grab my shoulder and try not to cry.

Everything feels different now. But none of that matters. We're going to have to hide out in the settlement and figure out how to get out before anyone catches us. I'd much rather not end things with me being fried as a witch. Which could happen to him too if he sticks with me too long.

I just need to focus on surviving this last leg of our journey. If I can save Matthew from Nantasket then my job here will be done.

CHAPTER FIFTEEN

I know I should be focused on our survival, but that dream I had has swirled around my brain, pushing out any other thoughts. My mind wars between Thomas and Matthew, even as my lips tingle with the memory of Matthew's in-case-we're-dying kiss.

I can't believe he kissed me. We were going to die and he kissed me. That's probably no big deal, right? But what if it isn't? I shake my head, thick strands of drying hair slapping my face. I shouldn't care. I've never cared before. Not that I've had a lot of experience with kissing. Just a few experiments in junior high. But kissing those boys never did anything. I couldn't care about them so I didn't want to kiss them.

Matthew held his hand out, stopping me in my tracks. "Wait."

"What is it?"

Heavy footfalls pound against the bare earth. Looking through the dense forest, I glimpse dark shapes moving through the trees. Crouching down behind some shrubs, Matthew makes his way back and pulls me to my knees.

"Stay quiet, just in case," he whispers, face close enough to my ear that I can feel his stubble on my cheek.

He smells like the ocean as he puts his arm around me and we hunch close to the ground. I focus on Matthew's steady breathing.

A branch snaps and the footsteps scatter further into the woods.

Matthew stands slowly, pulling me up with him. "Probably just a deer."

Nodding, my cheeks warm as his hand stays pressed against my back. He turns to face me, his chest rising and falling with heavy breaths. The memory of his kiss spreads tingles through me and I force the thought away.

"Do you think we should keep heading to the settlement?" I attempt to ignore my beating heart. "Like, is it safe?"

"You would know more about that than me," Matthew says with a laugh, his hand falling back to his side.

"I just don't know what everyone's schedule is like. How weird is it going to be when we come out of the woods when we both just left?"

Nerves settle into my stomach as we plod farther into the woods. I don't know what is scarier at this point, what's happening with Matthew or having witch hunters find us.

"It doesn't really matter what they think about us coming back. We won't make it if we try to go back to the city, and honestly, that would be stranger. People in the city know we got on that ship. What would they think if we showed up again but the ship was still gone? We are much more likely to be accused of witchcraft if anyone sees us."

We walk along for a while, each of us consumed in our own thoughts. I steal a glance and notice the look of peace covering his handsome face. "I'm surprised you're not freaking out I'm a witch."

"How could I? You used it to save my life. That is so different from what the church has said, that it must be wrong."

"That's good to hear. I mean, I know if I were with someone else, I'd most likely be burning from a stake right now."

"More like hanging from a rope," Matthew corrects me with a crooked smile.

I bite my bottom lip. "You're just so calm about it."

"I do not believe calm is the right word. I have a lot to think about."

"So, what should we do now that you know about it—"

"I would rather not," Matthew cuts me off with a frown. "I shall appreciate you saving me by not saying anything and you shall appreciate me not turning you in by not talking about it. Deal?"

"I guess so." I say it but don't really mean it. My body feels heavy as I trail after him, my hands hanging limp at my side.

I can't help but wonder if he regrets that kiss now. The kiss that sends a blush creeping up my cheeks just thinking about it. He can't be that happy knowing he's kissed a witch.

"We're almost there." His back muscles are tight in the weakening light.

"So let's just sneak back into your house until we've figured out when we are."

"That is not a bad idea. I doubt they will have done anything with it yet anyway if we're in the recent past."

"Just taken your goat, right?" I ask with a smile he doesn't return.

"I doubt they let her sit there alone long. Thomas most likely appropriated it."

Matthew branches off the path, onto a patch of land filled with leaves and branches and sticks poking up between dark patches of rich earth and rocks. "Let us try to go straight for the house. No need to alert everyone to our hideout. Are you going to be able to get through the woods without making an outrageous amount of noise?"

My mouth screws to the side. "I'm not making a lot of noise."

"Anyone within fifty feet of us would know you are a person and not an animal with the amount of noise you make."

"That's not a very nice way to talk to a lady," I grumble but watch where I place my feet with more care.

Matthew gives me a grin. "I would worry about that, but I am pretty sure you are not actually a lady."

Gaping, I miss the root jutting across our makeshift path and tumble over into the leaves. He hooks my arm with his and heaves me to my feet. Heat blooms where he touches me and I forget for a moment what I was going to say.

"Wh-what do you mean?" I finally manage as a blush spreads up my neck.

"In the future, do you still call women 'ladies'?" He lets me go and continues forward into the tangle of pine branches, releasing the crisp scent of its sap.

"Not really. But you're still a gentleman, so shouldn't you still treat me like a lady?"

He glances at me over his shoulder. "I am not a gentleman."

"Obviously," I breathe to myself, but I catch the start of a wry smile as he turns back around.

Wind whistles through the trees, rustling the leaves still clinging to their branches. I shiver in my damp dress and goosebumps break out across my skin. The trees grow closer together and Matthew slows. His footfalls silent as we make our way through the dense foliage. I follow, my shoes crunching on the dead leaves.

"We are close now," Matthew whispers, holding out a hand. "I shall help you until we get into the house."

I slid my hand in his. Warmth envelopes me, sending a shiver down my spine. "If you can call it that," I whisper, trying to not think about the butterflies fluttering in my stomach.

His eyes narrow but there's humor in them as he tightens his grip and leads me through the woods.

The clearing spreads out in front of us. We're still hidden by a healthy amount of trees, but the path is much more worn here than before. I see Thomas's house and my heart tightens.

My foot slips on a pile of wet leaves. Before I can stop myself, I gasp, the sound loud even to my own ears. Matthew drops down next to me, sinking into the leaves with a squelching sound, his finger going to his lips to silence me. He hauls me back to my feet but the damage has been done. The shifting leaves were loud even to me. Matthew glares at me as we sink close to the ground and wait.

Men's voices drift through the trees from the settlement.

The voices grow closer. "Think it was an Indian?"

Matthew's hand tightens around mine.

"I am telling you, it was just an animal. No Indian would be that loud."

"A young one could be—"

"And they would send a young one out to spy on us and get himself caught?"

"I guess not."

The men move away and the tightness in my chest loosens.

"Just leave it," a familiar voice calls. My heart seems to stop, my breath catching in my throat. "We have better things to do than worry about the squirrels that come close."

Thomas.

Matthew stands, listening to the footsteps of the men fade away.

"Soph?" he whispers, coming closer to me. "We have to go."

Blinking, I force life back into my limbs. It shouldn't surprise me that Thomas is here. He lives here. I just didn't plan on seeing him again.

I follow Matthew on numb and silent feet. We're not far from Matthew's house but it seems like forever before he finally stops.

"This is the clearing behind my house." His eyes are far away as he stares through the trees and into the shaggy grass beyond. "We shall have to move quick."

"Shouldn't we wait for nightfall or something?"

He shakes his head. "I just want to settle down for a bit. Staying out here for another hour does not sound very comfortable."

His mouth tightens as he moves through the trees toward the settlement. Creeping after him, my gaze travels to the right, toward where I heard Thomas. It's ridiculous, but then so much of my life feels that way these days.

I miss my mom. She'd know what to say. I'd love to have someone else to talk to about all of this. About Matthew's kiss and the way Thomas makes my stomach flip. It doesn't make any sense. But Mom would understand and she'd know how to make sense of it. And if she couldn't then one of my aunts could. I just know it.

"Ready?" Matthew asks, pulling me out of my thoughts.

We break through the treeline. Matthew's sad little shack sits only a hundred feet away.

He scans the area. "Let us go."

We sprint across the dry grass growing in patches between the slanted shack and the woods. My dress rustles with every heavy step as I try to keep up with him. Glancing back once, Matthew motions me to move faster before speeding up himself.

Looking around as I run, I make out the back of Thomas's house through a thin patch of trees. There's no one back there, but I know that just moments ago he stood there, staring into the woods.

My foot sinks into a hole. I pitch forward, my ankle twisting. Gasping, pain blooms from my ankle up my leg. Matthew is almost to the back door of his squatty house. I stand and start limping after him. Pain flares with every step.

Matthew reaches the door and turns. Frowning at my struggle, he runs back.

"Hurry up! What are you doing?" he hisses as he comes closer.

"It's my ankle." My face twists in a grimace.

After a quick scan of the area, he scoops me up, my body pressed against his chest, and books it for the house. As I jostle against his bare chest, the pain is temporarily forgotten. The sensation of being so close to him overrides everything else and a blush creeps over my cheeks.

He shoulders open the back door. Stale air rushes out, filling my nose.

"If the house is stale, we must have gone back in time only a few days," I say.

Matthew sighs and sets me down in the wooden chair. A pang of longing rushes through me and I push it down.

He slides down the wall, hitting the ground hard, stirring the dirt covering his hardwood floor. "It would appear so," he says, resting his head against the wall.

"Do you think anyone saw us?"

Matthew glances up at me with a tired smile. "I do not believe so."

"We won't be headed to the noose today!" I wave my arms and give him jazz hands, his smile growing.

"You still do not know when we are?" Leaning over, he opens his abandoned chest and rifles through its contents.

Curious, I bend over toward the chest. Pain shoots up my leg and I hiss between my teeth. "No, I don't know. We'll have to actually talk to someone else to know exactly when we are," I tell him in a grunt.

"How bad is your ankle?"

"It's nothing serious."

"Let me look at it." He crawls over and lifts my skirts a little, taking my foot in his hand.

My breath stills in my chest as he unlaces my ankle boot and slips it off my foot. The swelling is already visible through my stocking.

He pulls off my stocking. My heart pounds in my chest as his fingers trail across my skin. This is nothing. He's just looking at my injury and it's only my ankle, but after our kiss, every touch makes my body go crazy.

I don't trust myself to speak, my tongue too big in my mouth for anything coherent to come out. He unties my garter, just a simple leather strap Aunt Tanis probably found somewhere in the house. He drops it and the room is quiet as we listen to the soft thud of it hitting the floor.

His hand grazes my calf, sending shivers down my spine. I watch his throat work as he grips the top of my stocking and rolls it down. Is he feeling the same thing I am? He presses against my ankle and I hiss through my teeth as it sends a spear of pain all the way up my leg.

"Apologies," he murmurs.

"It's not your fault. I should've been paying more attention when we were running. I did this to myself." I laugh in an attempt to lighten the mood, the pressure in my chest building as he runs a gentle hand down my ankle.

"I should have waited for you." He frowns. "I should have made sure you were right behind me instead of worrying so much about making it to the house without being seen. It would matter little if no one saw me if they still saw you."

"It's not like we're attached at the hip. It's possible I could go places without you. I mean, it's happened before," I ramble, my mouth spouting words my mind has nothing to do with as Matthew rubs small circles into my ankle.

He hums his agreement, hands still working on my leg. Closing my eyes, I focus on how much better my ankle is starting to feel instead of the fact that Matthew is touching me. He knows I'm a witch and he's still touching me.

Warm heat travels up my leg, spreading tingles through my body. Grabbing my leather garter, he works it around my ankle and ties it in place.

"Thank you," I breathe, eyes closed.

"It is no trouble." His low voice rumbles in his throat. "I think you shall feel much better now."

He sits back and I put a little weight on my ankle. It barely even twinges, and I glance up at Matthew with wide eyes. "That's incredible!"

"Like I said, I think you shall feel better now."

His father is a warlock, is it possible that he's . . . no if he were a warlock too it would have shown up before now. He wouldn't hide it from me after I told him I was, right?

The sun dips lower, the light burning orange through the window. "Do you think we could just eat something and sleep? Maybe? I don't know about you but I'm exhausted."

"That is what I was looking for, something to eat." He turns back to his chest.

"Is there somewhere else I could look?"

"There is a basket in the corner over there where I kept the food that went bad the quickest." He pauses. "That might actually be a good way to find out how far back in time we are."

"You didn't take all your perishables with you when we left?" I test out standing on my ankle. It holds firm, the pain a distant memory.

His voice is muffled as he digs farther into the trunk. "I cannot carry everything. Plus, I was starting to stock up for winter. There should be some potatoes and apples still here."

"You were stocking up on perishables?" I ask with a laugh, walking with ease towards the corner he'd pointed out. "Does that sound as weird to you as it does to me?"

He doesn't rise to my taunt, the sound of him shuffling through the trunk increasing as he digs further down.

The basket is as forlorn as the rest of the house, a ring of dust sitting on the opening. Hesitating, I don't reach in right away. I hate mold and squishy things and basically anything on the verge of going bad. I can't even run the garbage disposal in the sink without wanting to throw up.

"Is there anything in there?"

With a frown so tight it wrinkles my nose, I reach blindly into the basket. Waiting to hit something nasty, I'm happily surprised to brush against the firm skin of an apple.

"I've got something," I announce with a grin as I pull out the fruit.

Matthew glances up. "What ho! Are there any more in there?"

I pull out three more apples and an onion. I set them on the table, Matthew bringing a small hunk of cheese he's found.

"We have found a feast," Matthew says with a smile. "You sit down, and we shall feast."

"Yes, Mom," I whine as I sink back into the chair, but Matthew just keeps grinning.

"We cannot have been gone too long because these would have gone bad in here, or been looted," he hands me one of the apples.

I bite into the thick flesh of the fruit, its sweet juices the best thing I've tasted in weeks. "So, you think we're out of danger then?"

"We are as safe as we could be considering you brought us right back to Nantasket. You could not have chosen a new place to go?"

"I got distracted. Plus I didn't know where you wanted to go. Should I have taken you to England?"

Matthew frowns. "I never wanted to go back to that place."

"So why Nantasket? Why stay here when Thomas didn't want you to?"

"I got land here, which made it the obvious choice. All I ever wanted was to make something of my own and Nantasket offered me that."

"You couldn't do that in England?"

"Not in the same way." He sighs. "There is no room to breathe there. This was going to be different. I was going to survive on my own."

"What happened then?"

He runs a hand through his unruly hair. "I had an altercation with Thomas and then my house did not live up to his standards. It made it easy for them to get rid of me."

I glance around the sagging house. "You have to admit, they had a point about the livability of your house."

"Maybe so," he concedes. "But it was still mine. Something I created with my own two hands."

"It must be beautiful to make something all on your own like that. I've never done it before." I lean back in my chair, staring up at the ceiling where a few spots of the fading sunset peak through holes in the roof.

He leans against the wall. "It is beautiful. I loved every minute of it."

Apples forgotten, we sit in contented silence until the last of the light slips away. Matthew's bare feet shuffle across the floor as he goes back to the trunk. Riffling around in the darkness, he pulls something out with an exclamation.

"There is no way we have been gone very long, because someone would have gone through my stuff and definitely taken this." He tosses what he's found at me with a grin. Warm, scratchy material hits me across the face while Matthew laughs. "With winter coming they never would have let blankets sit here unused."

I'm glad of the darkness to hide the stain of my embarrassment as it travels up my neck. "Well, that's good news for us."

"Very good news," Matthew steps close enough that I can see the shine of his teeth in the weak light. "We might even be able to say that we never left Nantasket, just hid out for a few days. There is not really anyone that would refute us. All the people we knew on that ship are long gone by now."

Dead.

He doesn't say it, but I know that's what he means. Everyone we met on that ship is dead now. Lost to the depths of the ocean after that terrible storm. My heart beats hollowly in my chest but Matthew doesn't notice my deflating mood.

"So." He claps his hands together. "Should we discuss sleeping arrangements, or . . .?"

His single bed sits back against the wall, appearing much as it did the first day I got here. That seems like a lifetime ago now.

"What about them do you want to discuss?"

He shrugs. "Well, I only have the one bed, and I was not interested in sleeping on the floor."

"So, you want me to?" The words come out sharp and Matthew takes a step away from me.

"I was not saying you should sleep on the floor, but I thought that maybe things were different where you come from and you would not be totally opposed to sharing." His voice trails off in an embarrassed squeak as though his saying the idea out loud made him think less of it. "I mean, we shared a bed at the inn and we will need to lay together to stay warm. There's not enough blankets for both of us."

"Fine." I run a hand through my hair, fingers getting caught in the snarls and half curls that have formed there since our ocean excursion.

Matthew shrugs as he steps around the table and toward the bed we'll share together. He doesn't look at me as I join him, but his heavy breathing fills the room.

"We do not have to do this if you are not comfortable," he says, staring at the bed.

I give him a soft shove. "We're not doing anything. We're just sleeping, right?"

"Right."

"Do you want inside or outside?" I hope he chooses inside. Being pinned between him and the wall has my mild claustrophobia flaring up just thinking about it.

He starts climbing into the bed. "Inside."

Thank goodness. I wait for him to settle and then climb in after him, throwing the spare blanket over the top of us.

There's no room in the bed, not even enough spare space for an inch between us. Now that I'm in the bed, I'm not sure it could even be called a twin. We lay packed in on our sides, my back pressing into his chest. I can feel the rise and fall of his chest with every breath he takes and the warmth I feel is only partially from the blankets.

"Are you comfortable?" he asks, the words a heavy rumble between us.

I nod and he relaxes a little more. We lay together in the darkness, our breathing the only sound in the room which seems to grow louder the longer we lay awake.

"Soph?" Matthew asks, his breath in my hair a soft breeze. "Thank you for today, for saving my life."

"Well, you know, it's why I'm here."

Matthew leans up on his elbow. "Why are you here for that? I doubt I am any more special than the other men who died when our ship went down."

"I just go where I'm told." My throat is thick as I try to swallow around all the deaths that happened today.

"You are not going to tell me, are you?"

"No matter how many different ways you find to try and get me to answer you, I won't do it. Time traveler confidentiality you understand."

Matthew laughs. "Time traveler confidentiality? Is that a real thing?"

"I'm the only one I know, so it's a thing if I say it is."

"You must not know a lot of witches for you to be the only time traveler you know, right?"

"I actually do know a lot of witches," I tell him, my mind traveling to my failure at the coven meeting.

"So, there are a lot of witches in your time?" Matthew asks. "If there are a lot of you, does that mean you do not have to hide?"

I dig farther into the blankets. "We're not in hiding exactly, I mean there hasn't been a witch hunt in at least a hundred years. No one will kill us for what we are, but that doesn't mean they accept us."

"That is incredible," Matthew breathes. "Who needs the acceptance of the masses when you are no longer in danger of dying just for being yourself. You did not ask to be a witch, it is something that happened. I shall never understand why so many have been killed for who they were born to be."

Rolling over, I meet his dark eyes. "But your people believe it's the work of Satan we've been doing, with gifts given to us from the devil. Doesn't that affect your opinion at all?"

"I have known plenty of accused witches and with the exception of a few, I have never known any to be close to the devil," he says with a shrug that bounces against my shoulders.

"How can you be sure?"

Moonlight gleams through the oil paper window, revealing Matthew's small smile. "I would say that it would be pretty obvious if someone were Satan's close friend, would not it be to you? None of the accused I have known have had any level of darkness in them that I would associate with him."

"How many have you known who have died?'

His face clouds. "Witch hunts are very prevalent where I'm from in England. I assume it is only a matter of time before they make it over here."

"Haven't there already been some here?"

"Yes."

He clenches his jaw so tight I can see it in the weak light. Reaching out, I place my hand on his shoulder as he closes his eyes. "I'm so sorry."

I don't know what happened and I'm not sure I'll ever ask, but he's been hurt. And based on the way he talks about his family and England, I'll bet the answer as to who hurt him lies there.

And I hate it.

CHAPTER SIXTEEN

I lay awake in the darkness for a long time, listening to Matthew's breathing as it evens out and becomes heavy. Still, I can't sleep.

Would Matthew save me if the witch hunters found me? I'm one misstep away from big trouble and the longer we stay here, the more likely I am to be caught.

Staring at him in the dark, I can just make out the thick curls lining his forehead. I'd love to believe that he'd come back for me. The kiss we shared makes me want to believe that he'd come back.

But it doesn't matter. I don't care, right? I can't care, I've never cared. And yet, I could leave at any moment but I'm still here. What does that say about me? All I had to do was save him from the boat, and that's been done. Curse broken, family happy, go home.

I try to build up my power, the rush of it flowing through my body feeling more like a trickle. The door appears across from the bed, its form wavering and sending off purple sparks. Before I can even get out of bed, it fades from view, disintegrated by my weakened state.

Sighing, I lay back in the bed. I turn so I don't have to look at Matthew's calm face, but that doesn't change the fact that I know he's there.

The longer we've been here, the more the stale air is replaced with the salty tang of the sea. If I close my eyes, I can pretend I'm safe at home with Mom and we've rented a cottage on the beach. It's a scenario that would be easier to believe if Matthew didn't snore so loudly.

I don't know what breaking this curse will do to us, and I'm worried about going home to find out. What if we decide it's too much? What if it's too much to be able to actually have to love people and really open our hearts for the first time in our lives? Could I reverse breaking the curse? I've never had to face being vulnerable like this before, and I don't know how to handle it.

Matthew shifts in his sleep, moving closer to me. He throws an arm over my side, fingers lay curled across my stomach. I can barely breathe, air coming in short gasps that have nothing to do with the pressure of his arm. Closing my eyes, I let myself lean into him.

He tenses, pulling me tighter against his chest. Suddenly I'm lightheaded, whether from the lack of air or I don't know what. Matthew grumbles in his sleep, the nonsense words blowing into my ear.

Relax, I just have to relax.

Irritated with myself, I throw his arm off and wiggle as close to the edge of the bed as I can without falling off. It's a bit precarious and any adjustment in my sleep will send me toppling to the floor, but its better this way. Already I can feel my head clearing.

Closing my eyes, I imagine the images of my mother, my aunts, my grandma, and let them stand guard over me and my burgeoning feelings until I fall asleep.

***

"Hey." Matthew nudges my shoulder. "Get up. I have to get out."

The chilly air seeps into my back where he's already pulled his side of the blankets down. "Then get out," I grumble, pulling the blankets back over my shoulder.

"I cannot get out without climbing on you. I figured you would rather get up on your own than wake up to me on top of you."

Even in my groggy state, his words send a blush burning across my cheeks. I slip out of the bed, toes curling as I stand on the frozen floor.

Matthew gives me a curt nod of thanks then pushes open the back door. A burst of cold air rushes in the room before he closes the door firmly behind him. Teeth chattering, I clamber back under the blankets, burying my head to soothe my numbing ears.

His footsteps tromp around the back of the house. A loud sigh penetrates the thin walls and I hum to block out the sound of him relieving himself.

When he comes back inside, I'm completely cocooned inside the blankets still warm from his body. This time I barely notice the cold draft circling the room.

Matthew sits, the chair creaking under his weight. "What should we do next."

"Get out of here?" I mumble from my sanctuary.

He sighs. "And how do you want to do that?"

"If it's left to me, we're going to have to travel my way. There's no way we'll be able to walk anywhere without supplies. Plus, you said we can't go back to the city."

"Staying here is not an option though. We do not have enough food to just hide out through the winter," he says as the flesh ripping sound of his bite into one of the last apples draws me out of the blankets.

I poke my head above the warm cocoon of safety. Matthew watches me, chomping on his apple.

"Save any of those for me?" I ask, keeping the rest of my body submerged in bed.

He shrugs. "There might be one left, but it would be for someone ready to get up and tackle our current problem with me."

"Can't I just relax for one moment after saving your butt yesterday?" I groan as I peel away the blankets a layer at a time.

"Only if you do not mind if I end up dying today instead," Matthew says, a smile betraying his serious tone.

Swinging my legs over the side of the bed, I keep them suspended above the floor as I reach out for my apple. Matthew rolls his eyes but hands it to me anyway. The sweet crisp taste is better than anything I could've imagined, and I know it will ruin apples for me when I get back to my own time.

"So," I say mid-swallow. "What options do you think we have?"

"The way I see it, we can either pretend that we never left or pretend we changed our minds and came back."

"The first one is too risky," I point out. "What if someone did come around while we were gone? How would we excuse our absence then?"

"Staying here would not mean we could *never* leave. They could have just come over when we were gone."

"Gone doing what?"

He lifts a shoulder in a shrug. "I do not know. Finding food or something."

"That's a weak explanation and you know it," I tell him, finishing the apple, core and all, as I wait for him to respond.

He puts the rest of his fruit on the table. "The other option will have Thomas sending us packing again. I do not know about you, but I am not eager to try the crossing to England again so soon, or ever."

"Like I told you before, he can't make you leave. Tell him you're going to stay and you're going to do it on your own. There's nothing he can do about that."

"I do not think I can," he says while watching the slow creep of the sun cresting the horizon out the window. "Not without my goat."

My feet hit the ground as I sit up and I bite back a curse. "So, get your goat back."

"She belongs to someone else now. I have no claim to her after I left her like I did."

"So, find another way to survive," I say, ignoring the pain creasing his forehead. "I'm sure you could if you wanted to. You seem pretty capable."

Matthew looks at me with a grim smile. "You could just use your magic and take us somewhere else where I don't have to worry about this at all."

Coming here was more than foolish, but there's nothing I can do about it now. He doesn't need to know about the image of Thomas that brought me right back. It might hurt him. And I really didn't want to do that.

"I don't have enough magic to take us anywhere right now. Consider me tapped." *Which is the only reason why I'm still here.* Even in my thoughts I can't make it feel true. Why am I still here then?

He sighs. "So, we have to go through with something then. No magicking our way out of this one."

"Because you've been so helpful with that thus far," I say, bristling. "I don't need any more guilt about how short my power reserve is or how much better it would be if I had more gifts. Enough!"

It's not like I've had to deal with everyone being disappointed in my gift my whole life and now to have Matthew give me a hard time . . . it's too much.

"That is not what I was saying," Matthew frowns. "I figured I would make sure there was nothing else we could do about our situation before we just charged out there and announced ourselves."

"Is that what we're going to do then? Just charge out there and what?"

"I do not know. We could tell them we missed the ship and had to come back."

My mouth gaps like a goldfish as I realize how stupid I've been for not thinking of that sooner. It's so obvious!

"That! Let's definitely do that!"

He nods and pulls on more clothes from his trunk. Swinging open the door, he steps out, leaving me alone. Shivering, I struggle with cold stiff fingers to pull on my own shoes, then hobble on frozen limbs out the door after him.

His footsteps leave warm outlines in the crunchy frozen grass as he marches to the center of the green. Picking up the pace as the movements warm me, I catch up with him as he veers toward the large building at the end. No matter what happens now, we're in this together. No matter what either of us thinks.

Life comes to the settlement with the spreading light as the sun comes up over the trees. People make their way out of homes, trailing the warm smell of chimney smoke as they straggle together towards the end of the row of houses. Whispered conversations fill the settlement with the hum of civilization.

Matthew picks up the pace. "It is the sabbath. How fortuitous! If we can make it inside the church, perhaps we shall receive more mercy."

Maybe Matthew's right. This will all be fine. We'll get the supplies he needs, and I'll be able to get out of here no harm done.

I'm finally coming around to this stupid plan when Thomas stomps out his front door. My chest seizes, feet faltering as he instantly meets my eyes.

"Soph?" his voice is quiet as our gazes meet.

His steps are steady as he crosses the green. I cross and uncross my arms, feeling more and more faint the closer he gets to me. This is not good. Now that I've spurned his offer of marriage, is he more likely to inspect me as a witch?

"Soph?" he repeats, stopping a foot away from me. "What are you doing here? I thought you left."

"Turns out I was not as ready to leave as I thought I was," Matthew says.

Thomas cuts his gaze toward Matthew, his jaw grinding as if he is biting back a retort. He turns back to me. "Is everything well? Are you all right?"

"I am fine." Thomas's hands hover in the air between us as though he might just reach out and grab me. "Honestly, everything is fine. Matthew just decided he didn't want to leave Nantasket after all."

Thomas glares at Matthew as he crosses his arms over his chest. "I thought we agreed that it was not your choice whether or not you stayed."

"Well, we missed our ship, so the choice is lost to both of us. Plus, Soph here reminded me that if I do not take resources from anyone else and make it on my own, then I do not need your approval."

I give Thomas a weak smile as his sharp gaze whips back to me. "I said he shouldn't leave if it wasn't what he wanted." The hole I'm in keeps growing as I speak. "Not that I wanted to go against your wishes or anything."

"Soph, go on in with Mercy. I am positive she can fix you something up to eat. I cannot even imagine what you must have been eating the last few days. You look so thin." He gives me a small smile before turning his attention to Matthew. "And you are not welcome here."

"I do not need your welcome," Matthew practically growls.

My feet feel like lead as I trudge towards Thomas's house. I know I should stay with Matthew, help him through this fight, but all I can think about is the warm bowl of pottage I know Mercy will whip up for me.

"The witch!"

I freeze in place at the young voice that silences the rest of the settlement.

"The witch!" it calls again.

Neck stiff, I pan over the people in the green, looking for the source of the commotion. A small girl stands outside her house, a shaking finger pointed at me. Her coif is lopsided and the ties on her petticoat are loose, but her back is straight as she meets my gaze.

"There is the witch!"

Thomas's feet crunch in the frost-coated grass as he turns towards me. There's a hesitation in his steps now as he gets closer. "Come with me," he says, voice low as he grabs me by the arm. His soft touch gives me hope.

"Where are you going with her?" Matthew stumbles to keep up with us.

"Sophronia will have to face her accusations. She shall be in holding until we can gather a court together," Thomas says as he leads me into his house and shuts the door in Matthew's face.

"What's going on?" My arms shake in Thomas's grip as he leads me to a chair.

He sighs and leans against the fireplace as he looks at me. "That girl came forward a few days ago saying she knew what caused that devil's circle in our woods. We found another one yesterday and the same girl said she had seen who had caused that one too. When we pressed her about it, she didn't have any answers about it. She just kept repeating that she did not know the witch's name. If she's been thinking it is you, then that would make sense. Very few outside of Matthew and myself know your name."

My head spins. How could she have seen me? I never saw the girl when I arrived. Or when Matthew and I arrived yesterday. So how could she have been there both times?

"What's going to happen to me?" I ask, voice quiet.

Thomas scratches the stubble on his chin. "Well, we shall get a court together, hear both of you out, and then make a decision."

"Make a decision?"

"We shall have to decide if you are a witch or not, well I will. I am the constabulary, remember? It will be my choice to make."

The pressure in my chest eases up. "I'm going to be fine then."

"It is not that simple." His ruffled hair stands on end. "I have to listen to all the evidence and make a fair decision. I cannot let my feelings for you influence my decision."

"Your feelings for me?" I ask in a small voice. My mind travels to Matthew for a second before slamming into the present.

Silence descends on the house. Mercy stops stirring the pottage.

Thomas shakes his head. "Like I said, it does not matter."

I don't know if it matters to me either.

My heart pounds in my chest. Thomas pushes off the fireplace, paces a few steps and then leaves the house, slamming the door behind him.

"Well," Mercy says with a small smile, wiping her hands off on her apron before handing me a bowl. "I never thought we would see you again."

"I didn't think I'd ever be back again either," I mumble into my bowl as I drink up the pottage.

Mercy sits across from me. "It has been a rough few days without you," she says, leaning forward. "It shall be good to have you back."

"If I get to be back," I sigh. "I have to go to court."

She waves my words away. "Do not let court bother you. Thomas would not let anything bad happen, no matter what Charity Goodrite says."

"So, this isn't serious?" I can't keep the images I've seen in books from entering my mind. There was a man accused of witchcraft in Salem who was pressed to death. Will that happen to me? Will I have stone after stone placed on my chest until my lungs can't expand and I suffocate?

"I would not worry too much about it. Thomas is very fair."

It doesn't matter how fair he is when I'm guilty. By their standards at least. Curling into myself, the pottage sits in my stomach like a warm brick.

"Soph?" Mercy lays a hand on my arm. "You really have nothing to worry about. Thomas will take care of you. I know he will. We do not believe every accusation flung by children."

Giving her a small smile, I swallow the lump building in my throat. "I'm glad to see you again," I say, changing the subject.

Her cheeks redden. "Like I said before, I am glad to have you back too. It is always nice to have another woman around." She leans forward. "So, where have you been the last few days?"

"We traveled to the city and missed the boat." I laugh but there's little humor in it. I'm just grateful Matthew came up with a plausible story. "Then we had to come back. We got here last night and stayed in Matthew's house."

"You must have been so cold! I cannot even imagine trying to sleep in that shack!" Mercy gets up and grabs a blanket from her room, throwing it around my shoulders.

"Do you know when Thomas will be back?" My face burns and I cough to hide it behind my arm.

"We have never had a witch trial here before, so I could not tell you. Thomas takes his job very seriously, so I imagine it will take him some time to get all the testimonials he needs to get started."

I grab fistfuls of my skirt, the material stiff from the salt water. A cheap version of starch, I guess. The thought makes me laugh and Mercy glances up sharply at me.

"Is there anything I can do to help?" If I have to sit here all day waiting to learn my fate, the anticipation might kill me before any flame could have the chance.

Mercy chuckles. "After the way you 'helped' Matthew the other day, I think we are all a lot safer if you do not."

"I just . . ." I clench and unclench my fists. "I can't sit waiting for them to decide my fate."

Mercy sets the spoon down and frowns. "Worrying will not help anything, you shall only distress yourself. Just relax and enjoy being home."

Home. If only I was. As tempted as I am to try and conjure another door, it wouldn't be a good idea in front of Mercy. I'll just have to wait and hope this trial ends up being nothing or I'm left alone long enough to use my magic to travel anywhere else. But it should be fine. I mean they can't convict me based on one little girl's testimony, could they?

"So, what brought Matthew back?" Mercy asks, her face carefully blank.

"He just likes it here. He loves that stupid house he built and wasn't ready to see it torn apart or left to rot. I imagine anyone would feel that way about something they slaved away on like he did on that house, sad as it is."

"Do not let Thomas hear you talking about Matthew having pride over his home. I think it is for his house alone that Thomas decided Matthew had to go," she says in a whisper with a knowing nod. "It does not reflect well on our settlement."

"Then why didn't anyone help him? I'm sure someone could have lent a hand to make sure he had a decent place to live."

"He built out of turn. We were all waiting, living in hovels while the men built house after house. When Matthew got here he just started building right away, did not even ask if he could help build the one all the men were already working on. Then when they finished that house and decided to help him out so he could assist in completing the rest, he refused them. Point blank said he would rather live in a shack built with his own two hands than in a palace the community built for him. As you can imagine, it made Thomas pretty mad."

I'm sure mad is an understatement. Matthew refusing his help probably sent Thomas into a rage. "Well, he's living in a shack created by his own two hands after all."

"I thought Thomas was going to set it on fire the day you left. I have never seen him in such a mood." Mercy shakes her head. "It is a good thing he did not since you both ended up back here."

"Yeah, very convenient," I murmur, wondering what we would have done if the shack hadn't been here. I don't know that I would have lasted through the night without the safety of those four ramshackle walls.

Standing, I shake out my stiff skirts and follow Mercy to the table. She hums to herself as she takes a few apples out of a basket on the floor and begins chopping them into slim wedges.

"This settlement must be pretty new. How did you guys end up with apple trees?" I'm surprised I didn't make this connection before. Apple trees take years to produce anything.

"We got lucky. There was an orchard already here. It was part of the reason why we settled in this specific spot. We have all loved having the fresh fruit, it really boosts everyone's morale."

"I bet." My mouth waters as she rolls out a dough, pressing the fruit into it before pinching it closed.

Mercy smiles. "Thomas loves these. I am hoping putting him in a good mood will help your case."

She winks at me as my chest seizes once more.

"I'm just hoping it won't come to that."

"He will have to take you before the court. It is the only way to make sure your name is officially cleared. I would hate to think people thought ill of you just because Thomas did not do his due diligence," she says, placing the apple filled dough into a pan over the fire.

My jaw strains. I want to tell her how it would not be in my best interest. But she'd never go against Thomas like that.

The front door bangs open as Thomas stands in the doorway. Mercy glances at me, her eyes haunted. Blowing out in frustration, Thomas comes in, his warm breath sending out white plumes in the air. Closing the door, he turns to us, forehead wrinkled.

"What is it, Thomas?" Mercy asks.

"There is nothing I can do. Charity's father has backed up her testimony. We are going to court."

CHAPTER SEVENTEEN

Thomas has my court assembled later that day. Mercy tells me it's because he wants to get it over with. She says no one really believes Charity but I don't believe her. I know she's just saying that to make me feel better.

Regardless of whether or not they believe I'm the witch, they all know about the devil circles in the woods. With two sitting out there, the settlement's unease has to be growing.

I'm led into the church with a crowd at my back. Five rows of wooden pews fan out on either side. The first two rows are full of my accusers, their stares hard as they turn to watch me come in. Mercy clutches my hand in hers. For all that she's told me not to worry, her handshakes in mine.

"It shall all be over soon," she whispers, leaning close to my ear.

My reflection looks small in her eyes, my appearance more haggard than I realized. My hair hangs in limp strands, the dark circles under my eyes growing deeper, my dress wrinkled almost beyond recognition.

I pat my hair down, wishing I had my coif to hide it under. Too bad it's at the bottom of the Atlantic, along with the rest of the ship.

"Do not worry about it." Mercy stills my hand. "You look fine."

"I look a mess."

She curls her fingers around my hand. "They do not care how you look. They only care if you are innocent."

Thomas marches in, a group of men following him, their faces gruff as they look me over. They sit in the pews opposite me as Thomas settles behind the podium.

"Thank you all for meeting with us on such short notice. I thought it best that we determine the truth of the accusation in a timely manner for everyone's sake." He leans over the podium. "Is the accuser present?"

A small girl I didn't notice before emerges from behind the thick wall of men. "I am here, sir."

"And the accused?"

"Here," my voice wavers and Mercy grips me tighter.

Thomas stares through me, his eyes dark. "We shall hear from the accuser, after which the accused will have time to speak."

Charity walks to the front, hands clasped before her, pressing into her blue petticoat. "I was playing in the woods a few days ago. I know I am not supposed to go that far, but I was not paying very good attention." She looks at the row of men, one of them, presumably her father, scowls. "While I was playing, I heard a loud crack in the sky. It caught me off guard and I stumbled, falling back into a pile of leaves. Then she," she points at me, "fell from the sky, the trees around her breaking into the circle the men found."

"Why did you not say something about this sooner?" Thomas asks.

"I-I didn't think it was my place."

"But it was your place to accuse her in the middle of the square with no provocation whatsoever?"

"I could no longer hold it in when I saw she was back and another one of those circles formed," she says, wringing her hands together.

The lines in Thomas's forehead deepen. "Is there anyone who can corroborate your story?"

Charity glances around at the men gathered. No one steps up for her. "I guess not, sir."

"What have you to say?" Thomas turns his attention towards me.

Charity scrambles back into her seat, moving quick as if she didn't want to share the aisle with me. I approach the stand.

"I'm not sure what I'm supposed to say." There's nothing I can say. Not if they want the truth. "I disagree with what she said."

It's a weak defense. Not even a defense. Mercy shakes her head and Thomas clears his throat. "On the days Charity claims to have seen you create the circles you were not even in the settlement yet. Is that correct?"

"Yes."

"Would you share with us where you were?"

"The first time I was traveling to Nantasket in search of Matthew, as you can attest. You found me in the woods that day."

Thomas steps away from the podium. "Yes, I did."

"And when Charity found the most recent circle, I was hiding out in Matthew's house." I try to keep to the truth. That *is* where I was, it just wasn't the same time as the circle was made.

"Is Matthew here to verify that?" Thomas glances toward the line of men.

I follow his gaze, but Matthew's curly brown locks are nowhere to be seen. "No, sir."

Where is Matthew? Did no one tell him I was going to be tried today? Did he know about it and just not care? After all we've been through, I would have expected him to be here. To be here for me. A cold tingle spreads down my back.

"Without Matthew here, we cannot confirm your story."

My stomach rolls and my throat goes dry. Glancing up at Thomas, I give him a shrug to hide my shaking.

Mercy raises her hand and Thomas shoots her a glare. "Yes?"

"Well," she coughs. "With no one to corroborate any of the stories, aren't we at a standstill?"

Thomas scratches his chin and opens his mouth to answer her before being shut down by one of the men in the front row.

"So, you are implying my Charity is a liar just because she was playing alone?" He wrenches his hat off his head, revealing greasy, matted blond hair pasted to his round head. "I told you before, Thomas, I am willing to back up her testimony. Additionally, we all know Charity. We all know how honest she is. We cannot say the same for this stranger. What more could you ask for?"

Mercy surges up, her face red with anger. "You are supporting her testimony, but you are not actually a witness. What good does that do? Could not I do that for Sophronia? Then we would be even."

"Sit down, Mercy," Thomas says, rubbing his eyes. "You are causing a scene."

Mercy sits down reluctantly. I can't lie, her show of solidarity boosts my mood significantly. When I make eye contact with her, I give her a smile, but she doesn't return it.

"Now." Thomas leans over the podium like an old man on his cane. "What are you suggesting should be done Goodman Goodrite? Without being able to act as a formal witness, your stance in this case is quite weak."

Goodman Goodrite grinds his teeth together. "As I am supporting Charity's testimony, I am expecting this witch to be taken care of."

The crowd around him murmur to each other, each one taking careful glances at me with narrowed eyes. Standing helplessly in the middle of the room, I just want to run away. Or at least run to Mercy. Her eyes are red rimmed where she sits on our bench, a glare directed at her brother.

Thomas doesn't say anything, and Goodman Goodrite's face grows redder. "This is usually the way of things, is it not? Are you letting your closeness to this girl cloud your necessary judgment?"

Straightening out his back, Thomas glares down at Goodman Goodrite with a face like thunder. "Are you trying to imply something?"

"You know exactly what I am saying, sir. If you cannot find yourself able to convict this girl as we both know you should, then perhaps we should wait until another constabulary can come and hold a real court," Goodman Goodrite says with a sly smile pressed into his thin lips.

"I do not believe that will be necessary," Thomas growls.

"So, you are going to go through our usual and necessary rites to rid our settlement of this parasite of a witch?" Goodman Goodrite asks with a voice like honey.

I bristle at his accusation, the first one that I feel has actually impugned my character. Why must being a witch mean I'm a parasite? I've done more parasitic things as a non-witch here than I ever did back home in my full and relatively open state. I mean, it's not like I told everyone I was a witch, but most people knew a few of my aunts were witches. And they never latched on to anyone.

Taking a deep breath, I let go of my anger even though it's a weird comfort. I'd rather be angry than have to deal with the very real fear of heading to the gallows.

Thomas's loud sigh draws me out of my thoughts. "Are you sure we cannot go another direction with this? After all, we would hate to harm an innocent girl over the bloated claims of a child."

"I would rather kill a hundred innocents than let one witch be free among us," Goodman Goodrite says evenly.

Sounds like a perfect Satanist to me. I glance around the room. Doesn't anyone else think that's weird? Apparently not. The group around him all nod their agreement. A glance at the back row reveals a man tossing a large stone from hand to hand.

"I guess that is settled then." Thomas's shoulders slump. "We shall hold the accused for two days during which people are welcome to come forward to prove her innocence—"

"Or guilt!" Goodman Goodrite shouts.

"Or guilt," Thomas concedes. "And at the end of the two days, if nothing has changed, then we shall proceed toward the customary hanging."

My jaw drops and my hand twitches. Seriously? That's all it takes for someone to be found guilty of witchcraft? The accusation of a child and the strong arm of her father? I glance back at Mercy, eyes wide. She paces over to me and throws an arm around my shoulders.

"Press her!"

"Stone her!"

I close my eyes against the voices clamoring around me, each one obviously upset with the idea of a simple hanging. My body shakes and my eyes burn as I try to stand. This can't possibly be happening to me.

"It is not so bad," Mercy whispers, hugging me tightly. "Thomas is giving Matthew two days to step forward and corroborate your story. This is the only way it will be able to be dismissed."

"Really?" I ask with a teary smile. "Are you sure?"

"Most definitely. He has not abandoned you yet."

But as the men file out one by one, several spitting at my feet and a few of the gruffer looking ones even going so far as to throw stones that land at my feet, I can't help but feel completely abandoned. Why did Thomas let Goodman Goodrite strong arm him like that? Why didn't he just throw the case out if he was so unwilling to believe it?

Rubbing my hand against my throat, I imagine what it will feel like with a thick cord of rope tied around it. Thomas watches me, looking away with a grimace as he notes the motion of my hand.

Mercy is wrong. I have everything to worry about. I am alone. Thomas has definitely abandoned me.

~eeeeee~

They decide to keep me in a root cellar that makes Matthew's shack feel glamorous, for the two days until I'm officially sentenced. It's nothing compared to a modern root cellar, basically just a hole in the ground with a wooden door secured over it.

Down in the dank earth with baskets of potatoes and apples, I let the tears I've been holding in slip free. Mom was right. It was dangerous to come here, far more dangerous than I understood. Now my ignorance will be the death of me. Ironic I guess to die as a witch when I actually am one. Very few people can claim that.

How lucky am I?

Hot tears roll down my frozen cheeks in buckets. My shoulders shake and I curl farther into myself. This is it now.

I'll never see my family again.

For all the power of being a constabulary, Thomas looked so powerless when he escorted me down here. He didn't even touch me, just watched as another villager threw me down into the root cellar and closed the door. His even footsteps as he walked away were the only distraction from the pain caused by the fall. Mercy was told to go home, her tears a mirror image to the ones imprinted on my cheeks.

Salem makes a lot more sense to me now. I always wondered why they relied so heavily on the testimony of young, obviously unstable, girls. Apparently, it wasn't something they did only in Salem.

The damp ground seeps into my skin, the smell of the apples mingling with the taste of my salty tears. I wish they had at least let me stay with Thomas again. Let me see daylight and the stars in the last few days afforded to me.

Cold clutches at my skin, drawing it into goosebumps where it's exposed to the air, and even where it's not. If they don't bring me a blanket, hypothermia might get me before the noose does.

Think positive, I need to think more positive. I'm positive I will freeze to death out here. No, no, no. That's not what I meant.

Huddled down amongst the baskets in the root cellar, I work on my plan. I'm alone now, I can leave anytime I want to, as long as my gift agrees. Focusing on my reserves, I'm happy to feel them filling back up with magic. At this rate, I should be able to leave before the two days passes.

Footsteps crunch through the layer of leaves coating the ground around the root cellar. Glancing up with dull eyes, I wait for the mocking to start. I may not be an easy target, hidden down here as I am, but I'm sure they found something rotten somewhere in this town to throw at me.

"Soph?"

Hope flickers in my chest. "Matthew?"

The wood slats covering the root cellar creak as Matthew lifts a few.

"Where were you today?" I hiss through chattering teeth.

He shifts on his knees. "I could not come. Forgive me."

"Well I'm sorry too but I'm still here in this hole. Didn't you think I might need you today?" The sour feeling of being alone in that courtroom still permeates my skin.

"Forgive me," he repeats but doesn't look at me. "I wish I had been there for you today."

Huffing, I lean back into one of the baskets. "Fat lot of good that does me now."

"I apologized."

"'Sorry' won't get me out of this hole. You do realize they're planning on hanging me, right?" I pin him with my gaze. He doesn't say anything, and my fury only grows. "Did you come here for a reason? Because if it was for this weak apology then I don't want it. Go back to your shack and remember the girl who saved your life that you couldn't be bothered to save in return."

"That is not fair. You do not know what I was doing or why. You have not even asked me to talk to Thomas now. Did you even think about that while your ruminated in your hole? No? I bet not. You are so content to sit down there safely wrapped up in your assumptions that no one cares and everyone is out to get you. Did you stop to think that maybe *Mercy* sent me over to find you? She cannot come herself but could not stop worrying about you down here. Think about that the next time you are so willing to throw the rest of us away."

He throws the blanket I used while staying with Mercy and Thomas into the pit with me. It lands in on my lap in a comforting heap. I bury my face in it, letting my chin drop into my chest.

"Mercy sent you to bring me this?" I choke out through the thickness filling my throat.

"Among other things," Matthew says, brows lowered as he drops a basket into the hole.

I open the lid with trembling fingers. Inside is the most unassuming package I could probably ever be given, but tears flood my eyes. Half a loaf of bread, a bowl of pottage, and an apple sit cozily wrapped in a cream tea towel.

Matthew's voice is soft. "I cannot stay, but I will be back. Is there anything else you need?"

I can't speak past the lump in my throat, so I shake my head and Matthew sighs.

"You shall be all right. I promise," he says as he lowers the root cellar's ceiling back down on me, blocking out the faint flecks of starlight that had been coming in.

Clutching Mercy's basket to my chest, I grab the bowl and drink the bland pottage greedily. The still warm sludge slips down my throat and heats me from the inside. With the blanket wrapped around my shoulders, the shivers have almost completely subsided.

I don't know what Matthew's planning, but I'm not sure I trust whatever it is, not after he left me on my own. Mind whirling with the possibilities, I wonder if he will talk to Thomas now. The court stuff may be over, but that doesn't mean he couldn't change his mind, does it?

The darkness filling the root cellar grows and I fall asleep thinking about how maybe I won't have to stay the night down here after all.

The darkness filling the root cellar grows and I fall asleep thinking about how maybe I won't have to stay the night down here after all.

Matthew isn't my only visitor. Men pass by the cellar, the glow of their torches staying with me long after they're gone, the light that should have been comforting making me sweat as I think about what comes with the daylight.

I'm going to hang tomorrow. At least that's what one of them said as they stood gawking.

When they first showed up to come poke at me, I was relieved they didn't set the cellar on fire with their torches. But with the sure knowledge of what's coming tomorrow, I wish they had just gotten it over with.

I pick at Mercy's bread, each piece harder to swallow than the last. Will Mercy's basket be my last meal? Will my mother ever find out what happened to me? Maybe even at this moment she's flipping through a book of early American history and finding my name listed among the early witch trials. How helpless she would feel to find me there, almost as much as I feel.

My magic has built up, but I'm not sure how far it will take me. I'm a little worried that using it to take Matthew with me has ruined it. What if it never builds all the way back up now? Forever stunted by the one big jaunt I was forced into. Not that I'd blame Matthew, I guess. He didn't make me take him, didn't even ask me to take him. No, it was his father. His stupid warlock father.

Where the heck even is this guy? He has the power to curse my family for centuries and across generations, but can't bring himself to come and help his own son?

Irritation burns in my chest, warming my body and bringing life back into my limbs. Just because my gift isn't working doesn't mean I can't get out the old-fashioned way. I'll find a place to hide for a little bit and then I'll risk using whatever is left of my magic and get somewhere if not home.

Using my blanket as a strap, I sling the basket over my shoulder, a few more apples from the cellar filling the void of what I've already eaten. Approaching the smoothed earth wall, I glance around for something to help me climb out. There has to be something down here. They wouldn't build a cellar no one could get out of.

When I was brought here last night the townsmen flung me in, and honestly, I was surprised the fall didn't break my leg.

The wall of the cellar is a good three feet over my head. Not even the tips of my fingers can reach the ledge. Sighing, I turn to the baskets of apples and potatoes lined up behind me. Eyes straining in the darkness, I search for a wooden box, anything that isn't a basket and could support my weight as I clamber out.

A quick search reveals nothing tangible. I guess they wouldn't waste their time building boxes for their food storage when they still have houses and churches to build. That would've been too easy anyway.

Making a leaning stack of baskets, I give up on trying to keep their food safe. Eat a few bruised apples this winter, but I'm not dying down here. Or out there I guess since they have no intention of waiting for me to die on my own.

I step on the first level of my basket pyramid, checking if it will hold my weight. The wicker basket cracks, folding under my weight. It's precarious but holds. Unwilling to press my luck, I move quicker over the pile until I get to the top. A symphony of cracks follow me up the makeshift ladder. My fingers dig into the earthen rim, dirt burning where it's shoved into my nailbed.

Muscles heaving, I pull myself out of the root cellar. I was never any good at these kinds of activities in gym. The teacher would ask me to do a pull up and I'd just hang there until he told me I could leave. Today is probably the first time I've ever regretted not taking those exercises seriously.

My leg pushes against the wall of baskets as I angle for leverage. All my flailing does is send down the damaged baskets. They tumble to the earth in a crashing heap as my body hangs suspended from where my hands dig into the ground above.

The shoulder I damaged during the shipwreck screams and slick trails of sweat drip down my neck. Groaning, I heave myself up again, my forearms now out of the pit.

I'm not stupid. I know that without the baskets to keep me up I'll soon join them on the floor. My twiggy arms were never meant for such strenuous work. This was a long shot in the first place, but I refuse to let myself drop now.

I won't go quietly to the noose.

My teeth grind together as I lift myself again. I make minimal progress. My arms are still the only part of me that's gotten out.

Swinging my dangling legs, I dig my toes into the smooth walls of the root cellar. The soft patter of falling dirt hitting the baskets fills me with hope, my feet becoming more secure in the wall as I dig farther in. Maybe I won't need my upper body strength as much as I thought I would.

Weight securely planted on my toes, I step up with my right leg and dig in further. With just this little movement, my torso clears the lip of the cellar. Laying against the cool grass, I take the time to breathe deeply before trying again. Lifting my other leg up next to the first one is much less challenging than I thought it would be and with a final press I'm scrapping my back against the wood-plank ceiling as I crawl away from my prison.

Turning onto my back, the pooling sweat sticking to my skin, I stare into the bright afternoon sun. Dry laughs rock my chest. Looks like I won't be hanging tomorrow after all. Now all I need to do is find a safe place to lie low until my powers regenerate enough for me to leave. Matthew is safe now. I don't need to be here a second longer. I certainly don't need to wait around and find out what a witch hanging is like firsthand. The trial was enough for me.

I need to get moving. As nice as it is to lay here, it won't take long for someone to find me if I never leave the vicinity of the root cellar.

All around me are the silent specters of trees. I've never been over here before and as I spin in a slow circle, everything continues to look the same, nothing but trees as far as I can see. I could choose a direction that leads me right back to the settlement without realizing it. And if there's anything I've learned in this journey, it's that the settlement is dangerous. Not even staying with Matthew is an option for me anymore. I wouldn't be surprised if I showed up there and he turned me in out of spite for last night. Okay, maybe that's a little far, but I'm still pretty irritated with him.

The sun sits directly above me, scalding the skin where my hair is parted. I need to make a decision and I need to do it now. Glancing around my surroundings again, I start off at a fast clip into the trees on my right where the forest looks thickest. In theory that should at least keep me away from Nantasket.

Roots and low growing brambles snag at my feet and grab at my dress. Tired after a night spent against the freezing ground, my reflexes are too slow to avoid most of the branches I encounter, allowing them to scrape across my face. My arms burn from constantly tugging my skirts free, which have filled with several holes both large and small, and my knees sting from scraping them with every fall.

Glancing behind me, I realize I've left a clear path. I'm an easy target with all the broken branches trailing behind me. Tears burn behind my eyes and in my weakened state, surviving this escape feels insurmountable. I just want to sit down in my warm kitchen with my family there. Mom filling me up with food and my aunts plying me with questions they know I won't be able to answer before they're off asking me the next one. Everything about my life before felt pretty ordinary, but I've become so much more here that I wish I could share with my family.

"Soph?" Mercy's voice is distant as it travels through the trees.

I hide behind the large trunk of an oak, heart pounding in my chest. In the silence every step hits my ear like the shattering of glass.

"Soph? Are you here?" Her voice sounds closer now. "It does not look good that you have left. We need to get you back in the cellar before anyone else can find you."

What did she think? That I was just going to wait in that hole until Thomas came back to tell me I'll hang tomorrow? I don't think so.

Dry leaves crackle under her feet as Mercy continues down my path. "I am not jesting. You need to get back right now. Leaving makes you look guilty."

Or makes me look like I want to live. I already had my trial, I already appeared before the court and they decided I was guilty. What I do now has no bearing on that. The decision has already been made.

"Thomas is working to clear your name with the town elders right now. You need to get back here!" I can hear the frustration in her voice, and she's probably only a few feet behind me now. "Please stop playing around, I am here to help you."

A hand shoots around from behind the tree, wrapping around my wrist with a firm grip that has me gasping.

"There you are." Mercy's fingers dig into my skin. "Why did you not answer me?"

"I don't care what you say," I cry. "I'm not getting back into that hole to wait for them to hang me tomorrow."

Mercy starts, eyes wide. Clearly she didn't think I'd know that little piece of relevant information.

"I am not asking you to wait to die. I am telling you to come back so you can prove yourself innocent when Thomas convinces them Charity's testimony is full of holes. He is working to sway the settlement's opinion."

Based on what I know of history, that's not going to work. People used to have a crazy blood lust. Like, people would bring their children to hangings. It had been considered a form of entertainment.

"I'm not going back there."

"I am not going to give you a choice," Mercy says. She moves quicker than I would have expected and I don't even realize what she's done until her shoulder hits me in the gut, knocking the wind out of me, and throwing me over her shoulder.

"Put me down," I wheeze into her chest, swaying with each step as she plods back to the root cellar.

"I am trying to help you. Please try to understand."

I hate her. I can't help it, but that's the thought running through my head as she approaches the clearing where my prison is so patiently waiting.

"If you leave now, you will always be running, you will never be innocent. I am not going to let you sabotage yourself, at least not more than you already have."

I struggle against the building pressure from her shoulder. Mercy pulls back the slat roof of the root cellar, my body hanging precariously on her shoulder.

"This isn't helping me!" I can't explain the falling feeling in my heart or the tears that prick at the corner of my eyes. Frustrated, I brush them away with the palm of my hand and use Mercy's distraction with the roof to rip free from her grip.

She lunges and grabs me around the waist, pulling me tight against her. Struggling against her, she squeezes tighter, the pressure around my chest tight enough that it gets hard for my lungs to expand.

"Please." Mercy stares into my eyes as I continue to wiggle. "Please let me help you. Just trust me."

But I guess that's the problem. I don't trust anyone here. She must see that too, as she stares into my hooded eyes.

She seizes me by the wrists and lowers my struggling body back into the hole. And the only stupid thing I can think as it happens is *Wow, I didn't realize Mercy was this strong.* Stupid. Especially stupid as she drops me the last two feet. I'm not prepared to hit the ground, my body crumpling into the cold earth.

"Forgive me." Mercy wipes her hands off on her apron. "But I mean it when I say I am trying to help you. I hope you realize that, and even if you do not . . . I have to do this."

She pushes the wood slat roof back over the root cellar, plunging me into semidarkness despite the high sun. Heart racing, I take in what's been left after my escape attempt. But there's nothing left. I've ruined everything. My wall of baskets had been kicked over as I tried to get out and now lay crumpled in a long pile against the wall.

Screaming my frustration, I dig my fists into my eyes as I try to breathe past the panic building in my chest. I can find another way. I can find another way. I'm not going to sit here and wait to die. I won't stay here on their terms. I won't—my thoughts are interrupted by my gasping breaths. My body knows what my mind won't accept. There's no way out now.

So, I sit, rocking against the ground as the light fades more and more, leaving me alone with my ruined hopes.

CHAPTER EIGHTEEN

The sound of rough planks rubbing against themselves brings me blinking blearily to my knees. Above me, the morning light is weak like my limbs.

"Here lies the witch," a man's voice grunts as the plank ceiling continues to shift, revealing a bright burst of sunlight. "Told you, you had nothing to worry about. Ain't nothing gonna get this one out."

He steps into view, but between the backlit sun and the hat pulled low over his eyes, I can't make out who he is. Maybe he's no one. Just another person drawn to the drama of a witch hanging. My eyes deaden as I realize that will be today. My hand brushes against my smooth neck, feeling where the abrasions will be that'll cost me my life and a shudder goes down my spine.

"Yes, thank you."

My head perks up as a figure I'd recognize anywhere steps in front of the hole. "Thomas," I whisper through dry lips.

"Did you remember to bring the rope with you?" Thomas asks, head turned toward the gruff figure he'd brought with him.

A pile of rope hits the ground at his feet, sending up a cloud of dust. Thomas shakes his head but doesn't comment. Who is this guy? Surely not someone he would have living in the settlement. If Matthew isn't good enough, I doubt this guy is.

"Good morrow." Thomas peers into the hole but doesn't look at me.

His eyes widen as he sees the damage I've caused to their food storage. I pull myself to my feet, staring unblinking into his smooth-shaven face.

"Thomas."

"I am going to toss the rope down, just hold onto it and we shall pull you back up."

What no ladder? Are they afraid that if I climb out on my own that I'll just take off? Not a bad idea honestly. I should do that with the rope anyway.

He lowers down a small length of rope and I wrap it around my wrists. I give him a nod and he starts pulling. Bracing my feet against the wall, I walk up it as he pulls, refusing to let myself just dangle helplessly.

Thomas steps back with every tug, so when I get to the top, he's standing a good five feet away from me. Despite the rope tying us together, I've never felt farther away from him. He stands there like a stranger, rubbing his shoulder with one hand while his lackey winds the rope back up. He still hasn't looked at me.

"Alright," he says, nodding to the other man. "Let us go."

With a smile that reveals more gaps than teeth, the man pulls a piece of rope out of his pocket. I jerk away but his grip is hard as he wraps it around my wrists. He smells of fish and BO, just like I'd imagine a pirate would. When he gets to the end of the rope, he pulls it tight, so the rough fibers dig into my skin. Satisfied, he ties it off but keeps hold of the end. Thoroughly trussed up, he tugs the rope so that I stumble after him.

At least we're walking in the opposite direction of where I tried to go yesterday. If it hadn't been for Mercy's interfering, I could've been gone by now. Even in these circumstances, I'm absurdly proud of myself. Without knowing where I was, I didn't head right back into the heart of my enemy. Because that's what we are now, aren't we? I stare at the back of Thomas's carefully combed head. His shoulders tense like he knows I'm looking at him, but he doesn't turn around.

No matter what Mercy said, Thomas isn't here to help me. The time of his protection is over.

The rope chaffs against my wrists as the man continues to tug on it despite the fact that I'm keeping up with him. It bites into my skin, a lovely precursor to what is about to come.

I wear the blanket Mercy gave me like a sash, unwilling to leave it behind despite how useless it will be. I hope Thomas saw it. I hope he recognized the generosity of his sister and it's eating at him right now. Even if he thinks I'm a witch, wouldn't he want to let me go because I wasn't a bad one? I've lived with them, so wouldn't they know whether I'd been off committing heinous crimes and working with the devil?

"Is this how it ends then?" I call to Thomas, trying to look braver than I feel.

Thomas looks back at me with a frown. "I must do as the law says."

And I don't know why I ever for one second thought he would do anything different.

Tripping over an exposed root, the rope pulls against my wrists and draws crimson blood. The man leers at me as I struggle to stand, his gap-toothed smile like a black hole.

Thick, fat tears build behind my eyes and spill down my cheeks like a fountain. The man holding my rope laughs, a dry sound against my ears, and turns to keep walking.

Sobbing like I haven't since I was a small child, I follow behind him. It's impossible to see in front of me anymore with tears blurring my vision, but I don't care.

Maybe that's who this is. Did they have to hire out for a hangman? Do they have to look so disgusting? Is that just part of the job description: "Must look like someone has attempted to kill you too"?

Despite my tears and stumbles, all too soon I'm staring down the length of the clearing at the brutish skeleton structure being created in the middle of the settlement. So, this was why they had to wait two days to hang me, they needed to build their own gallows.

The structure went up surprisingly fast, people must have been excited to hang me. My limbs go weak looking at its solid structure, and I don't know if I can keep going.

Glancing around at the settlement for one of the last times, I try to take in the last moments of my life. When my eyes pass Matthew's house, a sob catches in my throat. There is no house there anymore. The front wall is gone, and through the gaping hole left there, I can make out the missing floor too. The house sags, the frame unstable with so many missing pieces and my chest tightens to watch the evidence of his broken dreams.

As we pass through the green, whispers fill the air around us. People flow out of the shelter of their homes in a clump to follow behind us. The crowd grows as we get closer to the gallows. Even with their hushed voices, it's impossible to miss the feverish joy-like atmosphere surrounding them. Reading about it was one thing, but seeing it is another matter entirely.

Glancing back, I take in their smiling faces, the jaunt in their steps, and I can't believe it. Something like this would never happen in the 21st century.

Reaching the gallows, Thomas marches up the hastily formed stairs, the wood creaking precariously with every step. I'm tugged after him, wishing the structure would just fall down on us. Maybe this was why Matthew was so busy. He couldn't show up to the trial because he was so busy dismantling his house for my hanging.

"If everyone could settle down," Thomas calls, projecting his deep voice across the crowd of people surging towards the gallows. "We have business to conduct."

Thomas turns his icy blue eyes towards me. They don't even so much as spark with recognition. I could be anyone to him, and the feeling makes me sink to my knees.

He turns to the other man and gestures for them to pull me up. Dragged by bleeding wrists that have already left a trail of fat red drops across the new structure, I stand on weak legs in front of a noose.

"Sophronia, you have been accused of witchcraft, namely creating devil's circles near our settlement. Do you deny it?"

"I didn't do anything! I didn't hurt anyone!" I can't deny being a witch but I have to say something.

"The men of this court have decided to deal with these matters the way we have always done, a public hanging to ensure you are dead and can no longer cause trouble for the good God-fearing people of Nantasket," Thomas continues, his face deadpanning.

The crowd cheers, the sound reverberating in my ears.

As they quiet down again, Thomas begins praying, quoting scriptures and praying for me to repent. That's not likely.

As they walk me into place, the noose waving at me from where it hangs in the slight breeze, the mood of the crowd picks up. A fat, half-rotten apple smacks against the side of my face. It slides down my jaw and sits in a jellied clump on my chest as laughter picks up in the crowd. It's quickly followed by a potato and several other foods too far gone to recognize.

Glancing at Thomas, I wait for him to say something, instead, he just folds his arms over his chest and stares at my shoes with a clenched jaw.

More food flies through the air. Some of it hits me, but a good portion lays splattered on the gallows floor. On Matthew's floor. The very same floor where we talked together just a few mornings ago.

Where is Matthew? Betrayal worms its way inside my chest. He lied to me. I thought he would help me. But here I stand, ready to die.

Wiping away my tears with the back of my hands, I push away some of the tomato slime too. Squaring my shoulders, I face my death. I had at least broken the curse that has plagued my family for years and finally my mother and my aunts will know love. I am standing in place for every witch, real or otherwise, who came before me. If they could do this with dignity, then so will I.

Closing my eyes, I envision my mother's face. Her soft, warm face that I will never see again. But it's okay. I will make it okay.

The smell of fish fills my nose and I open my eyes to see the hangman's empty smile. He reaches out and grabs the noose from where it flaps in the breeze next to my head. With manic eyes, he lowers the loop over my head, snagging it on my loose bun for a moment before yanking it down to my neck, pulling a few hairs with it. Blinking back tears from the stinging pain, I stare past him, stare past all of them into the trees beyond as the weight settles against my throat.

It will all be over soon.

He tightens the noose and pats me on the cheek, making me flinch. Stepping away, he puts his hand on a lever I didn't notice before. I stare at my feet and notice the trapdoor hidden there.

Closing my eyes, I start counting back from one hundred, knowing I'll never make it to one. There's nothing stopping them now, least of all Thomas with his cold eyes and hard jaw. I can't believe Mercy ever thought I should stay for him.

When I hit fifty, I know something must have gone wrong. Opening my eyes, I notice how quiet it's gotten, and not like the reverent quiet at church, but like no sound exists at all.

All around me, faces are still. Frozen in time, each one stands without moving. Dresses flap in the continuing breeze, but no one acts like they notice it. They don't act like they notice anything. A woman close to me stands with finger pointed at me, her jaw still hanging open as though mid-word. A man holding a burning torch precariously close to the platform leers into empty space with gleaming eyes.

Taking a step forward, I press my luck. Waiting for the hangman to yank me back into place, I lift the heavy loop of rope from around my neck. He still stands with a hand on the lever, dark eyes practically glowing as they stare where I was just standing.

"What the heck?" It doesn't matter what's happening, I know enough to get away from the danger of the gallows. I lift the noose from my neck and run for the stairs.

"Hurry up," Matthew hisses, waving from where he stands at the bottom of the stairs. "What are you doing?"

Gaping at him like a fish, I take the stairs two at a time. My foot lodges in the last one, ragged wood biting into my ankle as warm blood stains my stocking. Wrenching myself free, I stumble into Matthew, knocking him back a few steps.

He loops his arm through mine for support as he sets a quick pace into the woods.

Each step has my ankle throbbing, and I have to bite my cheek to keep from yelling out.

"What just happened?"

"I figured as soon as everything stilled you would have been out of there. You are a witch, right? Like this stuff should not faze you," Matthew says, pulling me along faster.

Favoring my right leg, I can only go so fast. "Maybe not when I'm expecting it! That wasn't me!"

"Well." He shifts, offering me his shoulder to lean on for better support. "I guess that would make it me then."

Distracted, my leg crumples under me with my next step. "What?!"

He shrugs, turning so I can only see the side of his face. Brows furrowed, he tries to explain himself. "Well, you see, I just . . ."

Struggling to stay standing, I grip him by the arm. "Are you," I pause, unable to form the words. "Are you—do you have—are you—?"

Of course. His father is a warlock. I feel like an idiot.

He glances at me with hooded eyes, hand clenched into a fist. "Yes."

I pick up my pace, trying to get to safety and away from my own idiocy.

"Soph, I—"

I hold up a hand to stop him.

"You . . . all this time you were a warlock and you never told me?" My voice is quiet and squeaky but at least I can get the words out.

He nods and I fall to my knees. The cold earth soaks up through my dress and into my bones. "All this time you could've done something, could've told me, could've at least helped me and chose to just stand aside and watch me struggle because?"

I don't know that I expect an answer and I'm not sure there's any answer I would accept. Matthew stares down at me where I kneel, my fingers brushing the tops of dry leaves where they sit waiting to rot against the ground.

"It is not like you were willing to tell me anything," Matthew points out, crossing his arms over his chest. "You did not tell me anything about you until you had to and neither did I."

"Except that you didn't have to do it this way." I bite back the urge to scream as I rise to my feet again, ignoring the stabbing pain going up my ankle.

Shoulders drooping, he pushes past me. "We need to keep going. I cannot hold them suspended forever."

"Well, isn't that good to know."

He's a warlock. A warlock that can hold people suspended in time. Well, isn't he just fancy? And I bet his coven would have taken him. He has to have more gifts than what I've seen.

Jealousy brews in my veins, tainting his rescue and filling me with annoyance.

We crash through the undergrowth as we head who knows where. We're not on any path that I can see, but maybe that's for the best. We'll be harder to follow through unmarked trails. Although, if his gift just suspends them in time, will it look like I disappeared when they come to again? How can they come after us when they have no idea which direction we've even gone? And I guess they don't even know there's a "we." As far as they know, I'm a witch working alone.

My head spins as I try to keep track of what little information I have and mesh it with all of the information I don't have. Stopping, I rest my hand against the cold bark of the closest tree. I close my eyes and try to breathe. I need to calm everything down. I'm not going to hang today, and that should be all that matters.

"Hey." Matthew rests his hand on my shoulder, startling me back into consciousness.

"What?" There's less snap in my retort than before. Matthew takes my arm and urges me forward.

Silently we plod along, the muscles in Matthew's neck are tense.

"Where are we going?" I ask after a while.

He gives me a sidelong glance. "We are just getting far enough away that you can do your little trip through time thing and go back to your own time."

"You're sending me home?" My heart falls in a way I don't understand.

Nodding, he gives me extra support as we climb over a boulder sitting in our path. "I think it is safest for you if you leave."

"What if I don't want to?" I didn't realize it until I said it out loud, but it's true. I'm not completely ready to go home, despite the fact that my gift hasn't regenerated enough to take me there anyway. Despite everything, I want to stay. I want to stay with Matthew even if he is a liar.

"Staying is not really an option."

"Isn't there anything you can do? I mean, you've been hiding your abilities from me this whole time, there must be something else you can do that would keep us safe," I point out under narrowed brows.

Matthew waves his arms at the trees around us. "What is it that you think I am hiding from you? The ability to change your face? The ability to make us invisible? The ability to change the past? Oh wait,

203

that is *your* gift." His chest rises and falls at a rapid pace that makes me want to shove him.

"You don't get to be offended with me!"

I hate the hot tears that course down my cheeks in narrow streams. I hate the softening in Matthew's face as he watches them. And I hate that I can't stop it.

Matthew scoops me into his arms, resting my head against his chest. Shoulders shaking, my tears evolve into sobs and he tightens his arms around me.

Everything is just so out of my control. It's never been like this before. I've never been like this before. I've never had to deal with emotions like this before.

"Shhh," Matthew breathes into my hair, running a hand down my back as my body continues to shake.

Maybe this has nothing to do with the curse and more to do with almost dying. I'll just pin it on that.

"This is probably far enough." He glances into the woods. "We can stay here for a bit until you can get back on your feet and go home."

"What will happen to you?" I'm still mad at him, I can't help it, but I'm not completely selfish.

"I was not supposed to come back here in the first place. I shall have to actually move on this time," he says with a shrug. "I will be fine. I'll just disappear like Thomas wanted." He chuckles but I don't join in.

A knot forms in my stomach. "Are you sure you'll be okay?"

"Yes." He glances down at me. "I shall be fine. It is you we need to get out of here, remember that all too happy mob waiting back there?"

He tilts his head and smiles. Despite the seriousness of the situation, I find myself wanting to laugh. He's right, I've got a mob probably searching for me right now and all I can think about is what Matthew is going to do with parts of the walls of his house missing.

I start laughing and he sets me down, watching me with wide eyes. Bent double, I just can't stop laughing. It's probably hysteria setting in, especially from the way Matthew watches me with an almost frightened expression, but I can't help it. I just have this image in my head of him sitting at his table under the sagging roof waving at his neighbors as they walk by.

Trying to pull myself together, I stand up but keep the wobbly smile. "Sorry, it's been a long day."

That's for sure. I'd venture to say that a little hysteria is perfectly natural right about now, but somehow I don't think that'd go over well.

"You have had a lot to take in," Matthew agrees, face softening.

"I just—" I stop myself before trying again. "I just don't understand why you didn't tell me. I mean, out there on the water when it was just me and you and I was telling you I was a witch, why didn't you reciprocate?"

And there it is, evidence of the vulnerable heart I'm trying too hard to bury. Too late, I guess.

He shrugs, not meeting my eyes. "I did not think it was the right time."

"Seconds away from death wasn't the right time to confess your biggest secret?"

"Who says this is my biggest secret?" His dark eyes are shadowed as he stares down at my mouth.

"How could there possibly be more?" I ask before I can censor myself. Clamping a hand to my mouth far too late, I watch Matthew behind the safety of my hand as he frowns.

"A few days together does not mean you know everything there is to know about me."

"Obviously."

He runs a hand through the waves of his hair. "We do not need to tell each other anything. It does not matter what you know or what I know because you are leaving. With any luck you are leaving right now."

Wincing, I duck my chin to hide watery eyes. "I still don't know if I can leave yet," I whisper.

"You will never know if you don't try." Matthew takes a few steps back from me.

The only person I'm really hurting here is myself. Matthew can fade into the distance and almost pretend he never knew me, especially if he has to start up somewhere new anyway. I have no such luxuries. Matthew is the first person I've been able to love. He's the only person anyone in my family has been able to love in hundreds of years. I will never forget him, no matter if he remembers me.

With a tear running down my cheek, I try to open the door to home. Its outline forms before me but puffs out with a sigh before it can solidify enough to use.

"Like I said, I'm still not back to one hundred percent after our little jaunt." The words come out soft, and I have to bite my lip to keep from crying more.

"Then I guess we shall just have to find someplace to hide you." Matthew gives me his shoulder and helps me hobble further into the woods.

My leg burns with every step, fresh blood coating my stocking. I should probably stop and look at it, at least make sure I don't have any splinters or anything stuck in it, but Matthew is moving at a quick pace to keep me safe, so, I keep pushing through the pain.

Matthew keeps me going, leaves crunching under our heavy footfalls. Silent tears course down my cheeks as the pain becomes too much to bear. I jerk to a stop, Matthew stumbling beside me.

His gaze travels from my face to my leg and breathes out slowly. I sink to the ground, unable to stand anymore.

Matthew sinks to his knees across from me. With gentle hands he lifts my chin, forcing me to look at him. "Forgive me."

His kind voice does nothing to help me get myself back under control.

"I am sorry I did not think about your leg. I am sorry I did not show up to the trial. I am sorry I never told you about me. I am sorry I got on that ship when you told me it wasn't safe. I am sorry for all of it." He pauses. "And I want to thank you. Thank you for saving my life even though it risked yours and thank you for learning I was a warlock and not turning your back on me."

Something about his apology relaxes me and releases the last amount of pent-up magic I needed. It fills my limbs, tingling as it rejoins the scraps I've been slowly building back up on my own.

"I'm sorry you've been hurt," I tell him, the honesty in my voice ringing true. "I just wish you'd trusted me enough to tell me what your plan was or what you could do, or really even that there was a backup plan in the first place."

He crosses his hands over his chest, chin tucked down.

"I found your . . . food. I knew what you were. I never turned you in. That is not abandoning. I just could not risk them turning their attention on me. Not when I am what I am."

Alright then. I'll just have to continue on and ignore the way my heart wrenches in my chest. I saved his life and he saved mine. We're even now and things can go back to the way they always were.

Except for me.

Life will never be the same for me again. The curse is broken, and I'll have to deal with whatever that will imply. Will people like me better now? Will I care?

"It's time to go."

"No Matthew, I'm not ready. Isn't there anything else you want to say before I go?" My voice is soft, almost pleading.

He backs away. "I thought you might want to head out before anyone came looking for you. Keeping you safe means getting you out of this time period—"

"And as far away from you as I can get apparently."

"That is not what it is. And I'd ask you to take me with you if I felt like it was something you could do. But I know, and you know, that just getting you out of here will be a trial in itself."

"You don't know that."

He runs a hand through his hair. "If you cannot leave right now, that is fine. We will just find another way to get you out of here."

Around us the bare limbs of trees curl in toward me, their branches like fingers ready to snatch and grab. Everything in this stupid time period is out to get me.

Matthew sighs. His footsteps crunch through the thick carpet of fallen leaves as he scoots closer to me.

"Let me help you. I am doing this for your own good." He sets me back down and takes my head in his hands as I try to stumble to my feet and get away.

His hands are firm, locking me in place. I stare into his eyes as his jaw clenches, lips thinning. He breathes out, and in a sensation like ink traveling through water, my vision grows dark, and I tumble into sleep.

CHAPTER NINETEEN

Everything comes back into focus slowly, the darkness leaving streaks across my vision as it drains out of me.

Matthew sits in front of a small fire. The woods are dark and quiet around us.

Struggling to sit up, my limbs are weak and about as reactive as cooked noodles.

Matthew glances at me, lips twisting to the side. "Sorry about that."

"What did you do to me?" I ask, my voice rasping.

"You are not going to feel up too much for a while. A shot like that should have held you down for at least a day."

So, he did have more than one power. I want to ask why he didn't tell me, but I didn't have the strength to argue. So, I push down the unwarranted jealousy and look around. "Wh-where are we?"

"A half-day's walk from the settlement." He pokes the fire with a stick, stirring the embers. The light from the flames dance across his face. "They don't usually come out this far. It is too unpredictable, you know with Indians and bears and stuff like that." My eyes widen and he laughs. "Do not worry, we shall be fine. I have traveled through this area often while scrounging for food."

Why does that not comfort me?

He leans forward, adjusting the blanket around my shoulders. "You should feel back to normal in the morning. Sorry I had to do that, you were not going to help yourself and you needed more rest."

I frown, not feeling up to responding.

He leans over the fire, prodding it with a long thin branch. I watch him. I want to be irritated, and there's a part of me that is, but through all the chaos, we've become friends. More than friends.

"I thought we could bunker down here for a few days if we had to, at least until you get enough magic to travel on your own." I must show some facial reaction to my panic because he laughs and reaches out to touch my shoulder. "I'm not sure what your experiences have been, but I know for me, rest and time are the best way to build my gift back up."

Wouldn't that be a great gift, to loan someone power when their reserves were low. I'm sure there's someone that has it, even if it's not Matthew.

He hums under his breath, poking at the fire again. A log shifts, sending up a plume of sparks. The gentle warmth seeps into my body, pushing through the blanket Matthew had spread over me. Thomas's blanket, I realize with a start.

How wrong I've been about everything. I can't believe there was ever a part of me that trusted him. Tears burn in the corner of my eyes, but I don't have the strength to brush them away. No wonder Mom didn't want me to come here on my own. No wonder she told me it was dangerous for me to be here. She knew I wouldn't know who to trust and would make the terrible decision to trust the first man I came across.

Leaning over my knees, I gulp down huge breaths to calm my heaving stomach.

"Are you going to be okay sleeping here tonight?" Matthew asks, watching me from the corner of his eye.

"Sure."

Feeling more under control, I lean back and wrap the blanket firmly around me.

"It is going to get a lot colder," Matthew says, adding another log to the fire as it sends up a stream of red sparks into the night.

"I'm sure."

The fact that I could see my breath when sleeping in Matthew's house does not bode well for what will come tonight, but if I could survive living in the root cellar, I can survive this.

My face flames as he hesitantly lifts up his blanket. I move over and lay down in front of him.

The warmth from his body cocoons me as he snuggles into my side. "Are you warm?" he asks, his breath tickling my ear.

I nod. Unable to speak past the emotion resting in the back of my throat.

I know it won't be warm like this all night, but between Matthew and the fire, I'm more content than I've been in weeks. I breathe in time with him, leaning into the sturdy planes of his chest. Despite everything, I find it easy to drift to sleep.

❧

I wake up to Matthew's arm wrapped around my waist, his face pressed into the back of my neck. The fire has died down and the sun is brightening the edges of the forest. A cool breeze swirls around us, but the heat from Matthew's body keeps me warm.

He shifts in his sleep, pulling me closer. My body burns where he touches me even as my limbs relax further into his hold. A sigh escapes me and I close my eyes. I start to drift off, comforted in a way I hadn't experienced before.

My eyes shoot open when a single thought worms its way inside of me.

Why did I wake up?

I blink all the remaining sleep from my eyes and look around. Everything looks almost exactly the same as it did last night. Yet something has my nerves on edge.

Steady quiet emanates from the trees. Is that what could have woken me?

A trickle of power runs through me and I realize immediately what woke me up. My magic reserves are full. It courses through the pockets of my body, alive in its own way with a power that dances across my skin.

Matthew stirs and my heart sinks. I'm not ready to go.

Matthew groans in his sleep, his arm gripping me tighter. I shift a little, just enough to maybe alert him that I'm awake. If I have to leave, I need to first say goodbye.

I feel the moment he wakes up. His body stiffens. Slowly, he eases his arm from around my stomach and rolls to face the sky.

"Good morrow," I shout.

Matthew starts so hard I expect him to fly out of his skin. "Good morrow." His voice comes out gruff.

I turn and get great satisfaction from watching the dark crimson blush spread up his neck and over his stubbled cheeks. "Sleep well?" I ask with a big grin.

He coughs to clear his throat. "Yes, quite."

The giggle that escapes me belongs more to an eight-year-old girl than to me, but it ripples through my chest anyway. Matthew's obvious discomfort has done more to settle me than any long, in-depth thinking about it ever could.

"So, uh, are you feeling any better?" he asks.

My laughter immediately stops. He still wants me to leave. Even after last night.

Why do I feel his rejection like an anchor in my stomach?

"Yes, much better," I whisper, pain infusing every word.

Matthew stares up at the sky as though there's something profound up there. "I guess this is it then," he says finally.

I sigh, all the warmth from earlier draining out my toes. "I guess so."

We both sit up. He doesn't look at me and I don't look at him.

"Do you have the energy you will need?" he asks, picking leaves off his shoulder.

"I'll be fine." I know it's true, but my heart drops even further in my chest, my body rocking with its hollow beats.

He chuckles a little. "Are you sure you do not want to try further in the past? I hear the dark ages are delightful."

"I think I could happily stay out of the past for the rest of my life." I give him a smile despite their being no joy inside of me.

"I can understand that. The past is not a place for us."

I turn away from him, a lump forming in my throat, and spot a place in the clearing a few feet away from us. Matthew follows me, both of us silent. I hesitate, searching for a way to prolong my stay. I don't want to leave him.

"Is there—" I start.

"I want to—" He reaches for me.

We stare at each other. The air between us charging with emotions and unspoken words. Matthew sighs and runs a hand through his hair.

"I have grown fond of you, Soph. And if there was any other way . . . I would . . ." He reaches for me again. A blush creeps up his neck, but he keeps his gaze focused on me, even as my jaw drops.

"What are you saying?" I ask, hope filling me.

He doesn't answer. Instead, he steps forward, taking me in his arms.

"I want you to know, that this was real to me. I know I have lied to you, but I never lied about this."

My eyes are wide, body frozen as he moves in closer, brushing his lips tentatively against mine. When I don't pull away, he grabs my neck and deepens the kiss, pulling me in closer. I let out a squeak of surprise, before opening my mouth to his feverish kiss. The smell of pine fills my nose.

I could stay wrapped in his arms forever.

When he releases me, we stumble away. I press my fingers against tender lips. His chest heaves as he stares at me out of emotion-filled eyes. It's almost as if he is trying to keep himself away from me. Just one single step toward him, and it would all start again. I have never felt this way about anyone. The longing is killing me.

"Say something," I breath out, hoping he would beg me to stay.

We stand there, staring at each other. I study his handsome face, committing it to memory—his short dark hair that curls at the ends, his deep brown eyes, his shoulders that seem so much broader than they were when I first met him. The way he can tower over me, even though I know we're less than a foot apart in height. The smell of earth and work that clings to him no matter where he goes.

His hands open and close, mouth doing the same like he has something to say.

"Thank you." I don't know what else to say. I turn from him. My heart seizes with pain. Is this what love feels like? If so, why would anyone want to go through it? I can barely breath past the sudden feeling of loss. Of knowing that I will never see Matthew again. Never be able to explore the connection between us.

Power flows through me as I create my door back home. It gleams in the weak forest light, the rough wood cracked and the handle a dull gold. It may not be much, but that's my door.

My hand touches the cool metal, its chill biting into my skin as I glance back at Matthew for the last time. He runs a hand through his hair and takes a hesitant step forward. A single tear slips down his cheek. "Stay." His eyes seem to plead with me.

"I have to." Vision blurry with tears, I open the door and step into the swirling cosmos.

CHAPTER TWENTY

I barely notice the swirling mists, the bright stars against a dark purple sky as I walk and walk and walk until there's nothing. Pulled forward on my own desires, I pass through time like I'm walking to my next class.

Reaching the door on the other end, I turn to look behind me one last time. I know I won't see anything, but it doesn't stop me from looking. From wishing. Hoping.

I've gone so far, I can't even make out where the other door sits, not through the kaleidoscope of space that sits between us.

Sighing, I open the door back to my time, leaving everything I've come to love behind.

CHAPTER TWENTY-ONE

I fall through the door and land on the uneven floor of my bedroom. My portal door slams, sinking into itself until finally disappearing. Cutting off my one chance to go back to return to Matthew.

Laying on the uneven floor, I gasp for breath, trying to come to terms with what I've done. I follow the lines in the cracked plaster ceiling, lines as familiar to me as my mother's perfume, while subconsciously reaching for my magic again. Why did I leave him?

I push up from the floor and look around. I'm home. Where I should be. So why does my heart hurt so much?

I push down the pain. There is nothing I can do about it now except wrap the memories of Matthew in a bright red bow to open when I'm more capable of handling my feelings for him.

The door to my bedroom flies open, banging against the wall. Plaster rains down from the ceiling, pooling on the floor. We really need to get our ceiling repaired.

"You're home? Iole! She's home!" a sob hitches in Aunt Agathe's voice as she peers at my prone form on the floor. "How are you, baby girl?"

I open my mouth but nothing comes out.

Aunt Agathe kneels beside me, scooping me off the floor with surprisingly firm arms. Lifting me into her lap, she wraps her arms so firmly around me, I worry for a moment that I won't be able to breathe.

"We were so worried about you! Are you hurt? What happened?" She doesn't bother to pause before asking her questions.

"She's here?" Mom stands in the doorway, her body filling the frame as she looks down at me with hitched breath.

Aunt Agathe shifts me off her lap and stands. Mom falls to her knees in front of me. With tears burning down my cheeks, I surge forward into her arms and bury my face on her shoulder.

She rubs a shaking hand down my back, like she really didn't think she'd ever see me again.

There's a scuffle down the hall and then the rest of my family pours into the room, jostling for space and trying to get closer to me.

"Did you not bathe the whole time you were gone?" Aunt Tanis asks with a wrinkled nose. "*That* wasn't necessary."

"Oh hush," Grandma says, a smile splitting her face where more wrinkles have formed just in the short time I've been gone. "She had more important things to worry about than bathing."

"I smell?" I ask Mom, still not ready for her to let me go.

"Only a little," Mom says with a relieved laugh. "Don't let Tanis bother you, she's just trying not to cry."

"I am not," Aunt Tanis protests before running back into the hallway.

Aunt Tanis was the one who always cried during the Hallmark movies and any commercial with animals. I'd have to tell her later that I'd managed to channel her in the past. All that weeping.

I burrow in closer to Mom, breathing in her lavender scent. I can't focus on our happy reunion like I know I should. I just keep seeing Matthew's face and the pleading in his eyes.

"You were gone two weeks," Mom says, pulling me closer and pressing her face into the top of my head. "We were so worried about you."

"Huh." In theory I should have been able to come back within minutes of when I first left, but obviously that didn't happen. Maybe time just knew I didn't want to come home.

"I'm so glad you're home safe," Mom says, my aunts pressing closer to us, as though they need to be able to touch me to know that I'm really here.

"I made it," I sigh. "I did what I needed to do."

"What happened while you were gone, sweetie?" Grandma leans closer, her eyes gleaming as she readies herself for a story.

Leaning against Mom, I tell them everything. About my rough start. About Thomas. About traveling and the boat and the witch trial. I tell them about everything except my relationship with Matthew.

"I didn't know if I was going to be able to make it," I confess, the tension of the last few weeks draining out of me.

"Well, let's remember that it wasn't me who wanted you to go," Mom says with a pointed glare at the hallway.

Mom pulls me closer, hiding my face in her shoulder, but she doesn't have to for me to know they've kept up their fight about me leaving the whole time I've been gone.

"You don't need to fight anymore." My voice is muffled inside Mom's shoulder. "I'm back and I'm safe, so everything's okay."

"It most certainly is not 'okay,'" Mom snaps, pointing an accusing finger at Aunt Agathe. "She ran back to that man she was seeing before you left and has been with him every day since you've been gone."

Agathe's cheeks redden, matching her sister's hair, but she holds herself up with a pride I've never seen in her before. "And why shouldn't I? Why shouldn't I try to make Soph's sacrifice worth something?"

"Because you should've been at home worrying about her safety with the rest of us," Mom says.

I push myself off her lap. "I have no problem with Aunt Agathe's interest in a gentleman caller, and I'm glad breaking the curse meant you got him back."

"Why doesn't everyone give her a chance to breathe and rest." Grandma ushers out Aunt Tanis and Aunt Daphne where they linger closer to the door. "I'm so glad you're home safe, sweetheart. I knew you could do it." She gives me a broad smile, and I can almost forget the permanent lines of worry I've etched onto her face. "Come along, Agathe, Iole."

Aunt Agathe gives me a smile and squeezes my shoulder, ignoring Mom entirely as she drifts behind Grandma. Mom lingers, obviously torn between following her mother's orders and being an adult herself.

She sighs. "You know how much I love you right?"

I nod as her eyes go glassy with tears. "Of course, Mom."

Straightening herself out, she holds her head high on her way out the door.

Left alone, I stare at the ceiling again. My eyes trail the cracks as the sun travels across the sky. I can't believe I'm here. I can't believe I did it. Grandma may have always believed in me, but I sure didn't. The idea that I was able to travel so far to the past, to travel *with* someone. I've done things I never thought possible. How will my real life possibly compare now?

I wish I had asked how Aunt Agathe's love life was going. Is she really *in* love?

I'm not anything special. I don't have a million gifts, my power isn't a limitless well that allows me to keep going through the folds of time over and over again. I'm just one, almost average person.

As average as a witch can be. And I broke the curse.

They leave me to myself for the rest of the day, Mom coming up only briefly to bring me food. They had stew for dinner, but the only thing on the tray that interests me is the thick slab of chocolate cake. Maybe it's the aftereffects of having basically just bread and cheese and pottage to live on for the entire time since I've been gone, but as I take bite after bite of cake, I swear it's never tasted so good. Sticking to the roof of my mouth and filling every taste bud with chocolate has me sighing in contentment. In this moment, I decide I never want to travel through time again. The present is just fine, thank you very much.

Stomach full and mouth happy, I sink into the real warmth of my insulated bedroom and thick blankets and fall into an easy sleep.

My dreams are anything but.

Vision after vision comes to me of Matthew.

My family and I crowd around the kitchen island, a shadowy Matthew watches from the hallway.

I sit in some boring class and Matthew sits at the teacher's desk while she stands at the front of the room lecturing us on World War I.

I walk through Nantasket, the settlement abandoned. Everything gone except Matthew's shack, his form standing on the front step.

When daylight comes, I'm already on my feet and ready to go. I've slept long enough.

Mom comes in as I tug on an oversized sweater. Her gaze travels over my face, noting the dark circles lining my eyes with a tight frown.

"You should be resting." She glances down at me. I've lost weight and I can see the concern on her face. "You also need to eat."

"I can eat at school."

"I think it'd be best if you took the rest of this week off. You need to rest after such a big jump like that. Just stay here and let us take care of you for a while." She holds my shoulder, stopping me from grabbing my backpack where it's slumped against the wall. "Just take a moment to process what you've been through. We can talk about what happened."

"I don't want to process." I shrug out of her grip, grab my bag and slip out my bedroom door before she can grab me again. "I'll see you after school," I call over my shoulder.

My aunts watch me from the living room as I drift past.

I have to get out of here.

Closing the front door behind me, I breathe in air that's so cold I can taste it. I let it fill me and cool my body before starting off toward school.

I can't talk to my mom, and I can't just sit in that house lingering on the fact that Matthew is dead now. Did he return to England? Get married? Start a family? Maybe he stayed. I can search the records for his name, but there are so many abandoned cemeteries throughout New England, it would be difficult to find him.

The library looms in the distance. Its old brick walls looking like a relic from long ago. Still, for the first time probably ever, I turn and look at it. Really look at it. And I realize it's the only place I want to be right now.

I have to find out what happened to Matthew.

Taking the crumbling stairs two at a time, I slam into the door before I realize it's a pull instead of push. Brushing back my hair with a hand, I quietly open the door and slip into the stale air of the building.

Silence drifts in from every corner. Rows and rows of books framed by lights that only illuminate the floating dust mites coating every surface greet me as I make my way toward the computers in the back.

"Can I help you?"

I almost jump out of my skin as a stooped woman with small glasses perched on her nose seems to materialize out of the shadows to my right.

"Do you have anything on the early settlements in the 1600s?"

The librarian nods, revealing a tight graying bun. "Follow me."

She drifts through the shelves, floor creaking as she leads me deeper and deeper into the library. It seems to stretch into eternity, bellying the appearance of the building outside. I never would've guessed it could've possibly been this big.

Just when I'm so turned around I doubt I'll be able to find the front doors by myself, she stops. I almost walk into her back, my mind wandering over what all these books could possibly be for before I notice her halt.

"These are our books on early America. We might have some slides too if you want, but I'd recommend that you start here." She smooths her sweater with wrinkled hands. "Let me know if you need anything else. I'll be at the front desk. And please remember to treat the books with respect and leave the library the same as how you found it."

She turns and walks away. The tapping of her shoes against the tile floor fades until I'm alone in silence once more.

I expect there to be a line of dust obstructing the titles of the books around me, I mean how many people could possibly want to research that time in history? But as I look at the shelves, I find the bindings to be practically beaming.

The first book I notice is *Settlements of Early America*. Perfect.

Sliding it out, I gasp as its weight. The binding is five inches across, and the book has to be at least fifteen pounds. What's it lined with? Lead?

There's a small table at the end of the bookshelf across from me, and I walk over to it and set the book down on the table. An echoing *shh* comes from my right, at least I know where the front desk is now.

Opening the book, the pages are so thin I can see the print of the next page underneath them. A headache threatens to bloom across my forehead as I lean over and try to read the small print. After a few minutes of deciphering in the weak light, I realize this book is referring to South America and the desire to slam my head into the desk is overwhelming. I return the book to the shelf and look for another one.

I grow more selective this time, getting pickier with the titles I run my finger over. I'm here to find Matthew, something I can't do just by winging it. Finally, I hesitate on a book titled *Early New England Towns* and pull it out.

Quieter this time, I put the book down on the desk and thumb through the first few pages. They detail the types of people that first came over, something I could care less about as its only taught in every history class I've ever had to take for school.

Flipping further into it, I find a list of the first settlements built along the coast. My eyes travel of their own accord, needing to see its name among the other more well-known places.

I don't see it.

I don't know what I was thinking, but there's no way I'll find Matthew here. Slamming the book shut, I march over and shove it back into its place on the shelf. This is ridiculous. I shouldn't be hiding in here looking for Nantasket. I shouldn't be in here looking for Matthew. I'm back in my own life now and I need to find a way to accept that.

I sling my backpack over my shoulder and practically sprint for the door. The cool air sears my lungs as I stand heaving on the front step. Suitably calmed, I straighten my shoulders and march towards the school.

◦◦◦◦◦◦

"Glad to see you're back," the receptionist says, snapping her gum with every word. "With how long you were gone, we thought you must be dying. Not that I've ever heard of anyone dying from mono."

"Nope, I'm just fine now, as you can see."

It makes sense that they would think that, but it doesn't stop the irritation from crawling across my skin. Mom had to tell the school something when I didn't show up for weeks, but it would've been nice if she'd called ahead this morning. Of course, she didn't think of it.

"Well, make sure you're not contagious anymore. The students here can't afford to miss weeks of school at a time," she says as she hands me my tardy pass.

"Of course." I give her a sickly-sweet smile as I snatch the pass out of her red shellacked nails.

Turning my back on her, I run through the abandoned halls, flyers for the upcoming fall harvest dance flapping as I pass by. Despite my detour to the library, I'm actually not that late. Maybe ten minutes.

The white sterile walls lined with brown lockers feel wider than ever before without the crush of teenagers to fill the space. I'm floating through a mile-wide emptiness just to get to my first class.

I stop in front of biology class. Mr. Robbins's thin tenor voice penetrates the thin walls and I can't help but scowl.

"You're late," Mr. Robbins snaps as I open the door. He glances up at me, face going a bit pale beneath his handlebar mustache. "Sorry, Ms. Magissa. I hope you've recovered well from your illness."

My classmates snicker as I step into the room, the back of my neck growing red. I swerve around desks to find mine in the back. The hum of gossip picks up around me. Faces turning to each other in eager haste to whisper what little they know about my return. I pick up the words "quarantine" and "pathetic" before they're quieted.

"Quiet down," Mr. Robbins yells, smoothing down his hair and turning to the half-filled chalkboard.

The hum continues but he doesn't seem to care. I drag my notebook out of my backpack, knowing I should be following the notes and his monotone lecture that insists on continuing despite the noise coming from his distracted students, but I can't. Instead my pencil curls over the blank paper as I mindlessly fill it with images.

When the bell rings, it shocks me enough that my hand shoots out across the paper, leaving a long dark smear across my doodles.

Or doodle, I realize as I glance down at the sheet. In my thoughtless state, I've left a pretty deliberate message to myself. Matthew stares back at me, his eyes a dark graphite grey. Despite the line, it's an incredibly accurate rendering, especially considering I wasn't even consciously thinking about what I was doing.

Running a shaking finger down the page, I know what I was looking for in the library. I want to know he really did make it. That he was okay after I left. I know that he's dead now, dead for centuries, but I want to know that he lived a long life, a good life. But no matter what I want, I doubt I'll be able to find the information I'm looking for. There will be no "Hey Sophronia, a book just for you detailing Matthew's life" waiting for me on those shelves. The most I can ever expect is his name, just his name listed as a resident of one of the early towns. And I'll most likely never find that because I don't know where he intended to go after I left.

Fat tears roll down my cheeks, splattering on my drawing and fading the pencil marks.

A cough interrupts my personal pondering. "Ms. Magissa, are you sure you're well?"

Glancing up into Mr. Robbins's concerned face, I shrug him off. Wiping away tears, I shove my notebook back in my bag. "I'm fine."

He taps a finger against his mustache but doesn't try to keep me as I grab my bag and make my way to the door. I'm glad. I don't know if I could handle trying to mask my all too overwhelming emotions if he confronted me.

So far, breaking this curse seems to have created nothing but trouble for me. I don't understand why my family wanted it at all, why even my Grandma was interested in having this pain back. I'm just a mess, crying all the time when I've never been one to cry before. I feel like I'll never recover from this, never get myself normal and back on track. Will this be the rest of my life now? Crying over a lost love anytime I have a minute alone to think?

Frowning, I march into my history class, sit in the front row, and start taking serious notes. If I'm busy with school, then I won't focus on my heartbreak or how I wish I could have brought Matthew with me.

My hand flies across the paper, math has never been so interesting. I don't even know half of what I'm writing, I see it on the board or hear it come out of my teacher's mouth and down it goes.

Time passes in a blur but when the bell rings this time, I'm ready for it. I go from class to class this way, filling my mind with meaningless facts to keep myself from actually feeling. When the final bell rings, I'm exhausted. I've never tried so hard to stay focused in class before, and it completely drains me.

My shoulders sink as I begin the long march home. My backpack digs into my shoulders, dragging me down towards the sidewalk. All I want now is a long nap.

Which of course I'm not going to get, I think with a sigh as I note all the cars lining the driveway. *Perfect.* I head up the familiar sagging front steps and into the packed house. Unfamiliar women fill the corners of the living room, their bright eyes snagging on me as I pass through to the kitchen.

"Sophronia," Mom calls out behind a tray filled with drinks. "Mind giving me a hand with these?"

Dropping my bag, I take the tray, eyeing the chipped glasses. "What's going on?"

"Last minute coven meeting." Mom waves a hand as she avoids making eye contact with me. "Nothing to worry about dear."

I barely stifle the groan rising through my chest.

"Take those glasses in, please," Mom says with a shove.

They barely even look at me as I enter the living room and hand out glasses from off the tray. A woman with red lipstick even sneers as I walk past, her eyes narrowing as she watches me.

In this oppressive atmosphere, all I want to do is leave. But as soon as my tray is empty and I'm about to bolt for the stairs, Mom wraps her arm around my shoulders, pinning me in place.

"I'm so glad you could all make it here on such short notice," she says, nails digging into my skin. So much for a random coven meeting, she asked them to come! "I just wanted to get you all together to discuss the matter of Sophronia."

"We've already discussed that matter. It's closed," Rebecca says, leaning forward in her chair, pinched nose high in the air. "I should have known this is why you called us."

"I know Sophronia is a topic we've already delved into, but recent events have made me think we should evaluate them again," Mom presses forward despite the tittering filing the room.

A stick thin woman perched in our old wooden rocking chair shoots to her feet. "You know the rules, Iole. We can't keep discussing your daughter just because you're ashamed she wasn't powerful enough to belong to a coven. It's a one-shot kind of deal and we've already decided her fate. To continue on this path is to embarrass yourself."

Mom flinches back, taking me with her. "Like I said, recent events have made me think we should reconsider her membership. I'm sure you all know that Sophronia's denial of membership was not caused by her lack of gifts, but by her lack of strength. And just like any other muscle, Sophronia has been hard at work building strength and I think when you hear what she's been up to, you'll agree."

The women shake their heads and turn, whispering to one another. It's like being in front of the PTA with all of their flower-printed dresses and cardigans. As a little girl, I thought these women just came over for tea parties, it wasn't until later that I learned they thought themselves to be a governing force. As if. Who could take a woman in a sunhat seriously?

Where's Grandma? I glance around the room but don't see her amongst the line of manicured nails. I thought she was a part of this, but apparently not anymore.

"I wish you hadn't done this," I hiss in Mom's ear as she digs her fingers further into my shoulder. "You should have at least asked."

She turns toward me with a pained smile. "I wanted to make sure we took care of everything while it was still fresh from your trip."

Peering around, I don't see any of the rest of my family. Odd. They're a part of the coven, even if Grandma may not be.

"Where is everyone?" I ask Mom, making sure to keep my voice down while the women continue to argue about me.

"They didn't like what was happening, so they left." The slight creases that could barely be called wrinkles when I left push farther into her face as she widens her smile. "Should we begin?"

Silence gradually falls over the group as they settle down.

"What is it that's new enough that you had to drag us out here?" asks a woman leaning next to the fireplace as she examines her nails.

Hummed agreement follows her remark and Mom's grip softens for a moment as she flounders. "A great display of her power is what's new. She's done something we never thought her capable of when we refused her entrance into the coven. I think that should be addressed."

"You just want us to change our minds because you're still angry she didn't get in based on being your daughter." Rebecca eyes Mom with obvious distaste.

"She's a witch, and I stand by my feeling that being a witch and having family ties should count for something, but that's not the argument I'm trying to have today."

"So you admit you're looking for an argument?" she asks with a poisonous smile.

Mom sighs, dropping her arm from my shoulders. "Can we just get back to the task at hand?"

"Yes, let's hear her out so we can get out of here," the one woman with grey hair groans as she sinks further into the sagging couch.

Mom hesitates, but Rebecca waves her to continue and it's all the encouragement Mom needs. "Sophronia has just returned from a mission, one that could have killed her if it had gone wrong and one that wouldn't have been possible without a great show of strength. She has traveled almost four hundred years into the past to change the course of history and save a man's life."

And there she goes. With it all laid out, Mom waits for the cue to continue. When no one immediately argues, she picks up again.

"Not only did she save a man's life, but through her actions, she broke a curse that has plagued our family for centuries. And in order to save that man's life, she had to take him through time with her." Mom pauses. "Now, I know what you must be thinking, 'despite all of this she still only has one gift' and that's still true. However, she displayed a strong grip on her power and an immense strength waiting to be used. It is my opinion that the vote to keep her out of the coven was done prematurely and should be reevaluated based on the new evidence of her skills."

"That's all well and good except for the fact that nothing has changed," the greying woman says with a frown. "She still exhibits the same issues we had concerns with before."

"But—"

"And these issues are still great enough that a few displays of power will not be enough to change our minds after all the tests she has failed." Rebecca's lips thin as her frown pulls deeper.

Mom takes a breath, shoulders shaking with restraint. "I understand your concerns, which is why I thought it would be prudent to meet together today to discuss them."

"What you don't seem to understand is that they've been discussed." Grey hair stands up and smooths the wrinkles in her skirt. "You already know that the biggest concern we had for keeping Sophronia from the coven was based on attitude. Despite what you say she has done lately, that factor has not changed.

"I'm sorry for your pain, I really am, but you can't keep trying to force us to accept her. It wouldn't be good for the coven or your daughter. Maybe after a few hundred years we can reevaluate, but you're expecting a lot of change in a few years from a young girl."

She gives Mom a sympathetic smile and walks toward the door, kitten heels clicking against the hardwood floor. The other women file out after her until the room feels spacious and empty.

Mom sags, her eyes welling with tears. "I'm so sorry, baby, that isn't how I thought things would go today."

"My attitude is a problem?" I ask, my voice rising out of public embarrassment. "You never said that was the issue. You've always said it was because I only had one gift. That my lack of power made me unfit to join a coven."

Mom twists her shirt in tight hands. "I didn't want you to think they were outright rejecting you. Saying it was something outside of your control made it less personal."

"So, you lied to me? You lied to me about the coven my whole life and then expect me to be able to make changes to join them? Do you not realize how insane that is?"

Shaking my head, I push past her for the stairs.

"Sophronia, I was trying to help you." Mom holds an empty hand out to me, face crumpled.

"Next time just stay out of it. I never asked to be a part of your coven anyway." I stomp up the stairs, the walls rattling with the force as I march to my room.

I never asked to be part of a coven and I don't need anyone else's approval. I know I'm strong enough. I can't find it in myself to care if a bunch of old women don't want me at their tea party.

Plus, my gift isn't something that's up for grabs. I know how that coven works, everyone working for each other. There's no way I want to spend my time traveling through time for them. I have so many better things to do, like learning better how to focus my power and actually finishing high school. And maybe learning what life is like now that the curse has been lifted.

Honestly, having the coven here proved that things haven't changed very much since the 1600s. We still judge each other in the same way and exclude each other just like our ancestors. I'm sure the covens of the past wouldn't have accepted me either, not that it makes it right. Mom's right, I have power and I have family, and that should be enough. And it is, for me.

What do I need a coven for when I have family?

CHAPTER TWENTY-TWO

I choose not to surface again until dinner. It isn't a hard choice to make when I don't even need to pretend I'm avoiding my mother when buried under a mountain of makeup work. Good thing all of my teachers decided to hold onto every little assignment from the last two weeks. It would be unreasonable to think they'd give a sick kid a break.

Aunt Agathe's thin knuckles rap against the door at around five thirty. She comes in without permission and leans against the wall with a tray of food in her tight hands.

"Thought you'd want to eat."

"I was going to come down, I just had to finish some things." I sit up and tidy the piles of papers into classes and complete or incomplete.

Aunt Agathe sinks into the bed beside me. "I thought you might want to be alone up here. I know what your mom did today was probably more than a little unsettling."

"I don't care if I'm a part of the coven or not." As someone who's survived a witch trial, I feel like I don't have to build myself up to anyone.

"We didn't ask her to do that, I hope you know that." Aunt Agathe peers at me with her big eyes. "We never would have pushed something like that on you, especially not so soon after returning from your . . . little adventure."

"That's one way to describe it." I grin at her as she slides the tray over to me and lies back along the width of my bed. "So, how'd you end up here with me? I would've thought it'd be Mom or Grandma."

"I didn't ask if anyone else wanted to do it. I just came up." She pauses. "Come to think of it, you might end up with more than one tray tonight."

I can imagine how thrilled Mom would be to come up with something she'd packed just to be shown up by her older sister. Grandma might not mind so much, unless she's hoping to corner me alone and lecture me on something I should've done while I was in the past.

"Well, I certainly hope that's not the case," I say, lifting the lid to reveal a smattering of leftovers, some of which I can't for the life of me figure out what they were once trying to be. There's something brown, and everything is covered in a layer of what looks to be a white gravy. The smell of fish drifts over the room despite the fact that I can't see any fish on the tray. "One serving of this should be enough."

Aunt Agathe lies back down. "No one felt much like cooking today, so it's a bit of a mess."

"No one ever feels much like cooking in this house." I laugh. "For so many women living under one roof, you'd think we'd eat better."

Aunt Agathe laughs with me, her voice like a tinkling of bells drifting up to the vaulted ceiling.

I bite into an old chicken wing, and Aunt Agathe turns to me, face serious. "I hope you know that your mother was trying to do right by you. She only wants to help you, and she's under the impression that a place in the coven will help her do that. Try not to judge her too harshly."

"That's not what I'm upset about." I sigh, knowing I could never hide my swirling mess of thoughts from a woman who's full of them herself. "I'm having a hard time adjusting back to real life."

"Give it time," Aunt Agathe says, patting my knee. "It's only been a day."

And yet each moment feels harder than the last when my heart keeps pulling back towards a time I should've never known, to people I should never have met.

"I miss them," I confess, letting her wrap her arms around me and pull me into her chest.

Closing my eyes, I listen to the steady beat of her heart and the echo of her voice. "I think that's normal, not that I would know much about normal, but I think it's normal to miss the people you love."

Love?

All these swirling emotions really are being inflicted on me by the stupid curse breaking. I should've held firmer to my belief that we didn't need it broken. Life was much simpler when the only people I had to care about were my family.

"How do I know if I love them?" My voice is quiet. I'm treading into unfamiliar territory, unfamiliar for all of us, and I don't know if Aunt Agathe can help me.

She leans back, my head shifting with the rise and fall of her breath. "I'd imagine love feels like what you're going through right now. Pain at separation, wanting the best for someone, that kind of thing."

"Do you really want to feel those things?" I ask, feeling very much like a little girl hearing a scary story.

"Of course I do," she says with a watery smile. "To live hundreds of years and never feel anything is an experience I wouldn't wish on anyone, especially you, Sophronia."

"So, you're glad I broke the curse?" My voice is muffled as I bury my face in her chest.

"I'm glad the curse is broken, I just wish you didn't have to be the one to do it. That's a big responsibility to lay at your feet at any age, and we all wish we could've protected you from that."

I sit up, brushing bronzed hair back out of my face while my jaw hardens. "You don't have to protect me from stuff, and I'm not that young."

"Sweet girl, someday you'll understand how precious this time is, how young you really are, and how wonderful that is. Never wish away your youth longing for the freedoms of the future. The tradeoff is really not worth it, my dear." She smiles with her faraway eyes. "Embrace your youth."

"Easy for you to say," I grumble. "You don't have to do all the homework forced upon me because of my youth."

Aunt Agathe laughs. "This phase will be over soon enough and then you'll be responsible for your own choices, although I can't see your mother ever giving up on you entirely."

Shoveling a mouthful of peas into my mouth, I don't bother swallowing before talking again. "Do you think things will change for you now? Think you'll feel that overwhelming desire to procreate? The curse is gone, you could even keep the father around if you wanted."

She squeezes my shoulder. "I think you're enough for me, darling."

I give her a half smile as I wolf down something that tastes suspiciously like stuffing despite the fact that Thanksgiving is still a month away.

"I love you, sweet girl, all of us do. No matter how breaking the curse changes us, that's one thing that will never change," she says with one last squeeze before rising to her feet.

"I love you too, you know. I never would have done it if you guys hadn't wanted me to."

"We know."

Tray empty, the food sits like a brick in my stomach. I don't bother trying to do more homework, I can't concentrate on it and I don't feel like giving myself a headache with the effort it would take.

Night seeps into my room through the big bay window, its dark fingers drifting across the floor and over my bed. I should be sleepy after the day I've had, but if anything, I feel more wired. Grabbing an abandoned jacket off the floor, I slip it on and creep across the hall and down the stairs. The light's on in the kitchen, but I turn for the front door without hesitation.

Fingers curling around the cold knob, rational thought kicks in for a moment, warning me against what I'm about to do. All I know is I have to get out of here. The door creaks open on rusty hinges and the crisp air hits my face and lungs like a brick. Still, I step out and carefully close the door behind me.

The porch squeaks under my feet as I walk across it, every sound threatening to alert my family that I've left. I let out a breath I've been holding when I cross onto the sidewalk, letting the small street-light penetrate the increasing darkness left by the drizzle of rain this afternoon.

Sneakers slapping against the damp ground, I take the opposite path that I usually do when I go to school, making sure to avoid the increasing density of downtown. A car speeds by, its headlights bouncing on the uneven road.

I feel out of place here, which seems silly after only being gone a few weeks. I've lived in this time my whole life, and yet I feel like I never truly lived until I ventured into the past. Being with Matthew helped me come alive. He pushed me and never acted like I was any-thing but what I was. I had to work for his trust and somewhere along the way he earned mine. Somewhere along the way he earned every-thing, even the emotions I'm not sure what to do with yet.

The streetlights spread farther and farther out the longer I walk, and I almost envy these quiet houses for their solitude. Maybe that's why I had to leave. I need some space and some quiet to come to grips with everything. Not that there's any real way to come to terms with what happened.

It's so stupid to get hung up on people I only knew for a short time but knowing that doesn't change how my heart twists in my chest just thinking of them.

Thinking of Matthew.

My breath comes short and I have to stop. Leaning against my knees in the narrow beam of a streetlight, I watch my shadow heave.

He's dead, long dead, and I need to let him go. Let him go or make the decision to go back in time. What would my mother say if I walked into the night and never came back? Just created another door and headed back to the lion's den. Because who am I kidding? I can't survive there. If I went right back, I'd be in the same situation I was in.

Running from Thomas.

Still, the idea of going back lifts my spirits to the point where I can almost make out the fluttering outline of a door a few feet in front of me.

"Pull yourself together," I hiss, straightening my shoulders.

Without my whirling thoughts to distract me, I finally notice the fall chill as it bites into my bones. Toes going numb, I turn, and start my journey back home. The pleasant darkness I felt before has completely ebbed away, the distance between the streetlight's beckons with ghoulish fingers.

"You are fine, you've traveled through time, you've faced down witch hunters, you can handle a little darkness."

The pep talk does little to buoy me, but I force my feet to keep moving. Its psychological, I know it is, but leaving the streetlight has me shivering.

I'm farther from home than I've ever been before, I didn't realize how long I'd been walking until now, when I want more than anything to just be home.

A car drives past, its headlight bright against the wet asphalt. I really should've told someone where I was going, the thought drifts across my mind as the car slows ahead of me, pulling to the side. Willing myself to even my pace, I get closer and closer to the car, it's red taillights bright like eyes watching me approach.

As I come even with the car, the driver's side window rolls down.

"Hey," a deep voice calls across the road.

Without turning, I pick up my pace. My breath rattles in my ears, my hands clammy where they swing by my side.

"Hey," he calls again, putting the car in reverse to keep pace with me. "Kinda late to be out alone don't you think?"

Body screaming at me to run, I force myself not to appear spooked. I remember some self-defense class in phys ed talking about looking like a victim being the first mistake most people make. *I'm not a victim, I'm not a victim*, I chant in my mind in an endless loop as the car's tires peel away from the street with a screech—the burnt rubber smell filling the air.

"Kinda rude not to talk to someone when they're talking to you. This age is completely devoid of manners."

I stop short. "Excuse me?"

A dark head appears from the open window. "I said, this age has no manners. There was a time when people wouldn't have ignored someone specifically talking to them. Can you imagine? I remember a girl who would've been completely lost if people hadn't listened to her crazy pleas."

My lips part, skin tingling. "Who are you?"

"I'm sure you know." His chuckle seems to brush against my skin, teasing in its familiarity. "It hasn't been that long, has it?"

The driver's door opens, long jean-clad legs unfolding as he stretches onto the pavement. Standing, he leans against the car's frame, running a hand through close cut curls.

"Wha—but you—"

Matthew laughs. "I thought I'd timed this pretty well. I didn't realize how hard it would be for you to recognize me."

Matthew grins at me, illuminated by the headlight beam. Resisting the urge to fall to my knees, I step closer, hand over my open mouth.

"Didn't think you'd be able to get rid of me that easily, did you?" he asks, hands slipping into the pockets of his leather jacket. "One little jaunt through time and you're free forever? I don't think so."

"But you—but you're—you should be dead."

He places a hand over his heart. "You wound me. Here I thought you'd be excited to see me, not insisting that I should be dead."

"It's not—I don't want you dead, I just, I don't understand." My voice is shrill, and I should be more embarrassed of it, but I can't find it in me to care right now.

"I thought you of all people would have no problem understanding what's happening. I mean, you're from a family of witches, right? How old do you tend to be?" He grins, teeth gleaming in the weak light.

"Well, old, but—"

"So, if they can live a long time don't you think maybe I could too?"

A smile spreads across my face as warmth fills my body. Closing the distance between us, I crash into him. I inhale his new scent of aftershave and stiff leather, but underneath all of that, it's still him. The same firm chest, the same lanky torso. I press myself further into him, the tears burning behind my eyes begging to be set free.

"It really is you," I murmur into his chest.

"Like I said, you can't get rid of me that easy."

I step back, peering into his night-blackened eyes. "But I don't understand, why would you bother looking for me? It's been hundreds of years, surely after all that time you wouldn't care about one disheveled girl who caused more trouble than she was worth."

"I wouldn't put it that way," he says with a grin. "More like, still thinking of a girl that risked her life coming to the past for him. A girl who followed his stubborn butt all the way onto a boat she knew was going to sink and then risked her life through exposure by using her powers to make sure he survived. That's not someone I could easily forget."

"I guess not when you put it that way." I give him a timid smile. "How did you know I would be here?"

"I tried the house first, but you weren't there, then I sat for a moment and considered what I knew of you and what you might do next. Then I saw you walking and had to flip back around before I lost you again."

He reaches out for me, but I maintain our distance. I need to keep looking at him, to keep *seeing* that he's here, he's really here.

"I was thinking about going back," I whisper.

He grabs my hand. "I'm glad you didn't. Surprising you was a lot more fun."

"I don't know if fun is the right word." My heart beats wildly against my chest, pounding in my ears.

Matthew pulls me against him. "Should I try harder to make it more fun?" he whispers, the air between us becoming heated with his breath.

"I—"

He doesn't give me a chance to respond before he presses his lips against mine, folding me against him so tightly my lungs can barely expand. Surrounded by his warmth and the rich smell of leather, I barely need to breathe. Fingers curling into my hair, he pulls me closer, our breath mingling in the lack of space.

Too soon, he pulls away. Running a careful hand down the side of my face, he lets out a slow exhale. "I've been waiting almost four hundred years to do that."

A grin splits my swollen lips. "I still can't believe this is happening."

"You will." He smiles. "I have an even bigger surprise waiting for you at your house."

"Bigger than you waiting for me?"

He grabs my hand and pulls me toward the car. "Just wait."

Matthew walks me around the car and opens the door for me. I slide against the cold leather seat as Matthew holds the door open for me.

He waited for me. I can't believe it. All this time he's lived and he's just been waiting for me. For this moment. It's like something out of a movie and the whole idea of it makes my toes curl.

He gets in and starts the car, sending a low rumble through the seats. "Ready?"

My fingers fumble in my seatbelt, the nervous energy coursing through me making me effectively useless. He stills my hand with a smile and latches the buckle himself.

"Just breathe," he whispers, running a finger down my jaw. "It's a good surprise, I promise."

I don't doubt that it is. If I could just have a few hours alone with Matthew that would be heaven.

The car crawls along the empty street, classic rock playing softly on the radio.

"So, you like soft rock?" I tilt my head at his leather jacket.

He glances at me and quirks his eyebrow. "Four hundred years is a long time. Is it so weird that I wouldn't be clinging to the clothes of my past?"

No. It's not.

"So, what have you been doing these last years, besides pining for me of course," I ask with a grin.

"That's definitely taken up a lot of my time," he says with a laugh. "But I've kept busy. Done a lot of traveling, got a few degrees, that kind of thing. I've been working as a doctor for the last few years."

My lips form an 'O.' After a pause, I say, "You know that I'm not that old, right? I'm still in my first life cycle."

"I know," he says with a dry laugh. "In the four hundred years I've been waiting, that thought has come up more than a few times."

Grabbing his hand, I force him to slow down and look at me. "Are you sure about this? About me? I'm still young compared to you."

"And you saved me when I was just a boy," he says with a wide smile. "Let's not ruin this moment for us, okay?"

"Okay."

Matthew pulls into my driveway and turns to me. "You ready?"

Nodding, I try to undo my buckle, but once more my fingers act like entities independent of me, and nothing happens. Matthew chuckles deep in his throat and presses the release button. Leaning closer to me, he wraps a hand in my bronzed hair. "It's just like I remembered it."

"Maybe because I came home yesterday." A hysterical chuckle bubbles up my throat.

"Maybe," he whispers, leaning in closer. Brushing his lips against mine, he sighs. "I've been waiting so long for you."

He gets out of the car, coming around to open the door for me. As I climb out, he takes my hand in his, lacing our fingers together.

Glancing down at our casual linkage, I wonder what Mom will make of this. After everything else that's happened, I'm sure she won't like it. Too much change has a tendency to make her go crazy.

"Matthew, I—"

He cuts me off as I try to disentangle myself from him. "Don't worry, they have bigger things to think about."

Bigger than this? Bigger than bringing home a boyfriend from the past? His surprise has to be pretty amazing to beat that.

We start up the stairs, their creaking suspiciously absent. "Did you—?" I shake my head, I can find out about all his gifts some other time. "Never mind."

Even from the porch I can make out loud voices coming from the living room. Heart pounding, I twist the knob and push open the door. My family turns as one to face me. My grandma is nowhere in sight.

"Hello." I wave awkwardly.

"I told you she was fine," a deep voice says behind the wall of women. "Matthew would never dream of hurting her."

"Forgive us for not believing you, warlock," Mom spits, adjusting her body enough that I can see the male figure seated on our couch.

With a touch of grey at his temples, his body long and thin, he could be anywhere from thirty to forty. His long straight nose reminds me of the man he used to be back in ancient Greece.

"Hello, Soph," he says, deep voice gentle. "Thank you for making sure my son made it back safely. The way he drives sometimes makes me wonder."

"I can't believe you found us."

"Once I found out about *you*, I had nowhere else I wanted to be." He chuckles. "Your gift made saving my son possible."

My eyes scan the backs of my family, but the one I'm looking for is missing. "Where's Grandma?"

"In her room." Mom shifts uneasily on her feet. "She doesn't know yet."

"Don't you think she should be here." I look at Matthew's father, sitting on my couch with a smug look on his face. "After all, he did curse her. The least he could do is apologize."

I let go of Matthew's hand. It doesn't feel right holding it while I sneer at his father.

"She will come down when she's ready," my mother says, looking between me and the warlock.

I shake my head and make my way to the stairs.

"Soph," my mom calls after me. I ignore her as I take the stairs two at a time.

Racing towards her room, I rap softly on her door. "Grandma?"

"What is it, dear?" She swings the door open for me like she's been waiting for someone to come up.

"There's someone from your past here."

Her face goes serious, the lines becoming more apparent. "I see."

She follows me down the stairs. The warlock watches her out of narrowed grey eyes.

The air grows thick as soon as they make eye contact.

"Damaris," he whispers, standing with open hands.

She sinks down on the steps, sitting suspended between floors. The warlock waits only a second before he vaults across the room. The stairs shake under his steps as he climbs past me and takes Grandma in his arms.

"Damaris," he whispers again, the words sounding like a prayer from his lips as he pulls her close. "I'm so sorry."

Grandma's head appears over his shoulder, eyes full of tears. "I never thought this day would come."

Giving them space, I finish my descent, eyes searching for Matthew. Seated on the couch, he watches his father with a quiet grin.

"He's been looking for her for a long time," he says as I sink in beside him. "He's always regretted his curse. Good thing finding your gift gave him the opportunity to lift it and to save me too. I mean I appreciate that for sure. You saved all of us when you saved me."

I lace my fingers through his. "And here you are."

"Just your modern happy ending," he says with a smile, enfolding me in his arms.

On the ancient phone with miles of twisted yellow cording in the kitchen, Mom leans close to the receiver as the dial tone rings.

"Hello?"

"John? It's me."

ACKNOWLEDGMENTS

As always, I want to thank my husband. Danny, without you none of this would be possible. Thank you for being so gracious when I needed time to write and for never complaining about not having dinner done . . . again.

Mom and Dad, you were right! I guess I did have more than one good story in me. I can't wait to see what else you might be right about!

Kristina, Megan, and Jake, thank you for always wanting to know what I'm working on and getting just as excited with me over every fun moment.

The Fellowship of the Ink, you guys are amazing. I really couldn't have done this without you. I'm so grateful for the day when I was able to manhandle you all into legitimate group, it was just what I (and hopefully many of you) needed.

Brandon and Alan, thank you guys for always being available whenever I have some crazy idea I need to discuss or query letter I can't write. Your support has been invaluable.

My Cedar Fort team, thanks for helping me get another book into the world. You guys are awesome and these books would have been nothing without you.

Heavenly Father, thank you for always sticking by me. Thank you for these talents and for helping nurture a small girl's dreams until they could come true.

And most of all (sorry family) thank you dear reader. Without you this book would be nothing. Thank you for continuing to support me and the wonderful dreamworld I live in. You are the hero of my story.

ABOUT THE AUTHOR

Elizabeth A. Drysdale, author of *Curse of the Forgotten*, won her first writing award at the age of seven and is an active member of the League of Utah Writers. She spent much of her childhood roaming through woods and climbing trees creating adventures to be someone else in. After graduating from Excelsior College, she's kept her nose in a book, either writing or reading, ever since. Elizabeth has a love of travel which often inspires her heroines to end up places very different from where they started. Originally from the back woods of Massachusetts, she lives in a small town in Northern Utah with her husband, three sons, one dog, and eight chickens.